STOLEN

RUBY SPEECHLEY

Boldwood

First published in Great Britain in 2025 by Boldwood Books Ltd.

Copyright © Ruby Speechley, 2025

Cover Design by Aaron Munday

Cover Images: Shutterstock

The moral right of Ruby Speechley to be identified as the author of this work has been asserted in accordance with the Copyright, Designs and Patents Act 1988.

A CIP catalogue record for this book is available from the British Library.

Paperback ISBN 978-1-83633-762-1

Large Print ISBN 978-1-83633-763-8

Hardback ISBN 978-1-83633-761-4

Trade Paperback ISBN 978-1-80656-061-5

Ebook ISBN 978-1-83633-764-5

Kindle ISBN 978-1-83633-765-2

Audio CD ISBN 978-1-83633-756-0

MP3 CD ISBN 978-1-83633-757-7

Digital audio download ISBN 978-1-83633-758-4

This book is printed on certified sustainable paper. Boldwood Books is dedicated to putting sustainability at the heart of our business. For more information please visit https://www.boldwoodbooks.com/about-us/sustainability/

Boldwood Books Ltd, 23 Bowerdean Street, London, SW6 3TN

www.boldwoodbooks.com

For my bookworm daughter, Sophie.
These words are for you,
with all my love.

PROLOGUE

Whatever is tied around her head covering her eyes is pulled too tight, digging into the sockets, pinching the skin across her temples. She's lying on her back, arms and legs bare and there's a gag in her mouth. Her arms ache from her hands being tied so tightly together in front of her. She's tried pulling at the string with her teeth but now her lips are bleeding. The metallic taste of her own blood turns her stomach. Nausea washes over her. How is she going to get out of here? Even with the blindfold on, she can make out a line of light around the door. She strains to hear if there's anyone there. Is someone coming to save her? What if they don't know she's here? She may never be found, and she'll die alone with no one knowing who tricked her.

1

VICKI

'I've said no, Lee, and I'm not going to change my mind.' I press my hand to my forehead then hitch my mobile higher against my ear.

'Just half an hour. To let me explain,' he pleads. My stomach tightens.

'You've used up all your chances.'

The last time he dropped the kids off their clothes stank of weed. To think he'd been driving at all, let alone with our precious children in the car.

'Look, I know I've messed up,' he sighs deeply. I wince at his discomfort. 'But I need them to know it's not their fault that we haven't spent time together. It's been over a month, Vicki.'

'Why would they blame themselves?' I straighten my back. He's always got an answer designed to make me feel bad for him. He could charm a saucer of milk from a cat.

'Because kids do, don't they?' He says it in that soft voice he uses when he's trying to get on my good side, but he's let me down so often it doesn't work any more.

'No.' I shake my head at myself in the dressing table mirror in case I give in. I mustn't. Much as I want the kids to see their dad, and as much as I know how important it is they have a relationship with him, he needs to grow up and stop behaving like this. 'I'm sorry but until you're completely clean, I can't risk it. I've told them you're ill, that you're getting treatment.'

'You've what? Can you actually hear yourself? Anyone would think I'm a monster.'

And here we go again, spiralling into the same argument.

When I first met Lee, I didn't mind that he smoked the odd spliff. It made him seem cool out of most of the boys I knew, most of whom were nerds. I presumed he was experimenting, but I soon worked out it was a regular habit. He had a handful of friends who smoked and a different crowd he went to the pub with, which is where I met him. I probably should have left him then, but I was already in love. He stopped once he got a good job, and he didn't smoke again until we had Alfie. Then when I fell pregnant a second time, he promised to stop again, and he did cut down for a while, but it wasn't long before he was back on it, even more than before. He said it was for medicinal purposes because he'd hurt his shoulder falling over.

I shouldn't have stayed for so long because now I'm full of anger and resentment. Marc saved me in a way, because for the first time in years I feel like I'm finally getting the life I always wanted.

'Come *on*, Vicki,' Lee shouts down the line.

'You're not going near my children in that state ever again.' My cheeks flush as my voice rises and sweat prickles under my arms. I blink at myself in the mirror.

'*Our* children.' His voice is hard. It doesn't take much for him to drop the charming act these days.

Yet again he's managed to upset me. It's like he knows Marc and I are about to go out for the evening and he's doing anything he can to ruin it. He needs to realise I'm not a pushover any more. I purse my lips and don't answer because right now he doesn't deserve to be their father. I shouldn't have to protect them from him.

'I told you I've cut right down, and I've got an interview next week.'

'I'm glad for you. Come back to us when you've sorted your life out.' I'm about to hang up when he speaks again.

'Is *he* behind all this, turning you against me?' It's his nasty tone.

'Why do you always blame Marc?' I should have put the phone down. Marc will be here any minute and I'm going to be in such a foul mood.

'You know why. You never used to be like this. *Before* him.' There's that bitter edge to his voice again. 'You need to have a serious look at yourself before you point the finger.'

I grit my teeth at the pang of guilt prodding my chest. If Lee knew how often Marc stayed over, he'd go mad. I've asked the kids not to mention it to their dad, especially Alfie as I know they still message each other, and they clearly haven't told him otherwise I'd certainly know about it by now. I can hear Lee's response in my head – *I do not want that man in my house.*

I can see how it looks from Lee's side, and a small part of me does feel bad, but he needs to take responsibility for his actions too. I didn't expect to meet someone else, but it felt like Lee and I were at the end of our marriage long before I met Marc. Neither of us was brave enough to admit it was over. After I began to work as Marc's personal assistant, it didn't take long for me to realise I wanted out of my marriage. Marc runs his own property business, Venture Properties. We hit it off straight away. He asked me out for lunch that first morning and within a few months Lee and I were officially over. I suppose Marc became his replacement. According to the whispers I've heard around the office, we're known as Bennifer, Ben Afleck and Jennifer Lopez. Although their relationship has broken down already, so I'm not sure that bodes well.

'I have to go, Lee. Call me when you're ready to step up and be a proper dad.' I cringe as my words spill out uncensored. It's true though, and maybe the truth will galvanise him into action. Without waiting for a reply or another excuse, I tap 'end call'.

I tug the lid off a bullet of scarlet lipstick and deftly apply a glossy layer to my lips. Lee will not get in the way of me moving on with my life. Marc is taking me to a fancy restaurant tonight, and I need to look the part. I'm hoping this new red satin dress will blow him away. We make such a gorgeous couple, everyone says so. Picturing him in his navy suit sends a flutter of butterflies rising in my stomach. Tonight could be the night he asks me, us, to move in with him. I'm not sure how Alfie and Bella will take it leaving the only home they've known, but I'm confident they'll adapt. They're good kids. Resilient. They've had to be with a volatile dad like Lee. I've done everything I can to protect them. I want them to have the best of everything in life, and with my new relationship, I'm hoping to achieve that. Which is why Marc must never find out about what I've been hiding. I draw in a breath. I don't want to lie to him, but if I tell him it will jeopardise our relationship.

Alfie and Bella haven't seen Marc's house yet, but once they've been there and seen how much space there is, with a games room, swimming pool and huge garden, they'll never want to come back to our modest semi-detached with its narrow strip of lawn.

I go to the window to pull the curtains but hesitate. There are a group of teenagers hanging around under the streetlamp at the end of the road. One of them runs out in front of a car and stands there, arms out, pulling faces at the driver. The horn sounds and in seconds, the rest of the teenagers have surrounded the car, pushing it and spitting on it. I'm about to call the police when the teenager in the road jumps out of the way and the driver speeds off.

I check my phone. Jess has texted to say she's leaving in a minute. I didn't think for a second she'd be involved with the teenagers causing trouble, but it's good to have it confirmed that she was nowhere near them.

> Hey gorgeous, are you ready for tonight?

Marc's text pops up.

> Yeah almost. Can't wait xxx

A hit of dopamine still shoots through me every time Marc messages me. It takes me back to our illicit exchanges in the office. I'm ashamed to say I was still married to Lee, but we were barely talking to each other by then. He was more interested in going out with his druggy mates. Having an affair with the boss was never on my radar, but I admit it's been exhilarating.

> Be five minutes. Was held up at work. Sorry!

> No probs. Babysitter is on her way xxx

I press send then grab my clutch bag and check on Alfie and Bella in their bedrooms to let them know Jess will be here shortly. I hope there's time before Marc arrives to have a quiet chat with her.

She swore not to breathe a word to anyone, but I just need to check she's not let it slip.

Because if Marc finds out what I did, he will kill me.

2

JESS

It's dark outside when Jess shuts her laptop and lets out a sigh. She switches off the ring light on her desk and changes out of her school uniform into casual clothes. One of her regulars is getting pushy, sending messages all the time and wanting to meet. But she doesn't do meet ups. She's heard stories and she does not want to be cooked.

At five to seven she leaves the house with her rucksack on her shoulder and locks the door behind her.

The cold air smarts her skin. She checks the local weather forecast on her phone app. Two degrees by midnight with a low chance of snow. She tuts out loud. There was a sprinkle last night which melted by breakfast time.

As she walks down the garden path, she opens Snapchat, more out of habit than anything, then stops at the gate. FeralCat9 has left another photo message. This time it's of the front of her house. It's taken at an angle from the ground up, so they must have been crouching in the front garden to take it. She shivers and looks left and right down the road, scanning the full 180 degrees before stepping onto the pavement. The hairs on the top of her head prickle. Their road isn't well lit but the light from the full moon shows it's deserted. Yet she senses someone is watching her. She automatically glances up at the identical semi-detached houses across the road. Occasionally she catches Colin standing at his bedroom window looking out at her, but he's friendly enough. He was in the year below her at school but now his mum home-schools him. She thinks he has a crush on her. It's kind of sweet. He has a lazy eye, but says it's not as bad as it used to be. His mum taped up one of his glasses when he was in primary school, but the bigger boys made fun of him. Jess and a couple of the other girls used to try and protect him, but it wasn't enough. He didn't go back after the pandemic.

There are plenty of parked cars on both sides of the road, so it would be easy enough for someone to hide and still keep her in their sights.

This feeling has been with her all afternoon, since she walked back from school. It's probably Fran or one of her gang, she decides. But deep down is the fear of someone knowing what she does in her bedroom, or what she plans to do tonight. Maybe they saw what she bought at the shops on the way home. She tries to swallow but her throat is dry. The box is safely tucked away in her rucksack with her English Lit revision as cover, just in case one of the kids wakes up or Vicki comes home early. She plans to do it as soon as they're asleep. But just the thought of what it could mean sets her heart drumming hard.

A pale blue camper van trundles past. It takes her only moments to walk from their semi-detached to the mirror image semi next door, through their garden gate and up the path to Vicki's, right on the dot of 7 p.m. All day she's been trying to avoid bumping into Fran and her mates, and somehow she's managed it and finally made it here.

Olly has been messaging her every five minutes wanting to see her but she's told him he can't come round tonight, she's babysitting, so when he tries to call a few times, she ignores it. It's one of Vicki's golden rules. No boyfriends and no alcohol.

She's been babysitting regularly for Vicki for the last two years, since Alfie was eleven and Bella was four. She was fifteen, and although things have changed now Lee has gone, she really needs the money so she can save up to go to uni. So she has no choice but to carry on babysitting for her, even though she really doesn't want to.

She glances over her shoulder as she walks up Vicki's garden path. There's no one around but the sense that someone is watching her won't go away.

3

VICKI

I sigh with relief when I hear Jess slam her front door shut. It always shakes our house slightly, but it's strangely reassuring living in a semi. Have done all my life. It's comforting to be near other people, know that life is going on no matter what you may be going through. Even when you hear the neighbours shouting at each other. And Jess's parents, Cassie and Dom, do that a lot. We went through plenty of drama when I was growing up, but nothing compared to them. I do worry about Dom's temper though, and my mind automatically springs back to the summer Jess fractured her wrist. I've never quite believed their 'accident' explanation.

I hurry downstairs and reach the bottom just as Jess rings the doorbell.

She's wearing a black cropped jacket which matches her long straight hair, a stripy jumper, jeans with a pair of Converse trainers.

'Come in, come in.' My mind instantly goes back to the day we were here together, alone.

'How are you?' Jess tilts her head with real concern on her face and a fresh coconut aroma is released from her newly washed hair. She's clearly thinking of that day too.

'I'm doing okay thanks,' I reply in a low voice.

She nods, keeping her eyes fixed on me.

I lead her down the hall to the kitchen and open the fridge. 'Can I get you some lemonade or a Coke?'

'Just water, thanks.'

I take a glass down from the cupboard and fill it from the tap. 'So for dinner, I've left a couple of pizzas and a garlic baguette for you and the kids. Apparently they want to watch something with you on Netflix; *Wednesday*, I think, so I don't mind them staying up a bit and eating on their laps. Just this once.' I turn and smile as I hand her the drink.

'Yeah, course.' Her face is powdered almost white, and her long lashes are lined black with perfect little flicks at the corners. Purple lipstick seems a bit over the top for school, although they don't seem to mind the older children wearing make-up these days. Or she only just put it on. It's Jess's signature look. There's a ring through one nostril but I don't know if it's real or some sort of clip on. I don't like to ask. They can't allow piercings at school, surely? I have all this to come with Alfie then Bella.

'Have your mum and dad gone somewhere nice this evening?' I ask her.

'Comedy club in town. Won't be back till late.' She nods.

'They're brave going on trains in this weather. Forecasting a storm later, but it's been sunny all day with not so much as a gentle breeze. We certainly don't plan on being out for hours anyway.' I fuss around straightening the chairs at the breakfast table.

'I don't mind, come back whenever. As soon as the children are in bed, I've got English revision to do.' She leans casually against the kitchen counter, her hands in her jacket pockets, rucksack at her feet.

'Good, good.' I hold onto the back of a chair and glance at the floor then up at her. 'I wondered if I could ask you something, about October half-term week?' I clench my teeth together.

'Yeah, of course.'

'It's nothing really.' I hesitate because whichever way I put it, it's going to sound needy. 'I just wanted to check that you didn't tell your mum about what happened, or anyone else actually.' I let go of the chair and wring my hands together – the way my mother used to, I suddenly realise. I'd be mortified if Cassie knew, or anyone come to that.

'No, absolutely not. I said I wouldn't.' She frowns and blinks rapidly a few times, probably wondering why I'm checking when we'd already agreed to keep it between us. But I can't help it, it's been playing on my mind.

'I really hate asking you not to tell your mum or anyone else about this, but I know you understand how... personal it is.' Jess picked the kids up from school then minded them for me that afternoon during October half-term. She saw the state I was in when I got home. She offered to stay longer than we'd planned, to keep Bella and Alfie away from me while I recovered. I was so grateful. I didn't want them to see me like that, so I sneaked up to bed and slept it off while she played games with them for the rest of the afternoon and cooked their tea.

'It's okay, I've not said a word to anyone, and I'm not going to, I promise.' She crosses her arms. I don't know if Jess is a little bit annoyed at me for not sounding like I trust her, or if she's bored of me talking about it.

'It would be devastating if anyone found out, that's all.' I rub the side of my head. The whole episode has made me so anxious. Just the thought of it gives me stabbing pains in my temple.

'That's okay, I understand, I really do.' She nods.

'Thank you, I'm grateful, especially for everything you did for me that day.' I'd like to think part of her agrees with what I did. I paid her well for the extra hours. But I'm just so paranoid that she might let it slip. Cassie would be shocked and disappointed in me. And then there's Jess's boyfriend Olly. She must confide in him about things and if she told him this, he might feel he needs to tell Marc, or even Lee, and where will that leave me?

I keep telling myself not to dwell on it, but Jess is just a teenage girl, how can I really expect her to keep it to herself forever?

Because the problem is, she's the only person with the power to blow my life apart.

4

JESS

Jess used to like babysitting for Vicki. It was easy money, in the nicest possible way. She started her online work to try and generate a new income stream and as soon as she's earning enough, which is hopefully soon, she'll be able to stop doing this completely. Alfie and Bella are lovely kids, and they like her, look up to her even, but Alfie has reached that age where he's started getting too much attitude and looking at her differently, like she's an object he can stare at. She does not want to babysit a teenager. But Vicki is friends with her mum, so she's going to have to think about how to tell Vicki she can't work for her any more, when the time comes.

Jess's dad doesn't like Vicki's new boyfriend Marc. Says he's too flashy and full of himself. Nothing like Lee in other words. Mum tells him he's getting grumpy in his old age. It always sparks a 'debate', as he calls it, which involves him being vocal about what a stuck-up arsehole he thinks Marc is. Vicki must have heard him through the wall. It's so demeaning. Why does he always think he's right? Jess used to think it could be jealousy because Marc is at least ten years younger than him and there's no doubt he's hot and fit, but she'd never dare say that to Vicki's face or to her mum.

Vicki opens the door and invites her in. She's wearing a tight red satin dress. A bit too tight in places but Vicki won't appreciate her mentioning it. She seems a bit anxious and shows her the pizzas in the fridge, then after getting her a glass of water, she randomly asks if she's told her secret to her mum. Seriously though, as if. She is not known for being a snitch. But fair's fair, she supposes; she'd be beyond nervous too if she'd done what Vicki has with no intention of telling anyone about it. But who's Jess to judge? For all she knows she could be facing the same dilemma one day.

Anyway, Vicki knows about *her* misdemeanour, so she'd hardly do anything to put their trust in jeopardy. Jess can't even tell Olly or her mum about what she did because she's so ashamed.

Jess is standing in the kitchen drinking her water when the doorbell rings. Vicki rushes to answer it. She checks herself in the hallway mirror before opening the door. Usually it takes her hours to get ready and she does look pretty hot considering she's recently turned forty. Jess's mum seems to have given up on wearing make-up completely, knocking about in jeans and trainers most of the time. But then her mum doesn't need to make that level of effort because she's naturally beautiful and Jess's dad adores her just as she is.

'Hi Jess, how are you?' Marc waves to her down the hall then hugs Vicki, still looking at Jess over her shoulder. He's holding a bottle of wine in one hand. The thought of drinking alcohol sets off a wave of nausea.

'Good, thanks,' Jess says in a tiny squeak. She tips her glass up and sips her cool drink, hand shaking. Sweat has gathered around her collar and her pulse is thudding in her neck. She hates that she's always like this when he speaks to her. It's so embarrassing.

She took a secret photo of him the first time she met him, and when she showed it to Dana at school, she agreed he looked like a young Tom Cruise but taller. They watched *Top Gun: Maverick*, then the original, at Dana's house. Now she can't get the comparison out of her head and it's driving her crazy.

The first time she went there to babysit after Lee left, and Vicki introduced Marc to her, he had held his hand out to shake hers. His rough tanned skin was warm, his grip firm and inviting, and she almost forgot to let go. Like then, he is wearing narrow taupe chinos and a pristine white polo top under a short brown leather jacket. Very Tom. Dana said he should start an account as a sexy older man.

He smooths back his quiff and follows Vicki into the kitchen, his pointed mahogany shoes clicking as he strides across the hallway tiles. Vicki takes hold of the bottle of bubbly, and for a couple of seconds they both have their hands on it, gazing into each other's eyes, laughing at some private joke. Then she takes it from him and puts it in the fridge.

Jess can hardly breathe. Marc smiles at her but she looks away, pretending she needs to check her phone. Her legs wobble but she manages to hold onto the back of a chair. Nausea washes over her again at the thought of Olly finding out how she feels. She's thought about telling Vicki sooner than she planned that she can't babysit for her any more, but she'd hate letting her down especially when Vicki's trying to get her life back on track after her break-up with Lee. And Jess really needs to wait until she's earning more money online. There are only a few families she babysits for, but this is the most regular. Maybe when she's more established online with a bigger fanbase, she won't have to babysit ever again.

Jess follows them out of the kitchen keeping her distance. Vicki calls up to the kids that they're leaving and to come and say goodbye, and soon after, Bella trots down and sits on a step near the bottom, wearing a unicorn onesie, her fair hair tied in plaits either side of her head. Alfie is nowhere to be seen.

'Alfie, did you hear me?' Vicki calls again. 'We're going.'

Silence.

'Alfie, come down now,' Vicki yells louder, hands on her hips.

Alfie appears at the top of the stairs and plods down three steps. He's swamped in his oversized Minecraft T-shirt and joggers, but he seems taller, more grown up than when she last saw him only a couple of weeks ago. His hair is a darker blond, cut shorter with a skin fade and on his forefinger is a plain silver ring.

'Why didn't you come when I called you?' Vicki snaps.

'I was in the middle of a game,' he mumbles and glares at his mum like she should know that and not interrupt him.

'Less of the lip,' Vicki says in a tight voice, probably embarrassed he's behaving like this in front of me.

Alfie over exaggerates a deflated sigh.

'We're going to head straight off.' Vicki checks her watch. She cups Bella's face and kisses her on the nose then puts her hand up to Alfie but he doesn't budge. At twelve years old, thirteen on Saturday, he's moved way past the age of wanting his mum to kiss him, especially in front of anyone.

'Now be good, both of you, and do what Jess tells you to, okay?' Vicki says.

Bella nods enthusiastically.

'Do I have to? I can look after myself, I don't need *a girl* to look after me,' Alfie grumbles in an agitated tone.

'Yes, you do.' Vicki shoots him a warning look.

'Whatever.' He turns away.

Marc holds her faux fur coat out and she shimmies into it, then turns to Jess.

'Please make sure he gives you his phone before bedtime.'

Alfie glares at the back of his mum's head then side-eyes Marc who winks at him. A little smirk appears on Alfie's lips.

'The restaurant details are on the fridge and if you need to call us for any reason, you've got my number,' Vicki continues, giving Jess a pointed look. Jess nods and Vicki turns to Marc and gazes into his eyes for a second before opening the front door. Olly looks that way at Jess and it's so lovely, but with university on the horizon she's not sure she's ready for a long-term relationship.

And after their argument last night, she's doesn't know if he'll want to stay with her, especially when she confesses to him what she did.

5

As soon as Vicki and Marc drive off, Alfie stomps into the living room and switches on the TV, immediately flicking through the channels. Bella perches on the edge of the sofa.

'Your mum said you wanted to watch *Wednesday* with me,' Jess says to them, standing in the doorway.

'That's for girls. I want to watch *Squid Game*,' Alfie says.

'Er no, I don't think you're old enough for that just yet,' Jess tells him.

'Who says? I've seen the first episode and it's not that bad.'

Bella looks round at him and her eyes widen.

'Really, where have you seen it?' Jess asks.

'At a mate's house,' he says and folds his arms.

'Oh yes and which friend was that? I'll make sure your mum knows.'

He doesn't answer and Jess suspects he's making it up.

'Do you realise how violent it is? I can't let you watch it, especially with your little sister here. You'll get me in deep trouble with your mum.'

'So what. I don't need you telling me what to do,' he grunts and tightens his crossed arms, and I click over to *The Simpsons*.

'Watch a bit of this while I cook the pizzas, okay?'

He slouches back on the sofa next to Bella who starts sucking her thumb, clutching a furry toy dog.

In the kitchen Jess switches the oven on and takes the pizzas out of the fridge. Once they're in the oven she sets the timer for eight minutes. She takes out three plates. While she's waiting, she makes herself a coffee and pours two glasses of squash and carries them in. Alfie has changed channel to a violent-looking cartoon where all the characters are depicted in red and black and fighting with swords and daggers.

'You cannot watch this, Alfie. Your sister is too young.' Jess jabs a button on the remote control taking it straight back to *The Simpsons*.

'You're not in charge of me.' He narrows his eyes at Jess and tries to snatch the control from her, but she swipes it out of his reach and carries it with her back to the kitchen. He never used to be so rude. He used to like her coming over, but he's become so moody and argumentative lately that it worries her.

She collects up the empty pizza boxes and opens the bin, but it's full so she unlocks the back door and takes them straight out to the recycle bin.

Outside, the wind has picked up and it's started raining. The ground is slippery under foot. She heard the local weather reporter explain on Instagram earlier that if the temperature hits zero the rain freezes the instant it hits the ground.

The bins are lined up down the side of the patio. Jess lifts the grey bin lid and chucks the boxes inside. As she shuts it, her eye is drawn to a clinking sound at the bottom of the lawn, like something hitting metal. Taking a step forward, she concentrates hard to hear it again but it's difficult with creaking branches and swishing leaves rustling in the wind.

A blur of movement catches her eye. Was it an animal or someone prowling around? She jumps at the distinct crack of a twig.

'Who's there?' she calls into the darkness, a tremor in her voice. She folds her arms around herself and glances back at the comforting pool of light from the kitchen window. Without waiting for a reply, she hurries back up the path, the growing storm filling her ears, heart banging against her ribs. Fear seems to pull her back so she can't move as quickly as she wants to, needs to. Someone could be moving closer behind her, but she'd never hear them. Stupid, stupid to have left her phone in the living room. She could have used the torch on it. And doesn't Vicki keep a torch on the shelf by the back door? Why didn't she bring it?

The oven beeper suddenly buzzes making her jump out of her skin. She thrusts open the back door and slams it shut, pulling the handle up sharply.

Just as she lets out a breath and goes to turn the key in the lock, the handle jolts down a few millimetres. Ice slides through her whole body. Someone is trying to open the door. With all her bodyweight behind her she leans against it and shoves the handle back up hard and turns the key.

A shadow emerges on the other side of the glass panel. Someone is standing there, staring right at her.

6

Jess jumps away from the back door and whoever it was runs off down the garden. All she can make out is someone dressed in black. They must have climbed over the gate at the bottom which leads onto an alleyway. It's accessible from the road and kids tend to hang out there smoking and drinking. She'll have to tell Vicki when she comes back. If it was a burglar trying to break in, they could well return. For now, she needs to calm down and concentrate on feeding the kids and getting them to bed.

She takes the pizza and garlic bread out of the oven. The cheese on top is a little browner than she intended, but it will be fine. She cuts it up and puts three slices on three plates and carries them on a tray into the living room. She hands one each to Bella and Alfie and sits on the armchair, leaving hers on the coffee table for now. Her appetite has vanished. It's dark outside and with the TV and lights on, anyone can see in but she won't be able to see them. Whoever was outside could still be snooping around. Her legs tremble as she stalks across the room. As she draws the curtains, she looks out but can't see anyone hanging around. It doesn't mean there isn't someone there though. She shudders. What if she hadn't managed to lock the door in time? Whoever it was would have forced their way in, and then what? There's nothing particularly valuable in here except laptops and presumably Vicki's jewellery. But they could have hurt the children, or her.

A knock on the door jolts her out of her seat and she goes to open it an inch. Colin from across the road is standing there with a bunch of pink carnations in his hand. She relaxes a little that it's only him.

'These are for you.' He thrusts them towards her and blinks. She frowns and leans back, slightly creeped out. She doesn't want to give him the impression she's interested in him romantically. But maybe she's reading too much into these little gifts.

'That's so kind of you, thank you,' Jess says automatically. He's just being thoughtful, she tells herself. Besides, he helped her out when she needed a friend. As she takes them from him, his fingers stretch out and he tries to touch her hand. She pulls away and their eyes lock. She frowns at him, and he bows his head. This isn't the first time he's tried to touch her. Once in church during Harvest Festival, she was squeezed in next to him and his leg wouldn't stop shaking next to hers.

She closes the door and takes the flowers into the kitchen and sticks them in a jug of water propped up in the sink. Was it Colin creeping around outside, trying to get in the back door? She shakes her head. He wouldn't do that.

She sits on the armchair again leaving Bella and Alfie to sit on the sofa while they eat. Bella is watching *Wednesday* while Alfie is flicking through TikTok on his mobile. Every now and again a Snapchat message pops up on her phone. More pictures of her, this time taken behind her when she's walking to school. It could be any of her classmates. The comments though are more menacing than before.

I want you to myself.

She pushes her phone under the cushion and tries to ignore it and concentrate on the programme.

Just as she's about to bite into her pizza, there's a knock at the front door. She's not expecting anyone. Maybe Vicki has forgotten something and doesn't have her key. She pushes back the living room curtain and sneaks a look out. Olly is standing there. He's rubbing his eyes as though he's just woken up. His short fair hair is tousled and sexy looking. She loves how tall and willowy he is. Opening the front door a few inches, she smiles at him through the gap.

'What are you doing here?' she whispers. 'You know the rules.'

'I want to speak to you. You're not answering your phone.'

'It's on airplane mode in my bag,' she lies, not wanting to admit that she's ignoring his calls. She can't afford to lose her job because of chatting on the phone or anything else. 'Anyway, I told you not to come here,' she checks over her shoulder then back at Olly. 'Was it you who tried to come in the back door just now?'

'No, why would I do that?' He frowns.

'Someone tried to force their way in while I was locking it.'

'Shit.' He shakes his head. 'Well, it wasn't me. How would I even get round the back?' He points to the side of the house as if she's not aware there's a locked gate there.

If it wasn't him, then who could it have been? A homeless person trying to sneak in for food? They're not far from a food bank; she helped out there a couple of winters ago. Maybe it's shut and whoever it was is desperately hungry. Even though it's a bit of a stretch, it's a possibility, and she begins to feel bad. They've had their milk and bread delivery stolen from their front doorstep before.

'I didn't want to leave things as they were. I needed to see you, make sure you were okay.' He glances at the ground. 'Sorry for what I said last night. It was out of order.'

'Yes, it was, but thank you.' She purses her lips, checks over her shoulder again to see if they've disturbed the kids. The sound level of the television is high, and the door is ajar. She steps aside and pulls it until it's almost shut. When she turns back to Olly, his foot is over the threshold. Could she sneak him into the kitchen, just for a little while? Better not. One thing could lead to another and she's not ready for that. Anyway, her job is to keep an eye on those two, especially with Alfie in such a belligerent mood.

'Are you going to say sorry to me too?' He leans against the door frame, his eyebrows raised and half a smile on his lips.

'Sorry for what?' She flutters her eyelashes.

'You know what.' His smile has gone.

'No, I'm not.' She holds his gaze.

'I don't like what you're doing. I told you, I think you should stop.'

'So you're not really sorry then?'

'I don't mean to upset you, but seriously, is this what you want to do with your life?'

'Yeah, why not?' She goes up on her tiptoes and kisses Olly's lips to try and pacify him, and his arms wrap around her as he kisses her back. 'Can I change your mind?' she asks, slipping a hand up his T-shirt onto his back.

'No, I'd never do something like that.' He pulls away from her. 'You're asking a lot, you do know that right?'

'But we'd be so good together, you agree with that don't you?'

'Yeah we would, but in private, not in front of a camera. And what about later, when we're both out there looking for serious jobs? I've heard of people being found out by employers, getting the sack or not getting the job in the first place.'

'It may not matter by then. It could become our full-time work if we want it to and we'd make mega bucks.'

He sighs. 'Really? It's not for me. I've always wanted to do something with cars, maybe work at Formula 1 someday.'

She pulls away. 'Alright. Well, I'm not saying you *have* to do it. I just thought we could try, that's all.'

He shakes his head and scrunches his nose up like he does when he finds something distasteful but doesn't want to say a load of ugly words. 'Anyway, your dad doesn't like me, so he's hardly going to let me go up to your bedroom.'

'Look, think about it. I need to get back to the kids. I'll speak to you in the morning, okay?' She tries to dismiss what he's said, but he's not wrong. Her dad has never liked any of her boyfriends, not since her first date back in year three. He always finds something about them to criticise, and he says Olly is too bookish and strait-laced. He expects all men to be macho like him.

'Fine.' He swings a kick at the bush by the side of the door and slopes off down the path. Sometimes it scares her how quickly his mood changes. Especially as her dad has the same trait, but is much more physical.

After he's gone, Jess watches the rest of the episode then sets about getting the kids to bed. Alfie complains as she knew he would, but she concentrates on helping Bella and in the end he hands his phone to her without any fuss. She wonders why he's not kicked off. Soon after she's turned their lights out, she goes back into his room and catches him on his tablet, so she takes that too and switches it to silent. She drops both devices in her rucksack and zips it up.

Downstairs, she takes her mobile out from under the cushion, ignoring any message alerts on the screen, and catches up on her social media, mainly answering questions and replying to her regulars. She's always strict with the time she spends on her phone, and when she's finished, she drops it back in her rucksack.

When she's sure Alfie and Bella are asleep, she pulls out the box she bought at the chemist. She lays the contents out and reads the instructions. Her hands are trembling. After a moment of deliberation, she stuffs it all back inside and closes the lid. Maybe another day would be better. But there's nowhere safe. It's too risky at home.

She carries the box to the bathroom and locks the door behind her.

7

VICKI

We park outside the gastropub and before we go in, Marc takes my hand and gently pulls me to him. His eyes roam over my face and deep into my eyes, then his arms reach around me, his body pressing against mine as he kisses me firmly on the lips.

When we move away from one another, we hold each other's gaze as though nothing else around us exists.

'Maybe we should skip the meal and go straight home; the kids will be asleep soon,' I say in a low seductive voice.

'But the babysitter is still there.' His smile lifts half his lips as though he accepts the disappointment.

'I can send her home early or we could go to yours instead?' I lift his palm to my lips and plant a trail of kisses.

'Sorry, I was going to tell you about that tonight, I've got workmen in, it's quite a mess,' he says.

'But your house is perfect; what could possibly need doing?'

'The roof leaked rain into one of the en-suite bathrooms causing a lot of damage. All the flooring was ruined and part of the ceiling, and the roof needs repairing.'

'Oh God, that's awful.'

'Yeah, it is. And so, it's not exactly a romantic setting.'

'I don't think I'd care or notice.' I smile.

He gives a weak smile and shakes his head. 'I mean it really isn't safe; it's like a building site.' He sighs and takes my hands in his. 'It's actually made me think about my situation and whether I really want to stay there at all.'

'Oh really? But it's such a lovely house and you haven't been there long, have you?'

'Four and a half, five years. But it's never felt quite my own. The décor is what my former partner chose and I've been thinking, why am I still living with my ex's ghost?'

Perhaps he thinks the house is jinxed because it didn't work out between them. We agreed not to delve too deeply into our past relationships, mainly because of my break-up with Lee still being so raw.

'Were you two together for long?' I can't help but ask.

He shoots me a curious look as though he can't believe I've crossed a line, but still answers obligingly. 'A few years but we grew apart. I wanted to get married and have children, but she wasn't ready to settle down. She was ten years younger than me. It didn't matter to start with, but after three years I brought up the subject of getting engaged and trying for a baby, but she shut down the conversation straight away. I suppose you could say the age gap had started to show. By the following year, she'd moved out with my blessing to go travelling the world.' He sighs and caresses the tips of my fingers. 'I was heartbroken of course, but fifteen months later, you walked into my life. The only problem was that you were married.' His grimace morphs into a smile.

'Good thing I fell for you then, isn't it?' I say and swallow down the guilt. I'd been so pleased to get the job as Marc's PA at his property business, Venture Properties UK. He started the renovation company about two years ago. I thought it would be a bonus working at the same place as Lee, having the same boss, although Lee was often out inspecting sites while I was based in the office. But starting an affair with Marc was never on my agenda.

'It certainly is.' He grins, touching my cheek with the back of his hand. 'Anyway, I've made a big decision.'

'Oh really?' A fizz of adrenaline bolts through my body. Could he be about to propose? Part of me would be flattered beyond belief, but I'm not sure I'm ready for a commitment like that just yet. I squash the thought down. We've only been together a few months. There's no way he would be considering marriage so soon.

'Let's go in and I'll explain it to you over dinner.' He holds out his hand and I take it.

8

The waiter shows us straight to our table by a window in a corner. Marc orders a bottle of Champagne.

'Are we celebrating something?' I ask and look down at my phone, checking in case Jess or Alfie have texted me with any problems.

'I hope so,' Marc says, his pale blue eyes glinting in the candlelight. He glances at my phone and raises an eyebrow.

'Sorry. I wanted to make sure everything was okay, but there are no messages, so I promise I'll put it away.'

He blinks at me and smiles.

'Okay, I'll switch it to silent as well.' I click the little button on the side then drop it in my bag and zip it up. Annoyingly he's right. If I don't put it out of sight, I'll be distracted every five minutes and then I won't fully enjoy my meal or the evening. I slipped into some bad habits after Lee moved out. Eating ready meals by myself straight out of the plastic container while doom scrolling on my phone, after the kids had eaten their proper cooked dinner and gone to bed.

The waiter shows Marc the bottle and another installs a silver bucket filled with ice by the side of our small round table. This is a bit over the top, unless he *is* going to propose. I swallow, my mouth dry. It's too soon. I can't possibly say yes.

The waiter skilfully covers the cork with a cloth and removes it with the minimum of fuss. With a flourish, he pours the bubbles into two tall flute glasses and hands one first to me and then the other to Marc, before retreating.

'Here's to us.' Marc clinks his glass against mine. I tilt my head and look him straight in the eyes, hoping to glean what this is all about.

'We've been together what, seven months?' he says. 'But it feels more like I've always known you. Do you think perhaps we knew each other in a different life?'

'It's not possible, I'd have remembered you,' I giggle, 'but I do feel the same way. It's hard to believe we only got together in April. You were so easy to talk to and get along with right from the start.' I shake my head at how lucky I am.

'I'm glad you think so because I can't honestly picture my life without you in it,' he says, taking my hand in his, gazing into my eyes. 'It scares me to think of you not being around.' He swallows. 'I want to spend my life with you Vicki, which is why I've decided...'

He hesitates and I hold my breath, trying to control the fluttering in my stomach.

'I've decided, it's time to sell my house.'

Relief floods through me that he's not popped the question, but then his words sink in.

'What, why?' It's hard not to sound disappointed that he wants to sell up, so I quickly add, 'But it's such a beautiful home.' My secret daydream about the three of us moving into his gorgeous house and being the perfect family evaporates in an instant. I lean back and my hand slips away from his.

'It is but I've made my mind up, as soon as the repairs are finished, I'll be putting it on the market.'

'I don't understand. Where are you going to live?'

'The thing is...' He purses his lips, trying not to smile, but the dimples in his cheeks give him away. 'I'd like you to consider selling your house too.'

'What for?' I frown and half smile, trying to read his face, work out what his plan is.

He stifles a laugh, then quickly adds, 'Hear me out, please.' He raises his hands. 'I propose that we both sell our houses and put our funds into one pot to buy somewhere jointly – to be *our* new home – together. What do you say to living with me?' He lifts my fingers from the tablecloth with his warm hand and plants a gentle kiss on them.

My mouth opens and I sit there, stunned. What do I say? I did not see this coming at all. Instead of moving into his house with his décor and who knows what relationship ghosts, I'll get to help *choose* a new house with him, as well as the style, the wallpaper, flooring, curtains, and all those personal little finishing touches to make it uniquely our own. I picture the beautiful show homes I've seen in magazines, the sorts of places a lot of money can buy. Something I've always dreamed of.

But on the other hand, buying somewhere together is such a huge commitment. Do I know him well enough? And should I even assume we'll have a healthy budget from the sale of both our houses? He could have a huge mortgage for all I know. And the amount I'll have from my sale won't be very much. But it doesn't really matter what size the house is, we'd be able to make it special and a wonderful home for the children. It is very tempting, but I don't want to get ahead of myself.

'That would be... incredible.' I cup my hands across my mouth then let them drop. 'You don't think it's too soon, do you?' I can't help worrying how Bella and Alfie will react, no matter how much *I'd* like to live with Marc, they've not known him as long and they miss their dad.

'I don't think it's hasty, and anyway why waste time if we know it's right for us?' He leans towards me. 'We're not teenagers, we know our own minds.'

'I know, but after everything I've been through over the last year, all the issues I've had to face with Lee, I need to think about it. It's tempting to dive in, but I don't know if I feel quite ready to make such a huge leap.'

The waitress comes over and we agree to share a seafood starter. Once she's gone, I sip my drink, contemplating Marc's idea. He takes a large glug of his Champagne and finishes his glass.

'That's completely understandable, of course. But it will take months for both sales to go through and for us to find the right property. You can change your mind at any point. I suppose because I'm already staying at yours three, sometimes four, nights a week, it felt to me like a natural progression. But I'm sorry if you think I've overstepped the mark and let my heart run away with me.' He holds his hand to his chest.

'No, it's okay. It's lovely that you're thinking of our future together. And I enjoy it when you stay over. It's just taking a while to get used to and don't forget, it's not only me I have to think about, it's the kids too, their welfare and stability. It's hard not letting their dad see them until he gets his act together.'

'I understand, honestly, but don't you think they're a little bit used to me being around?'

'I suppose so. Maybe I'm worrying too much. But Lee owns half our house as well, so he'll probably object to the sale. He definitely won't be happy that you've practically moved in so he'll probably try to block it just to spite me.' I take a glug of my drink. 'And another thing, I'm not sure that once our house has sold I'd have enough funds to contribute to the sort of house you'd want. I doubt if it's worth anywhere near as much as yours. And I'm not expecting you to be okay with that.' I take another mouthful, wondering if I've been too frank, but I need to be upfront with him if this is going to work. This is a long way from the office romance it started out as, especially when it involves my children.

'Don't worry about the finances, please. It's not a problem for me. I get that you've had a difficult few years, but I want everything to be equal between us. What's mine is yours and all that.' He smiles and holds his glass up.

And what's yours is mine? A cynical voice in my head finishes the saying as I tap my glass against his. After the break-up, it's been hard to learn to trust again. The truth is, there isn't anything I have to offer Marc in comparison to his wealth, whatever he says to try and reassure me. He's sole owner of the successful property business where we work. I can't match that. I'm just his PA. I own half my house, minus a significant mortgage, and a crappy five-year-old VW T-Cross. That's it. If I ever *had* to sell and give Lee his half, I wouldn't be able to afford a big enough place on my own, not with two growing children. I need to make sure Marc really is fully aware of how little I'd be bringing to the table. Even when Lee was working and we both had good salaries, we had to watch how much we spent so we could afford holidays, Christmas and little extras.

'Here's to us and our future together in whatever form that takes.' Marc raises his glass for a third time and drinks a large glug, seemingly oblivious to the extent of my concerns.

'To us.' I take a sip, keeping my eyes on him.

Would he still be so keen to live with me if he found out what I'd done? I never intended to keep secrets from him, but this is different, isn't it? I vowed I was done with men telling me what to do, yet if I own up, he'll probably leave me, and I don't want that either. So I have to keep my mouth shut and hope that Jess does too.

9

JESS

Jess takes the contents out of the box and carefully follows the instructions.

Just as she's sitting on the side of the bath waiting for the result to develop, the doorbell rings. She springs up. Who the hell is that? The sudden noise is bound to wake the children. She chucks the test stick back in the box and zips it up in her bag then runs downstairs and drops the rucksack on the floor by the coats. Is this Olly again, or maybe Vicki and Marc are back early? But they must have a key between them and would not want to wake the children. She slows her pace. What if it's whoever was prowling around out the back?

The doorbell rings again and again, as if it's urgent. But she's not going to fall for that, so she nips into the living room and peeks round the curtain to see who's standing on the doorstep. She frowns. It's Livi, a girl from school. What's she doing here? She's one of the quietest and most hard-working students in her year, but they've never hung out. They often see each other in the corridors or in the library at break times, but that's it. She's standing sideways, gazing at the ground as though there's something weighing heavily on her shoulders. Jess opens the front door a couple of inches. The wind catches the door, but she holds it firm. Livi's strawberry-blonde hair, twisted up in a bun, is falling apart in the wind. She's wearing cropped jeans and a short leather jacket. When she sees Jess, she looks up, startled as though she didn't expect anyone to answer.

'Are you okay?' Jess asks, trying to look her in the eye but she's still standing sideways. Jess frowns.

'Not really,' she sniffs and pushes her glasses up her nose. Her head turns and there's a small graze on the side of her face.

Jess thinks of Vicki and what she would say to Livi. It's her house after all. 'Is there something I can help you with? How did you hurt your face?'

Livi shrugs.

Jess still isn't sure why she's here because they don't have all that much to do with each other at school.

'Is it Vicki you're here to see?' Jess crosses her arms.

Livi shakes her head.

'Me then? But how did you know I'd be here?'

There's no one at home to tell Livi she's at Vicki's if she went there first.

Livi hesitates and her eyes slide downwards, to the right.

'Lucky guess.' But these words aren't from Livi's mouth. Fran Higson said them. Livi steps back as Fran appears from the side of the porch, beaming, showing her perfect white teeth and signature pink lip gloss.

Jess's stomach seems to separate from the rest of her body. Fran has been bullying Jess in and out of school for most of the year. She frowns at Livi, wondering what she's doing hanging around with her. Livi pulls a pained expression as if to say she had no choice, then stares at the ground and sheepishly retreats.

'Aren't you pleased to see me?' Fran says, tossing her sleek golden hair over her shoulder.

'What do you want?' Jess asks, hoping the slight quiver in her voice is undetectable. She folds her arms and stays firmly on her side of the threshold, but shutting the door will mean taking a step back first and Fran may take advantage of that. If she'd checked out of the other living room window, she may have seen Fran hiding in the front garden.

'I just want a chat with you, that's all,' Fran says, holding her palms up and taking a step forward. Jess can't let her in because she's bound to cause trouble, although she seems calm enough right now. She's used the bookish Livi to put Jess off her guard.

'About what?' Jess tries to sound casual, but her mind is going over how they knew to find her here. Did Olly put something out on social media about her babysitting, or maybe he mentioned he'd be coming over to see her? But he rarely uses social media and he's not the type to try and cause her trouble deliberately.

'To sort things out between us. Nothing to worry about.' Fran looks beyond Jess, down the hall. Livi tries to swallow but struggles to, as though her throat is too dry. Jess detects a glint of fear in her eyes.

'It's not my house, sorry.' Jess steps back to swing the door shut, but in that split second Fran raises a fist in the air and shouts over her shoulder, 'Let's go!' And with that, she marches straight towards Jess, pushing her out of the way as she enters Vicki's house, quickly followed by a group of kids from her school who appear from both sides of the front garden. In a unified cheer they stream into the house, tight fists held high above their heads.

'What are you doing? You can't come in,' Jess shouts, pushed back against the coats behind the door, but they ignore her and stomp right past.

10

'You need to leave right now or I'm going to call the police,' Jess says, but no one appears to be listening to her. There must be twenty or more kids from her year and above in the house, a few of whom she recognises. The ones in the kitchen are taking food out of the fridge, and someone has switched the oven on. The others are in the living room, lounging all over the sofa and on cushions tossed onto the carpet. Hip-hop starts blaring out of the Bluetooth speaker.

Fran spins round, grinning at her. 'They won't do anything; we'll just say you invited us, then you'll be the one in trouble.' Fran says it in such a blasé way that Jess can feel her face heat up with rage.

'We'd be gone by the time they got here anyway. Make you look very stupid.' Fran elongates the word 'very', then she abruptly turns her back on her. Jess stomps down the hall, grabs her rucksack and darts upstairs. How the hell can she make them leave? She's going to have to let Vicki know. Alfie and Bella must be awake by now with all the noise. Bella will be scared and wondering if *she* invited all these people and Alfie is bound to tell his mum word for word what happened. She needs to make sure they're okay. It's her job to keep them safe but she's failing miserably.

And in the middle of all this chaos, she needs to find out the result of the pregnancy test, although a big part of her doesn't want to know.

Upstairs, Jess finds Bella on Vicki's bed, huddled under a blanket.

'Are you okay?' she asks. Bella nods, her thumb in her mouth. Jess dips her head around Alfie's bedroom door. He's sitting at his computer.

'Why aren't you in bed?' she asks.

He gives a start and grunts a reply that sounds like a swear word. She can't see the screen but guesses he's watching a YouTube video because he's not on his Xbox.

'Come into your mum's room, please.' Jess doesn't wait for an answer and nips back to Bella. Alfie swears more distinctly and follows her.

'What?' He glares at Jess.

'Sit there and no more swearing.' Jess points to the bed.

'Can't tell me what to do.' He drops down on his side next to Bella.

'Actually, I can.'

'Who are all those people downstairs?' Bella says in a tiny high-pitched voice, the blanket pulled up to her chin.

'Mum didn't tell us you were having people round,' Alfie says in a narky tone. He probably can't wait to snitch on her to Vicki. He resents being kept out of the loop because he doesn't think he's a child.

'I didn't invite them; they forced their way in.' Jess sits at the end of the bed. She always tries to be truthful with them because she remembers what it's like to be their age, wondering at some of the things adults get up to. But she doesn't want to tell them Fran has been bullying her at school. She's ashamed of letting someone dominate her and she's aware it might make Bella worry that it could happen to her too. As for Alfie, she doesn't want to lose face in front of him or lose the low level of authority she has over him.

'Shouldn't you call Mum or the police?' Alfie says in a sarcastic tone.

'Don't worry, I've told them I will if they don't leave.' If Vicki turned up now, Jess would lose her job and she'd never forgive her for putting her children in danger.

'If you won't do it, I will,' Alfie says. He will do anything to try and get his phone back. Jess is tempted to take it out of the rucksack and chuck it on the bed, but she needs to deal with this herself, show she's in charge.

'It's okay, I'm dealing with it. I don't want to make things worse, and I don't want to worry your mum. If these people hear police sirens, they might start deliberately breaking things. I'm going to go back down in a minute and if you hear things starting to escalate, then yes, I want you to get your phone from my rucksack and call for help.'

Alfie rolls his eyes.

Jess is going to be in so much trouble as it is with the mess they're making. Vicki will be disappointed in her and when word gets round, no one will want to use her babysitting services again.

She carries her bag into the bathroom and shuts the door. Her mobile is almost out of charge. Her stomach tightens. Perhaps she should call Vicki now, tell her what's happened. But she'll be so angry with her for ruining her big night out. And she'll be furious that she let a bunch of teenagers rampage through her house.

She needs to do the right thing. She taps on Vicki's number. After a few rings the answer phone kicks in, so she leaves a message for Vicki to call her back as soon as she can.

Now what? She's still stuck with twenty teenagers taking over the house. It could be ages before Vicki replies. Olly will know what to do. She sends him a text telling him what's happened and to please come and help her.

While she's waiting for him to reply, she pulls the box out of her bag but doesn't open it. She can't bear to take it out and look. What if it's positive? Her whole world will come crashing down. Everyone will know what she did. Worst of all she'll have to tell Olly, and she knows just how devastated he will be.

11

Jess chucks the box back in her bag. Maybe it's still developing anyway. There's no time to wait around for a reply from Olly, she needs to go back downstairs and try and persuade Fran and her gang to leave. Music is thumping loudly, making the floor vibrate. If only her mum or dad were in. They'd come straight over and sort this lot out.

At the bottom of the stairs, she zips up her rucksack and dumps it at the back of a pile of shoes under the coat rack. She'll look at the test result later.

Pushing through the people hanging out in the hallway, she's confused by the annoyed looks they give her interrupting their snogging or deep conversations, like she's the stranger here not them. There seem to be more people here than there were when she went upstairs.

'There she is,' Fran shouts when she sees Jess. Jess's stomach flips over at the sight of Sean next to her. What is he doing here? He's the most popular boy at school and she's had a secret crush on him for months. He smiles at her in that seductive Timothée Chalamet way he has about him. Her breathing becomes rapid and she tries to tell herself it's because she's just run downstairs. Does she look a mess? She should have checked herself in the bathroom mirror. He's going to think she's so uncool making them all leave, but she doesn't have a choice.

'You and your friends really need to go now,' she says to Fran. She strides straight over to the Bluetooth speaker and switches the music off. When she turns around to the room, everyone has stopped what they are doing to stare at her.

'Don't be so hasty, Jess. I'm sure you like a party as much as we do,' Sean says, touching her arm, setting off fireworks all over her body. A ball of guilt tightens in her stomach. She never meant to be attracted to him, but she can't seem to control how her body reacts when he's around, and what makes it worse is he's been pursuing her for weeks.

'There are two children upstairs who are frightened. This is not my house so I can't let you stay.'

'Bring them down so they can join in,' Sean says, flicking his dark fringe.

'Yeah come on, they might enjoy it.' Fran laughs.

'I don't think so,' Jess says, watching someone rolling a joint on the coffee table.

'Okay but before we go, I thought we'd have a bit of fun, although some of the guys don't think you'll be up for it.' Fran claps her hands, playing to her audience.

'Up for what?' Jess tries not to be distracted by Sean blatantly gazing up and down at her body.

'I know you like to have a laugh.' Fran prods Jess in the side with her long pink acrylic nails.

'Don't let me down now, will you?' Sean eyes her from under his fringe.

'What are you talking about?' Jess is finding it hard to know where to look with everyone watching her. She crosses her arms, suddenly aware that the whole room is lined with people.

'We want you to make a reel for our socials. You'll do that for us, won't you?' he asks. Fran clicks her fingers once and grins at everyone.

'Bring me a chair,' Fran commands and a lanky boy carries one of the chairs in from Vicki's dining room.

'What? No!' Jess cries. How can Sean be involved in one of Fran's sick games? He should be stopping the bullying if he has any feelings for her.

'Scarf,' Fran says, holding out her palm. A girl with light brown hair smacks a red silk scarf in Fran's hand. Jess recognises it as one of Vicki's. Fran goes to tie the scarf around Jess's eyes, but Jess holds a hand in front of her face.

'You're not blindfolding me.' Jess steps back, right into two boys who look like they're from the year above hers. They shove her into the chair, and everyone claps and whistles.

'What are you going to do?' Jess cries and immediately kicks herself for showing how scared she is.

Fran pulls Jess's head back by her hair and runs a finger across her throat. Jess gurgles a scream. She thinks of the children upstairs and hopes they don't hear what's going on down here.

'We'll start with a taste test challenge,' Fran says. The lanky boy covers Jess's eyes with the scarf and starts to tie it.

'Stop!' Jess cries.

'Okay, fair enough, take the scarf off her,' Fran says in a matter-of-fact voice, and Jess lets out a sigh of relief as it's untied and pulled away from her eyes.

'Let's get one of those little kiddies down instead.' Fran waves her hand at one of the boys nearest the door.

'No, you can't do that,' Jess screeches and tries to stand up but a hand from behind pushes her down again.

It's already too late. Within minutes Alfie is being frogmarched down the stairs.

Sean fist-pumps him as he comes into the room. 'Hey buddy, wanna hang out with me?'

Alfie nods, then shrugs, trying to be cool.

'If you do as I say, you and I could be mates,' Sean says to him but winks slyly at Jess.

'Don't believe him, Alfie, he doesn't want to be your friend,' Jess cries. Alfie frowns and Sean points to a chair for him to sit in.

Fran swings round to face Jess, mock concern on her face. 'So, the choice is yours. You or him.' She grins.

12

VICKI

'How about this then,' Marc says over the seafood starter, 'I move into your place for a few months to see how we get on before committing to buying a house together?' He tears a mussel from its shell and eats it whole.

'Hmm, that could work.' I try to elegantly peel a huge prawn and not flick juice all over my new dress. I don't look up straight away because I'm not keen on being put on the spot.

'I'd pay you rent, of course. And contribute to the bills and so on. You could view me as the lodger if you wanted to, if it feels too much too soon. But you'd be helping me out, because I need to find somewhere to stay now the house refurb has started.' He rips a tentacle off a chargrilled baby octopus and stuffs it into his mouth. 'And if you ever felt you needed your space back or just wanted me to leave, you only have to say, it wouldn't be a problem. I can easily move to a hotel.'

I put my fork down and look at him, genuinely puzzled at his suggestion. It's not what I was expecting, but it could be the perfect solution for both of us. He must have sensed I didn't want to commit to selling up right now. Besides, I have a strong feeling Lee would block a sale as much as he could. He still can't accept that we're not together and he's sure to complain about Marc moving into 'his house' with 'his children' too, and could create all sorts of problems for us.

'I'd need to run it past the children first, and probably Lee as well if I'm honest.' I wince, not expecting a good reaction to that. 'It's still technically half his property and they're his kids too.' I hesitate. 'I've not mentioned to him that you stay over as much as you do because I have a strong feeling he wouldn't like it at all.' I wince again, imagining Lee's reaction if he found out.

'Yeah, of course. I understand. I wouldn't expect anything less from him.' Marc averts his eyes and dips his fingers in the bowl of lemon water. He wipes his fingers on his napkin and lets out a sigh as he puts it down next to him, clearly a little pissed off.

'But on the upside, the children seem to really like you, so I think they'll give you the thumbs up.' I smile, hoping it will make him feel a little less rejected.

'They're fantastic kids. A real credit to you considering the difficult circumstances you've had to deal with.'

'Thank you.' I glance down and catch sight of my handbag at my feet. I'm itching to check my phone for messages; Jess will have taken Alfie's away by now and be busy doing her revision.

'Just to warn you, if I were to move in soon, I'd need to pop back to mine every day for a while because Milly had puppies a couple of weeks ago.' He grins widely at me.

'Really? That's lovely. Are they all doing okay?' I thought his little spaniel would make a lovely pet for the children, but I hadn't realised he was going to breed her.

'Yeah they're all good, thanks. I've already sold two of them to neighbours, but the earliest they can leave their mum is eight weeks.'

'Are they okay on their own while you're at work?' I frown.

'Yeah, they're still being fed by their mum for now and won't start weaning for another week or two. My old gardener says he'll pop in and feed them when they're ready. He checks on them for me most days. He's got a key to my side gate anyway. I've made a bed for Milly in the summer house at the bottom of the garden and there's a dog flap in the door for her to get in and out.'

'That's good. I'd love to see them when they're a bit older. Bella would love that too, but I won't mention them for now otherwise she won't stop pestering us about it.' We laugh and Marc tears off the last piece of bread.

He glances up at me before he speaks. 'Look, like I said, if it makes it any easier, I could sleep in a separate room so you can tell the kids I'm the lodger.'

It's sweet of him to be so thoughtful. It just makes me like him even more.

'There wouldn't be any need for that, they know you're my... boyfriend.' I smile. 'Anyway, it's not that I don't want you there, it's just a little tricky.' It sounds odd to me calling anyone my boyfriend after fifteen years of having a husband.

'Because of Lee?' He tips his head forward an inch and sighs again.

I nod.

'It's hardly your fault though. It's him. I could have a quiet word if you want. Tell him not to be such a dick.'

'I'm not sure that's a good idea after everything that's happened between the three of us.' I pick up a prawn and peel the shell off.

'Fair enough, but at some point he has to accept that your life has moved on. That he's not the centre of your universe any more.' His eyes crease as he tries to contain his frustration.

'I will talk to him about it, I promise. And for the record, I would like you to move in, but I need a bit longer to get used to the idea.' A crackle of excitement runs through me. Does this mean I'm in love?

'That's fair. It makes me want to pick you up and twirl you around.' He takes my hand and kisses it then gently rubs his thumb in a tiny circle across my palm, sending a tingling feeling all over my body. Lee did something similar once when we first got together. I sigh. Maybe one day I'll stop referring everything back to my life with Lee. But we were together for so long, it's hard not to. My brain is hard-wired to memories with him. Marc is slowly waving a hand in front of my face.

'Oh sorry, I was miles away.' I shake my head and my face flushes.

'It's okay, I was just saying that it's a shame Lee has taken this dark turn. He was considered a highly valuable member of the team.' He picks at the bed of fleshy peeled cold-water prawns with his manicured fingers, dropping one after another into his mouth.

'To be fair to him, I'd never known him to blur the lines between work and recreational drugs before, so it was a shock when Belinda found that baggie in his drawer,' I say.

'I know what you mean. I was as gobsmacked as everyone else. I wasn't aware he was into that kind of thing out of hours let alone during work time. He hid it well I'll give him that. But I guess things were getting bad at home?'

I nod, not wanting to say too much about it.

'The whole episode is heartbreaking really. I had him down for promotion at one point.' He shakes his head slowly.

'Really? I didn't know that. I feel there should have been a proper investigation because he denied ever having taken drugs into work and honestly if he had, he's the sort of person who would have just held his hands up and admitted it.' The shameful moment Lee was frogmarched from the office premises replays in my head for the hundredth time. I could barely watch him protesting, looking at me, appealing for my help, saying out loud what a stitch up it was.

'Isn't it the drugs talking though? They make you lie and do things out of character because you're so desperate to get that next fix. And maybe he thought he'd be able to hang onto his job if he outright denied it, because he knew the rules – instant dismissal. Don't forget that little detail.' He blinks at me.

'Ultimately, it's all because of us though, isn't it? We drove him to it. His smoking wasn't out of control until we got together. It was only ever recreational, occasional. I feel desperately guilty about that.'

'You shouldn't. And I've said before, don't listen to the office gossips. Other people's lives are like a soap opera to them. It'll be someone else next month. Anyway, you and Lee were heading for the rocks already from what you've told me. So no one is to blame. We met. We hit it off. That's it. If you'd been in a happy, stable marriage you'd never have looked my way. It's not your fault or mine that Lee decided to smoke weed, then bring it to work so he could have a sneaky spliff at lunchtime or whatever he was planning to do with it. He could have been dealing for all we know.'

'It just feels a little unfair.'

'Um, how exactly?'

'If pints of beer were his poison, no one would have taken any notice.'

'They would, but they're not illegal.' Marc shrugs and refills our glasses.

'Which is why it's so harsh that he lost his job over it. It's not like he was smoking it in the middle of the office.'

'I couldn't bend the rules for him even if I'd wanted to, otherwise others would expect the same treatment.'

'I know, and I don't mean to stick up for him because you know how much I despise drugs. It's just so frustrating having to deal with his addiction and practically parent the children on my own. I shouldn't be the only one paying the mortgage, bills and a babysitter on top of it all.'

'Which is why, if I moved in, I could look after them for you once in a while, if you wanted me to.'

I purse my lips, weighing up the pros and cons.

'You could go out with the girls or pop over to your mums on your own. Have a bit of freedom. When was the last time you had that?'

'I can't remember.'

Marc digs into a half side of lobster and pulls out a solid piece of white flesh. He holds it out for me, and I seductively slide it off his fork.

Much as I like and trust Jess, they'd be so much better off spending time with a dad who was completely there for them. Then Marc and I could go off for weekends away, maybe even exotic holidays – he's shown me his friend's yacht he sailed around the Med in last summer. It would be amazing to go with him next year. Perhaps I should let him move in, see how we get on living together *and* going on holiday before we commit to buying a house jointly.

'Look, as long as the kids are okay with you moving in, we could trial it for a month, see how it goes.'

His eyes light up and he reaches across the table for my hand. 'Fantastic, if you're absolutely sure?'

'Yeah, why not?'

No doubt Lee would tell me I'd be making the biggest mistake of my life.

Well, it's my life, my choice, I'd say to that.

13

JESS

After playing three so-called games which were pure torture for Jess, she escapes to the kitchen and pours herself a glass of tap water, downing it in one. She has never been so humiliated. And in front of Alfie and the kids from school too. She cringes at him witnessing all the gross things Fran made her do. Sean was filming every second and has already posted up her licking the cat bowl on social media. Showing his true colours – what a two-faced creep.

Fran took Alfie's phone off him and saw he'd been texting Vicki, pleading for her to come home, so Fran texted her too, pretending to be Alfie and saying everything was okay. Surely, Vicki will think that's odd. Hopefully she's already on her way. How else can Jess make everyone leave? And where's Olly? She hoped he'd come and save her. All she wants to do right now is hide away in a dark corner and cry.

As she puts the glass on the draining board, something resembling a person catches her eye out of the window. She leans across the sink and stares beyond the flooded patio, half-lit in the moon's eerie glow. The storm has picked up. The trees are swaying, and the swing is jangling around, but there's no one there.

She needs to get back to check Alfie isn't being corrupted any further by Sean and Fran, but as she turns, the back door starts to open. Her body jolts. She's certain she locked it. One of Fran's lot must have gone out for a smoke. But the door swings wide and a man in a black hoodie and mask bursts in. Jess shrieks and leaps backwards. His dark menacing eyes squint at her through tiny slits. He makes a grunting sound as he waves a bent metal bar at her. Jess gasps and raises her hands, trembling all over.

'What do you want?' she says in a strange out-of-body voice.

The man indicates with the bar for her to move towards the hallway. Her whole body is shaking violently now as she opens the door and slowly steps out of the kitchen, the man following close behind her. Jess leads him into the living room like she's walking to her fate and he's the executioner. Then she stands aside so he can see everyone, and they collectively gasp at the sight of this masked man dressed in black. The girls start screaming at the sight of him, waving a metal bar above his head.

He yells, 'Get out of here now, the lot of you!' His deep booming voice fills the room. Alfie screws his eyes shut and clamps his hands over his ears at the noise of people screaming all around them. Jess makes a beeline for him to move him out of the way.

'What the fuck?' Fran yells and is one of the first to head for the front door. She gives one last look at Jess and Alfie, digs in her pocket and tosses his phone at him. It lands at his feet. The phone lights up with a message on the screen. Alfie crouches down and picks it up, trying to read it at the same time. Jess wants to see who it's from but she's too busy directing him to stand behind her, trying to keep him safe. Inch by inch, she moves them backwards towards one of the full-length curtains and they hide behind it, hopefully unnoticed.

Through a tiny gap Jess watches the man chase everyone out of the front door, the bar raised high above his head. He continues to roar at the few remaining kids who are running in and out of the kitchen grabbing drinks to take, and makes them drop the bottles of beer, then watches them run for their lives out of the house.

Jess backs up further behind the living room curtain and stands beside Alfie, whispering to him to stay still and silent. She hopes Bella is hidden under the duvet upstairs and doesn't move. Hopefully she's still listening to *Paddington Bear* on her headphones or has fallen asleep. If Bella wasn't here, Jess would have fled the house with Alfie, run down the street with the rest of them. But she's paid to keep both children safe; they're her responsibility. She never imagined she'd ever be in a life-or-death situation. She won't leave either of them alone in the house with this maniac. What the hell does he want? She shivers all over. He must be the one who tried to get in the back door earlier, which means he's been stalking around the premises all evening. She's seen plenty of horror movies to know what could happen next, but she can't let herself think too hard about what he might do to them. She needs to focus and stay strong for Alfie and Bella, *and* herself.

The front door slams shut after the last teenager has left. She holds her breath, not daring to move because she can't tell which direction he's moving in. Then his coat swishes past the coffee table. Right in front of them.

A chilling dread creeps up her throat; he knows exactly where they're hiding.

14

VICKI

I'm not sure if I've upset Marc with my indecisiveness. Was he hoping I'd be more excited about the idea of living together? A large part of me is, but I'm also in two minds about having a man in the house again, giving up my freedom. Perhaps I should have sounded more grateful for his suggestion that he move in and essentially be my lodger because I could certainly do with the extra money. Lee hasn't paid me any child support for weeks.

While Marc is in the bathroom, I reach in my bag for my phone to check everything is okay at home and to message Lee. I need to arrange a time to speak to him about when he intends to pay me and gauge how he feels about the house being sold. Maybe it would benefit him too to have a lump sum. It could help him get back on his feet. I'm not sure where he's living, he hasn't told me, but he's probably sofa-surfing at various friends' houses if they'll have him in his drugged-up state.

I tap my screen and several missed calls register. One from Jess and five from Alfie. There are texts from him too: *People here making trouble, come home please!* And another one a few minutes later: *Don't worry, Mum, all gone now.* How odd.

'Sorry, but I need to call home,' I say to Marc when he returns to the table. I move my chair back. 'I've had a strange message from Alfie and several missed calls.'

'Can it wait? The main course will be here any minute,' Marc says as I stand up.

'I'll be two seconds, I promise.' Not waiting for his answer, I dash out to the privacy of the porch and dial Alfie's number. It tells me his phone is switched off and my call goes straight to his answer phone. What could have happened? Does this mean everything is okay and he's gone to bed? I dial Jess's number, but it rings out then goes to her answering service.

'Jess, what's going on? I saw you tried to phone me and I've received two strange texts from Alfie and several missed calls. Has something happened? Are you all okay? Please call me back as soon as you receive this. Thank you.'

I slope back to the table, not sure what to think. If it was up to me, I'd go home right now, but the main meal is on the table and Marc is patiently waiting to start eating.

'Don't wait for me, you tuck in,' I tell him as I sit down.

'Are you sure? Everything okay at home?' He digs his fork into the rare steak and cuts a slice of essentially raw flesh with the serrated knife. I look away, nauseous with worry. How can I even eat?

'I'm not sure. Something isn't right.' I stare down at my lasagne still bubbling in the terracotta dish.

I leave my phone beside me even though Marc won't approve of it being on the table. I wish I hadn't switched it to silent in the first place. I understand his not wanting us to be interrupted, but when you have children and you're away from them, it's never that straightforward. And now something has happened that they needed to contact me about, and I wasn't there to answer let alone help them. I hope they are okay. I trust Jess to look after them, but all I want to do right now is go straight home. My appetite has completely vanished, my stomach a tight ball of anxiety. But I'm going to have to try and eat some of it. Marc hates waste, especially food. He doesn't have children so I can't expect him to understand.

'That looks too hot,' he says, pointing at my sizzling dish with his fork.

'I'll have to let it cool a bit more.' I put my fork down and glance at my phone.

'What's wrong then, didn't they say?'

'Just some cryptic message from Alfie about people being there causing trouble, then another one shortly after saying they'd gone. Who do you think they mean?'

'I don't know. Perhaps Jess opened the door to a cold caller or maybe it was something to do with what was going on outside earlier? You said there were some kids hanging around at the top of the street.'

I clench my teeth. 'God, I hope it's not. I should really go home and find out what was wrong, make sure they're safe.'

'You need to eat first. They'll be fine with Jess, she's trustworthy, isn't she?'

I nod.

'There you are then. And they said whoever it was had gone. You deserve to enjoy your meal,' he says, stuffing another overloaded fork of steak and chips into his mouth.

'I can't. I feel sick.' I rub my hand over my brow but the disappointment on his face makes me pick up my fork.

'You're not... are you?' He grins, pointing to his stomach, then mine.

'No, of course not,' I snap. Is that seriously all he can think of when I'm worried about my children? My face is burning as I dig into the soft texture of the pasta and layers of oily meat smothered in bechamel. The smell of melted cheese and the rich sauce brings on the nausea even more, but I manage to put a tiny mouthful of food in my mouth.

As usual Marc finishes his food long before I do which makes it even more obvious how slow I am. I eat a few more tiny mouthfuls from around the edge, forcing myself to swallow them. I just want to go home.

'Shall we have coffee?' he says gently, when I finally give up and push my plate away.

'I'm sorry, I need to try Jess's phone again. She's still not replied.'

'At least have a small coffee?'

'Okay, if you want to.' I pull up Jess's number.

'We don't get that much time alone without the kids.'

I stare at his face but he's not joking. He really means it. I didn't know he felt like that. I thought he was on board with having my children in his life. He seemed excited about it as he doesn't have any of his own. He even hinted that he'd like us to have at least one together. How can I let him move in if he feels like this? While Marc calls the waiter over to order coffees, I tap Jess's number again. It rings, but then it goes to her answer phone. Why wouldn't she have checked by now? She usually keeps it with her when she babysits for me, and we often exchange little comments or emojis to let each other know how our evenings are going. The first date I went on with Marc was nerve-racking and I texted her a couple of times when I went to the loo, then when he did, sending a thumbs up and a love heart emoji to let her know it was going well. Perhaps I am worrying about nothing, and she's let the children stay up later because they're watching another film? But Jess is the sort of girl who'd have checked with me first to see if that's okay. No, something doesn't feel right.

'I want to go now. I'm worried. Something just isn't right,' I say as soon as the coffees arrive. I stand up and start pulling my coat on and turn towards the main door. It sounds windy outside. I hadn't noticed how much until now.

'That's fine, I'll go and pay.' Marc grabs his jacket off the back of the chair. He looks hurt but I can't help that he's upset. My children are more important to me than anything. If he can't understand and accept that, then this isn't going to last. I go and stand in the porch and try Jess's phone again, willing her to pick up this time. It rings and rings and once again the answer phone kicks in. I plead with her to call me. Then I say the same to her on text.

When I've finished, I peer out of the porch windows at the gusty wind and driving rain. It wasn't this bad when we arrived. It must have rained heavily in the hour we've been here because there's water gushing down the pavement. A man trudges past, leaning forward at an angle, shoulders hunched, ploughing through the deep water.

I check my phone. Still nothing. My stomach twists into a tight knot. Now I'm convinced something is wrong otherwise Jess would have phoned me back by now. She knows how much I worry about the children when I'm away from them, especially since I broke up with Lee. It's not like her to ignore my messages.

But I don't know how we're going to get home quickly in this weather.

15

JESS

The man in the hoodie yanks back the curtain and looks down at Jess and Alfie with hard dark eyes through the narrow slit in his face mask. Jess draws in a breath and holds it. The light sound of footsteps on the landing makes them all look up. Jess wants to cry out to tell Bella to hush, to go back to her mummy's room and hide, but she comes to the top of the stairs and stops.

Jess can't bear Bella putting herself in danger like this, so she runs past the man to the bottom of the stairs and waves her hands at her.

'Go and hide, please!' Jess shouts, but Bella doesn't move, gripping the banister with both hands. Jess jumps at a touch of her arm. She spins round to face the man, glancing down at the tube of metal he's holding, fearing this is the end of her, he's about to attack her. But instead, he chucks it on the sofa. Jess steals a look up at Bella again and tries to shoo her away. Alfie cracks a strange laugh, probably nervous of what the man will do, but when she swings back to speak to him, the man is back over by the curtains and has his arm around Alfie's head in an armlock.

'Get your hands off him,' Jess shouts and takes a running kick at his ankle. The man yelps, loosens his hold on Alfie and swipes to catch Jess's leg but misses. To her surprise, he laughs as he stumbles forwards. Once he's steadied himself, he pulls the mask down beneath his bearded chin then throws the hood of his sweatshirt back. He ruffles Alfie's hair. Jess frowns, confused.

'Daddy!' Bella cries, her face instantly brighter as she runs downstairs.

'Lee?' Jess examines his face. 'I... I didn't recognise you.'

'You'd better not say a word about this to Vicki.' He frowns at her.

'Okay...' But she can't keep this from her. Vicki would go mad if she knew he was here. It's been months since the split and the last time Jess saw Lee he was wearing a suit and his hair was cropped short. She's never known him to have a beard before or look so rough. Her mind immediately lands on the secret she's keeping for Vicki, and she can't look him in the eye. He didn't seem like a bad person to her until everything came out about what he did at work.

'Thanks for driving the intruders away,' Jess says, trying to lighten the mood again. He's putting her in an impossible position asking her to lie and she won't do it.

'It's still my house too. Little bastards coming in here pushing all of you around. Yeah, I quite enjoyed scaring them off.' He lifts his chin so his jaw juts out. Alfie grins up at his dad, his eyes fixed on him, full of admiration.

'How did you know they were here?' Jess asks him and looks directly at Alfie, who immediately averts his eyes and tries to brush away a grin with his fist.

'Don't go blaming him,' Lee says. 'The situation was out of control. I'm not blaming you either. It's Vicki's fault. You shouldn't have been left with such a huge responsibility. An adult should have been here. Alfie was merely calling me for help.'

'But Fran checked his phone; how did she not see your message?'

'We used Snapchat, so there's no trace. Look, Vicki wasn't answering her phone, and the kids haven't seen me for over a month, which is not their choice or mine. I couldn't *not* come.'

Jess nods. Thank God he did. It's hard enough when Fran and her mates are bullying Jess at school, but in front of a crowd, and Alfie? It's embarrassing and unforgivable.

'It's been hard on them as well as me,' Lee says, hugging Bella to his side. Her arms are wrapped around him as far as they can reach. She looks up at his hairy face adoringly with her big brown eyes. He brushes her cheeks with his thumb, and it sinks in how much they've missed each other and how different he looks because of how run down he is. No wonder she didn't recognise him straight away. Sore red patches cover his cheeks on his otherwise pale grey skin. His hair has grown long and wiry, and it's a lot whiter. She wonders where he's been sleeping because he doesn't exactly smell fresh.

'You know you shouldn't be here though,' Jess says gently, not wanting to be the one to lay down the law. He owns half this house but has lost his job; how is he even getting by?

'I just want to see my kids, Jess.' His eyes squint as he speaks, emphasising the lines and dark circles. He doesn't look like he's slept for days.

Jess is about to say she can't let him, but stops and exhales a breath instead. She remembers something Olly said about him after he came back from work experience, what a good bloke he was and that he hadn't deserved to lose his job. She'd asked him what he meant, but he wouldn't say.

'You can let me stay with them for a little while can't you, just so we can catch up?'

'Please,' Alfie and Bella say at the same time. She suddenly sees them as the close family they were before the split, and the younger Alfie, before the backchat and rudeness of teenage-hood crept in, and she wonders if all his bravado is covering up the pain of not having his dad around.

'I suppose so.' Jess wonders if this visit was planned between him and Alfie long before Fran and the others arrived. 'I mean, I'm going to be in so much trouble already.' Jess's eyes scan the room, at things tipped over, cushions in places they're not meant to be, and empty drinks left on the floor and table. 'Vicki's going to go ballistic, but you did get rid of them and I'm grateful, even though you scared the shit out of me.' Jess doesn't have much choice. She can't exactly kick him out of his own house. 'Could you give me a hand clearing up this mess?'

'Yes, we can,' the children chant in unison, and Lee nods.

'Come on then,' he says and starts by straightening the sofa and chairs in the living room while Bella plumps up the cushions. Jess takes Alfie aside, gently holding his wrist. He shakes her off.

'Fran said you texted your mum. Has she replied yet?' She holds her hand out for his phone.

His eyes dart about. He's clearly contemplating lying but Lee intervenes.

'Let her do her job and check your phone, son.'

Alfie slaps his mobile in her hand. She checks through his message list and reads the text Fran read out to everyone, and the reply she sent pretending to be Alfie. It clearly didn't fool Vicki because there's a missed call from her about twenty minutes ago. Jess closes all the open apps and is surprised at a video Alfie's been watching on YouTube. She frowns at him. He blushes as she hands the phone back. It's not something she's willing to cover up for him. She glances at Lee who has his back to them. Alfie shakes his head, pleading with his eyes for her to stay silent. But Vicki would want to know.

There are missed calls on her own phone, so Jess texts her back saying everything's fine, and apologising for not picking up her message earlier, but she fell asleep on the sofa. She won't call her about Lee being here because she hates lying to her and doesn't want to lose this gig while she's getting her online work off the ground.

Vicki doesn't reply so it must mean they're on their way home. They'd better get a move on clearing up because otherwise she's going to find out what really happened here. And worse still, Vicki will know she let Lee in.

16

VICKI

Marc queues for what seems like forever at the till. 'How are we going to get home?' I ask when he comes back to the table. We watch through the window at the river of rain sweeping past the door.

'Shit. That's a lot of rainfall in a short space of time. You stay here. I'll walk up and get the car and drive to the door.'

'Are you sure? Are we going to be able to drive in this?'

'We need to get a move on before it gets any worse.' He pulls on his coat and takes a baseball cap out of his inside pocket.

Marc opens the main door but the wind catches it clean out of his hand and forces him back. He pushes forward, head down and steps outside. I try to help him shut the door, but it whips out of my fingers and closes with a bang. Sheets of rain swirl around him as he battles against the wind; his cap is plucked off his head and blows away into the darkness. I watch until he turns the corner and heads up the street out of sight.

I check my phone. My battery is getting low. I'll have to charge it in the car. Still no reply from Jess. Nausea curdles my stomach with the memory of the rich lasagne smell.

I text Alfie's phone in the hope that because Jess will be looking after it while he's in bed, she might notice a message. But there's no reply. It's been delivered but not read.

I stamp my feet. It's cold standing here in the glass box of a porch with no radiator. I call Jess's mum's phone, but it's switched off. They're probably still in the Comedy Store so won't be able to look at their phones until the interval.

A couple of cars drive slowly past with the water high on their wheels, windscreen wipers on their fastest setting. Behind them, Marc's car creeps around the corner and stops outside the restaurant. I flip my hood over my head and open the door, bracing myself as I step onto the pavement. A gust of wind sweeps swirling rain around me, blowing my hood off my head. My strappy heeled shoes sinking under water. I so wish I'd worn boots. I bite my lip and wade towards the car. My phone lights up in my hand and I can't help but glance at it. At last Alfie has read my message. I try to press the call button as I step forward, reaching for the car door with my other hand, but my foot slips from under me and I fall backwards onto the pavement with a heavy thud.

Marc jumps out of the car and wades through the rain to reach me lying flat out. He crouches down and looks me squarely in the eyes.

'Are you okay?' he asks, frowning. I gaze up at him and close my eyelids then open them again in reply.

'Anything broken?' Marc asks as he helps me to sit up.

'I don't think so. Oh no, where's my phone gone?' I hold up my empty palm.

'Shit.'

'It was in my right hand. I must have dropped it as I fell.'

We both scrabble about in the rain searching for it. It could have washed away by now and be heading for a drain. And if it's not, will it still work?

'There it is,' Marc shouts, pointing under his car. My phone has lit up almost halfway under the chassis. He lays down on his front and stretches his arm as far as he can with the tips of his fingers, just reaching it.

'Thank God.' I take it from him and try to wipe the rain away. 'It's still working and there's a message from Jess.'

Marc pulls me up to standing and opens the passenger door. I'm soaked through and start to shiver. He pulls a blanket from the back seat and lays it across my lap.

'What does she say? Everything alright?' he asks.

'Yes, says nothing to worry about, she fell asleep. Thank goodness.' Relief spreads through me.

'I told you they'd be okay.' Marc jumps in the driver's side of the car and starts the engine. I'm grateful for the warm blast of air from the fans straight onto my face.

We set off but as I'm in the middle of replying, my phone dies.

'Oh no. The water must have got in it after all. I'll have to try sitting it in rice to dry it out.'

Marc's phone lights up with a notification on the screen in the console between us. I can't quite see what it's for, but two seconds later it lights up again. He glances down then snatches it up and switches it off. I didn't recognise the logo next to the message. I'm guessing it's from social media or one of the selling sites he likes browsing.

Marc turns the windscreen wipers on to maximum, but the rain is coming down so hard and fast, it doesn't help visibility.

We're not far up the road before we hit a queue of traffic. I sigh. I can't believe it.

'Why don't you call Jess now you know she's got your message? It'll help put your mind at rest.'

'But my phone's dead.'

'You can use my phone. You put her number in the first time we went out, remember?' He switches his phone back on and hands it to me with Jess's number ready on the screen.

I press the call button, and she answers on the third ring.

'Hi Jess, it's Vicki, everything alright? How are you and the kids?'

'Hi Vicki, erm yes, all good here thanks. You okay?'

'We're stuck in traffic. The roads are flooded in all this rain.' Jess doesn't speak so I add, 'Have you seen how wet and windy it is outside?'

'Oh right, yes.'

'It came down so suddenly. We won't be able to get home for a while because of the weather and it looks like we're stuck behind an accident. I hope you're okay to stay until we get back. I'll pay you extra obviously.'

'That's fine. Just thinking that Mum and Dad will probably have a difficult journey home too.'

'More than likely. By the way, I had a strange text from Alfie saying something about a problem with some people there. Do you know what that was about? No one's been round, have they?'

'He probably meant some teenagers from school who came to the door. They've gone now but it woke Alfie and Bella up.'

'Oh no. What did they want?'

'To speak to me, that's all.'

'Oh, right.'

Jess stays silent.

'No other problems then?' I sense her hesitating, but then she says there's nothing else. 'Alright, we'll see you soon, hopefully.'

Jess doesn't reply and the call ends.

'All okay?' Marc asks, fiddling with the heating and checking the traffic on the satnav. I'm starting to shiver again.

'I'm not sure. Jess sounded a bit... distracted.'

17

JESS

Lee is in the kitchen with the kids when Jess finishes the call with Vicki. It's a relief they've been delayed because of the weather, but her heart is galloping not knowing how long they will be. She hopes Lee won't stay too long then she can get the kids back to bed and finish tidying up the house. All the time she's thinking of the test result in her bag. She's not properly looked at it yet, and she's not sure she wants to know.

Alfie is making his dad a cheese and pickle sandwich while Bella is sitting on a chair drinking a glass of milk. The bread slices are thick one end and thin the other. He must have cut them himself. At least he's making an effort. It's sweet of him. Lee takes the sandwich straight from the bread board with both hands and takes an enormous bite into it. Jess imagines what Vicki would say about not using a plate, because crumbs are falling all over the floor.

She leaves them to it and collects her rucksack from the bottom of the stairs and takes it into the living room. Bella runs past the open door, grinning, then runs upstairs. She probably wants to show her dad the latest set of friendship bracelets she's been making. Jess sits on the armchair and peeks inside the box at the test stick. She can't see it properly, so takes it out and tips it slightly to see it under the side light. She blinks and swallows hard.

'I'm guessing you don't want your mum and dad to see that,' Lee says behind her, making her jump. He snatches it from her hand.

'It's not mine, I'm looking after it for a friend.' She pulls it out of his fingers, stuffs it back in the box and shoves it in her bag.

'Yeah, pull the other one,' Lee says, 'I won't tell them, I promise.' He tilts his head and raises an eyebrow. Jess doesn't believe him, because he knows her parents well, especially her dad. But does Lee know what he can be like when he loses his temper?

Alfie comes out of the kitchen holding a mug of coffee, and hands it to Lee.

'Thanks, son. Go on now and get ready,' he says to him and strokes the back of his head. Alfie nods and runs upstairs. He's not normally so enthusiastic about going to bed.

'Who's the dad then?' Lee continues to stare at her.

'I told you; it isn't mine.' She holds his gaze, hoping he doesn't spot she's trembling. He wouldn't believe her if she told him the truth.

He shrugs. 'Whose is it then, someone I know?'

'I can't say.' Tears start to fill Jess's eyes.

'I'll get your dad on the phone and tell him he's going to be a grandad then, shall I?' He slides his phone from his pocket and holds it up to his face.

'No!' Jess shouts and lunges towards him as he starts jabbing the keypad with his finger, but he lifts it out of her reach.

'He'd do the same for me, I know he would. And if I don't tell him, it'll get back to him that I knew about it. I can't do that to a mate, sorry.'

'I told you it's not mine.' Jess begs him to believe her, otherwise her life may as well be over.

'So you keep saying, but until you tell me who it belongs to and why you have it, how can I believe you?'

Jess swallows. Oh God. Vicki is going to find out everything that happened here tonight. It's all been posted online. She's going to hate her for it. She doesn't want to betray her trust, but what other choice does she have right now? She can't let her parents find out. Her dad will crucify her, and her mum will never speak to her again.

She draws in a breath and says, 'I found it upstairs and I was curious.'

'Whereabouts?' he presses.

'In Vicki's bathroom.'

18

'You are kidding me, right?' Lee stares down at Jess. She shakes her head, holding her breath.

'No wonder she made me leave. It must be *his*.' He kicks the sofa and punches the back of it. Jess shrinks away from him. 'Show it to me again,' he demands, and she opens her rucksack with shaking hands and hands him the box. He rips it open and takes out the stick with the faint word *pregnant* in the little window.

'Maybe it's not hers,' she says lamely. But it's too late to backtrack, the damage is done.

'Who else would it belong to? Unless you're lying to me?' His fingers curl around his phone and Jess pictures her dad losing his temper like this too, only so much worse. Once, he'd pushed her up against the wall with such force, she'd heard the back of her head crack. Then her mum and dad had argued about her, throwing things at each other, and she'd run upstairs and shut herself in her room. After that she'd added a little bolt to her door to keep herself safe.

'Maybe she had one of her friends over, a mum from school, someone who needed to do the test in a safe place.' She's trying so hard to lean away from Lee, her ribs hurt where the armchair is digging into her side. She has a strong suspicion that when he's had a few drinks, he has a temper like her dad does.

They were buddies when Lee lived here. Perhaps he knows her dad's secrets, what he's really capable of. Maybe Lee's a liar too?

Since Jess caught her dad in a lie, she's never been quite able to trust him. He'd always said he couldn't go in the loft because of vertigo, but she heard him sneak up there when her mum was out one evening and she was in her bedroom with the lights off. Maybe he thought she was asleep. She'd been alerted by a tiny squeak of metal and a slight rumble of the loft hatch being moved and silently stole a peek round her door. In the dim light from the landing window, she saw the loft hatch open and her dad standing at the top of the step ladder in his socks, only his legs showing and a narrow glow of light moving around from what she guessed was his torch. She'd wondered ever since what he was hiding up there, but she daren't tell her mum because she wouldn't believe her and it would start another row where they'd both be shouting at her.

'Daddy, will I need my toothbrush?' Bella calls out halfway down the stairs. Jess shoots a look at her. There's only one reason why she'd ask that. Jess catches Bella's eye and she can tell the girl knows she is alarmed.

'Yeah, I don't mind, whatever, it's up to you, darling. I can always get you a new one.' Lee stumbles over his words, glancing at Jess out of the corner of his bloodshot eyes, the lids dark and heavy. 'And don't forget your swimming cossies.' He must have been smoking weed while he was hanging around the garden, that explains why he's so irritable and angry.

'What are you going to do?' Jess asks in an even voice, trying her best not to rile him. Now she hopes that Vicki and Marc get back as soon as possible.

Lee chucks the box back at her. 'What do I care if she's having his baby. He's welcome to her. They've taken everything else from me. I've got nothing left to lose except my kids, and they're not having them.' He leans closer to Jess until she can smell the weed on him and see the sweat on his top lip. 'If she thinks I'm leaving them here to be brought up by *him*, she is very much mistaken.' He straightens up, his jaw muscles clicking.

Alfie trots down the stairs with his rucksack on his back, and his sleep cushion hanging around his neck as if he's going off on holiday.

'Will I be able to come back for...' He stops on the stairs when he sees Jess, as though he didn't realise she'd still be there and what he's saying is not for her ears.

'It's okay. Jess won't say anything.' Lee flashes her a smile with his greyish yellow teeth and she glares back at him.

'Your Xbox? Yeah, we can come and get that another time, don't you worry.' Lee reaches out and pulls Alfie beside him. He's wearing his fleece, trainers she's not seen before and a baseball cap. A mini version of his father.

'Where are you going, Alfie? It's past your bedtime,' Jess says, folding her arms so Lee can't see her trembling. 'What will your mum say?'

He shrugs and looks to his dad for an answer. 'I... don't know... it's none of your business.'

Lee looks at her and grunts, 'Keep out of it.'

'I can't let you take them,' Jess says, getting to her feet. She holds up her phone, pulls up Vicki's number and is about to press the green button to call her when Lee whacks the phone clean out of her hand. It flies across the room and slides under the bookcase.

'What the hell.' Jess gawps at him confused. Alfie frowns at his dad then raises an eyebrow at Jess with a smirk on his face. Bella plods down the stairs and stands with Alfie, holding onto his arm.

'Ready?' Lee asks. Both children nod.

'You didn't need to hit me, did you?' Jess hisses at him, holding her hand where it stings.

'I didn't hit you, did you see anything?' Lee asks his son.

Alfie shakes his head. 'He was just putting you in your place.'

Bella frowns.

'What did you say?' Jess can't believe he said that, but Lee ignores it.

'Anyway, you were phoning her right in front of me,' Lee says. 'Bit rude.'

'Because you need to ask her permission before you leave. You know that. If you want to see them regularly, you need to be sensible and get her on side. You can't just take them.'

Lee leans in close to Jess, his warm sour breath on her face, bloodshot eyes boring into her. 'Do not tell me what I can and can't do with my children. Got it?' He grabs Bella's hand and makes a swift turn towards the front door.

'Daddy,' she squeals in pain, and he loosens his grip. Alfie follows them out of the door but glances back with a smug face at Jess, because he knows as well as she does, there's nothing she can do to stop Lee taking them.

Lee hurries them up the street towards some kind of van. Jess follows, not prepared to give up. She has to try and change his mind.

'Please, think about what you're doing,' she begs him. The van looks like the VW Camper she saw driving past earlier. She recognises it from the GB badge on the bumper. Her grandad had one just like it. Lee must have been watching the house, waiting for Vicki and Marc to go out. He must have been planning this. Did he see all the school kids come in? If so, why didn't he intervene earlier?

'Get lost, Jessica. They're my kids too. I have every right to take them with me, especially as she's stopped me seeing them.'

'But look at them, they're scared, they want their mum.'

'I'm not scared,' Alfie grunts at her.

'They don't need her or *him*. Between them, they've destroyed my life. The kids will be better off with me.'

'But where are you taking them, when are you bringing them back?'

He ushers the children into the body of the van. Jess tries to coax them towards her but Lee pushes her away. The two children sit in silence on the back seat.

'Phone, Alfie.' Lee takes it from him and checks his latest messages, probably to make sure he's not texted his mum. He slides it into the central console.

'Just so you know, I'm not bringing them back,' Lee says matter-of-factly.

'What do you mean?' Jess clamps her hands either side of her head. 'You can't be serious.'

'She stopped me seeing them for a whole month. It's Alfie's thirteenth birthday in a couple of days, and I want to spend it with him. I've tried to be reasonable, reach out to Vicki on the phone, but she won't budge. She has no remorse or regrets whatsoever. Well, two can play at that game. Let's see how she likes it.'

'But you can't do that,' Jess cries.

'Can't I? *He's* behind all this you know.'

'What do you mean, where are you taking them?' Panic rises in her throat. What can she do? This is all going to be her fault. What if he means it and he never brings them back?

He pulls the side door shut and climbs in the driver's seat. Jess bangs on the window but he ignores her. She peers in at the children sitting next to each other; Bella looks terrified, and both have long pale faces. Even Alfie seems a bit shaken despite his bravado earlier. Lee starts the engine and pulls away from the kerb, forcing Jess to step back. She quickly takes a photo of the number plate as he drives away, and the last thing she sees is the kids straining to see her out of the back window.

19

VICKI

The storm seems to have calmed down a bit, or perhaps it's just that the wind has dropped. I can't stop shivering because of my damp clothes despite the heating being on, and I'm aching where I hit the ground. I'm going to need a hot bath when I get home.

Marc is quiet and I wonder what he's thinking. It's been a disastrous evening so far, not the relaxing night out I'd hoped for and certainly not the moving-into-his-house scenario I've been quietly dreaming about. But the more I think about his suggestion that he come to live in my house, pay rent, then sell up both houses and buy somewhere together, the more it sounds like a sensible way forward. Although after tonight, he could be having second thoughts.

It's only three weeks till Christmas. Should we wait until after? I'm planning to put the tree and decorations up this weekend. Maybe the kids will be more accepting of him moving in if they're distracted by the festive season. We can all look forward to some quality time together over the holidays – playing board games, watching old films and all the new Christmas drama specials on TV. I've asked Marc to go up in the loft and bring the tree and decorations down. I'll mention it again later because I don't know if he's remembered.

I told him a bit about my childhood, so he knows how much Christmas means to me. More than any other holiday during the year, I like to go all out and make Alfie and Bella feel loved and special. And even though they won't have their dad with them this year, Marc will be there and he's gradually bonding with them.

As soon as we're waved past the crash site, we follow the one-way signs and end up on a road that will take us towards home. I let out a heavy sigh of relief. It's only then that I notice Jess has sent me a text message a few minutes ago on Marc's phone.

Vicki, please get back here as soon as you can!

20

Marc turns his car into my street at speed.

'Slow down,' I shout at him, 'someone is in the middle of the road.'

His foot hits the brake.

'It's Jess. I wonder what's happened for her to be out here? She should be inside looking after the kids.'

Marc doesn't answer but shakes his head. Jess steps onto the pavement as he pulls the car up to the kerb next to her. I wind down the window.

'What's wrong? Why are you out here?' I ask. She draws her arm across her face, pushing her wet hair out of her eyes. Her cheeks are pink, make-up smudged.

'I'm so sorry, Vicki, I tried to stop him, but he just wouldn't listen to me.'

'Who are you talking about?'

Jess gabbles it all again so fast I only catch the last two words: *Taken them.*

'Who has taken them?' But I know who she means. I need to hear her say it because I can't take this in on top of the evening I've had.

'Lee was here; he's gone off with the kids,' Jess says again, hand to her forehead.

'Where, Jess, where has he taken them?'

'I don't know. It was like he was on a mission to get them away from you.'

'Christ, how did he even get in?'

'The back door. I thought I'd locked it, but I must have forgotten. I'm so, so sorry,' Jess says, and cups her face in her hands.

I reach out to her. 'It's not your fault, Jess. He must have been hiding out in the garden waiting for his chance.' I turn to Marc.

'He must have known we were going out. I bet you anything Alfie told him. When I get my hands on him, he's never going to have a phone again! Where would he take them, did he give you any clue?'

'No, I'm sorry. He made them get in his camper van and then drove off.'

'We need to go after them.' I turn to Marc who is already shaking his head.

'You've had a bang to the head, and it's taken us over an hour just to get across town.'

'You can't be serious,' I say.

Jess frowns and I quickly explain about falling over.

'I'm fine and we were delayed mainly because of the crash.' I turn back to Marc. 'I need to go and find my children, now!'

'Look, he won't get far in this weather and neither will we. Much better to contact the police, let them go after him.' Marc turns the engine off.

'I can't believe you're doing this. You expect me to do absolutely nothing? How can I leave it to the police? By the time they get going, Lee will be long gone to who knows where. I might never see my children again.'

'Please just take a breath,' Marc says gently, laying a hand on my leg. 'What's the point in haring after him when you don't know where he's gone?'

'What sort of camper van was he in?' I ask Jess.

'A vintage one. Pale green. Looked like it's where he's been living too. It was quite a state inside and out.' Jess pulls a face as if remembering the smell. 'I took a photo of his number plate as he drove off.'

'Well done, Jess,' I say. She taps on her photos to enlarge them.

'It's a bit blurred, but I think you can just about make it out.'

'Did he say or do anything else before he left?' I ask. I need any clues as to which direction he's taken them.

Jess looks at the ground.

'Think, Jess. If there's anything, even if it seems trivial. I need to know.'

Jess kicks a stone with her boot and looks at me under her eyelashes.

'He made them each pack a bag and he told them they'd need their swimming costumes.'

'In this weather? And what else? Come on, please.'

'He took Alfie's phone off him and said something really chilling to me before he drove off.' She stops speaking as a sob catches in her throat.

'What was it? Come on, Jess, you're doing really well,' I say gently, not wanting to scare her into silence.

'As he was about to drive off, he said...' Jess presses her fingers to her lips. 'He said he wasn't going to bring them back.'

21

'Shit.' I smack my hand on the dashboard.

'I said we should call the police, the man is out of control,' Marc says.

'I don't want a bloody car chase and put my children in danger. Who knows what Lee will do if he feels cornered.'

'They won't chase him, but they'll be able to find out where he's gone using number plate recognition, make sure he doesn't leave the country.' Marc gets out of the car.

'He wouldn't do that. He'd need their passports and I doubt if he'd know where to find them.'

'I don't think you should risk going anywhere tonight,' Marc says.

'It's not up to you,' I snap back at him.

'I get that, but you're not going to be able to help anyone until you've at least had a rest.' He comes round to help me. I sway as I get out of the car. I silently curse myself for falling over. He holds my arm as we walk up the path to my front door as though I'm twice my age, but I'm still shaken, and I don't want to slip over again. My hip and knee are throbbing as much as my head. I could do with some strong painkillers. I'd like nothing more than to jump back in the car and drive after Lee like I'm some kind of super-mum. But I suppose Marc is right, I've had a bang to the head, so going off on my own wouldn't be the wisest move. He wants me to go to A&E for a check-up, but I don't feel nauseous, so I don't think it's necessary. I'm sure if Alfie and Bella were his kids, he'd have the same outlook as I do.

I sit in my living room and decide to at least tell the police, see what they say. They note Lee's car registration number and say they will alert ANPR, but as we're not yet divorced and there's no custody order in place for the children, the police can't treat this as an abduction by a parent. At least they'll be out there looking for them though. They advise me to try and call Lee on his mobile, which I do, but it keeps going to answer phone.

'He's just not picking up,' I say, but Jess seems distracted, her eyes darting around the room. I follow her gaze. The wall clock is hanging at a slight angle and the cushions on the sofa are in a different order to how I normally have them. I reach down and touch a dark patch on the carpet. It's wet.

'What's been going on in here?' I ask her, as Marc comes out of the kitchen with my cup of tea.

'It's a right state in there too. Did you do some cooking with the children?' Marc asks Jess, putting my cup on the smudged coffee table next to me.

'Um, yeah, sorry I meant to clean it up.' She shifts closer to the door.

'What sort of cooking?' I ask.

'Pizza and what else was it?' Marc says. 'There are smears of tomato and who knows what in the oven, and crumbs all over the place. Lots of dirty plates in the sink for only three people as well.'

'Did you have company?' I ask her straight. 'Not your boyfriend I hope.'

Jess can't look me in the eye. Dom won't allow her to have boyfriends at home, especially up in her bedroom. Says he does not want his daughter to get a bad reputation. She's invited Olly in here at least once before. I caught them kissing and fondling each other on the sofa when we came back from the theatre one night. I told her it was unacceptable especially when she was supposed to be looking after my children. Bella could have come down needing water or something and caught them, and that's not what I want her seeing at her age.

'Jess? Please answer me.' She's normally so grown up and sensible when I leave the children with her.

'I'm sorry, but a group from school pushed their way in, I couldn't stop them.' Jess winces as though there's a lot more to come.

'A *group*? How many? Can you give me names?' I ask.

'Fran, Sean and her gang from school.'

'The same girl who's been bullying you?'

'Yeah.' Jess starts to cry. 'I'm so sorry. They were eating out of the fridge and drinking your beers, and they wouldn't listen to me. They made me do all sorts of gross things like licking cat food, then posted reels of it on social media.'

'That's disgusting. How did they know you were even here?'

'I don't know.'

'I want you to write a list of all their names so I can go and pay a visit to each one of their parents.'

'Please don't, it will make it so much worse for me.' Jess dries her eyes on her sleeves.

'I can't let them get away with this.'

Jess blinks at me. 'They'd still be here if it wasn't for Lee. He was the one who got them to leave. He scared the shit out of them. Turned up with a mask on and chased them out.' Her eyes glisten as she recounts how Lee shouted at them, threatening them with an iron bar.

'Oh great, so now all their parents will be lodging complaints about his threatening behaviour, and probably me as well for having him here.'

'I'm so, so sorry. I'd better go home.' Jess picks up her rucksack. She mumbles about having to pick the right time to tell Olly something important, and how he's probably going to kill her when she tells him.

'Everything okay?'

She nods but looks completely crestfallen. I pay her in cash, but she won't take it.

'It doesn't feel right under the circumstances.' She shakes her head and won't look at me.

'Just take the money,' Marc says but she ignores him.

'Please let me know when you find Alfie and Bella. I'll understand if you want to find a new babysitter. I really am sorry for everything, Vicki.'

'There'll be no need for that, it wasn't your fault.'

After Jess has left, Marc covers me in a fleece blanket on the sofa and makes me a mug of hot chocolate. I ask him to put my phone in a bag of rice and bring me some painkillers and my tablet. It's gone 10 p.m. I check Alfie's location on Find My, but Jess was right, Alfie's phone has been switched off. Its last known location was outside our house. There's not much I can do in this weather and in my current state, but there's one person who may be able to help me. While Marc is out of the room, I stab a text message in capital letters:

> LEE HAS TAKEN THE KIDS WITHOUT TELLING ME. PLEASE COME AND HELP ME IN THE MORNING. I DON'T KNOW WHERE THEY'VE GONE AND HE SAID HE'S NOT COMING BACK!

22

JESS

When Jess gets in, she has a hot shower, makes herself a milky coffee, and carries it up to her bedroom. She's trying to work out who left a small ceramic cat on their doorstep. Was it Colin again? She instinctively looks out of her window at the glow of light in his bedroom across the road. It's kind of sweet of him really, especially the posy of flowers propped up next to it, tied with a band. Or are these gifts a little bit creepy as her mum keeps saying? She can't decide. Mum thinks this constant attention is starting to ring alarm bells, but Jess doesn't want to think of him like that, because she's put her trust in him. He's a good person.

She promised herself she wouldn't look at TikTok, but it's hard not to. Sure enough there are at least three videos of her, posted by Sean. Her stomach falls away from her. The one of her blindfolded, licking the cat's food bowl, has already been viewed three thousand times. She can't bear having no control over who sees it and who comments on it. There's nothing she can do except hope that by the morning, everyone has moved on to something new.

She checks her messages but there's still nothing from Olly. Has he seen Fran's posts and decided not to get involved? He won't approve. She hoped he'd turn up to help her, so it's hard to understand why he's chosen to ghost her instead.

She glances at the ceiling, at a scratching sound like a mouse. She shudders, suddenly cold. She can hear her nan's voice in her head: *You've caught your death of cold standing out in the rain.*

Pressing the on button on her laptop, it springs into life instantly from sleep mode. She has thirty-two messages, five from her VIPs. The first one is from Tonka10, one of her longest-standing clients, requesting a private show of her wearing his favourite outfit. He's offering to pay double if she shows her face, but she still can't bring herself to make that leap just yet. As it is she's underage by a year and if anyone found out her identity, she'd be kicked off the platform and lose her growing revenue stream. Not to mention how much trouble she'd be in with her parents.

She slides the lock across her bedroom door just in case anyone comes home when she's in the middle of her performance. Sitting in front of her mirror, she weaves her hair into two chunky plaits on either side of her head. Another light scratching sound from the ceiling makes her jump. That was definitely a mouse. It makes her skin crawl. There could be a whole nest of them up there. She shudders thinking of their bare whippy tails, and their long teeth gnawing at the wooden beams. She's told her mum about it, but her mum won't go up there unless she absolutely has to because of her fear of spiders and cobwebs, and her dad claims to have vertigo to the point where he can't even climb a ladder. But she knows that isn't true. Maybe he's secretly keeping a pet rodent up there.

Jess changes out of her clothes into a lacy white bra, short, pleated skirt and crisp white blouse, attaching a clip-on stripy tie over the top button. Out of her top chest of drawers, she selects a pair of hold up tights and carefully rolls one up each leg, making sure the tops sit level on her thighs. From her bottom drawer, she lifts out a sparkly blue and silver bunny mask which she pulls over her head and secures at the back with a thick black bow. Finally, she covers her bed in a deep red velvet cover, pulls the shimmering canopy around and softens the lighting.

Lining up the webcam with the centre of the bed, she checks the position of the camera until it's in the right position. She's about to message Tonka10 that she's going live exclusively for him in nine minutes when another message comes through from one of her other VIPs, Hestheboy18. Jess reads his message:

> Special request for my favourite girl: Please tell me
> your first name.

> You know I can't do that, much as I like you.

> Not even if I pay you double?

> Sorry no. You know I need my privacy.

> I'll pay you triple.

> No can do.

> Meet me and I'll pay you five thousand pounds.

Jess springs back from the laptop as though it's burst into flames. What is he playing at? Her fingers shake as she types.

> That's such a generous offer, but I can't meet clients,
> even VIPs, you know the rules.

> I'll pay you ten thousand pounds if you meet me
> tonight.

Jess clamps her hand over her mouth. Is he serious? That's an insane amount of money. She needs to think about this. It would get her through a year at university. She wouldn't have to do this for as long, although she kind of enjoys it. Olly would be pleased if she made a lump sum towards her uni fund in one go, but conflicted because he doesn't like her showing her body to strangers. She tried to get him to do a couple's reel with her, but he flat out refused and they argued about it.

> I sense you're thinking about it. Am I getting closer?

Jess doesn't know what to say. She can't risk her reputation by revealing who she is, but who says she can't turn up in disguise? He's only asking her to meet him. She hasn't said she'd be prepared to reveal who she is.

> Twelve thousand pounds. My final offer. Take it or
> leave it my sweet angel.

Jess buries her face in her hands. She can't even type her heart is thumping so hard. That is real money. There must be a catch. He's going to want a lot more for that price. And if she does meet up with him, she's leaving herself wide open to who knows what.

He's typing again...

> I think my final offer might be the one you won't be able to refuse, on top of the twelve thousand pounds, of course...

He is not going to give up. He must really like her. A new-found confidence blooms in her chest as she types her reply.

> I doubt it but go on, try me.

She's curious to see what else he's offering, what he thinks she won't be able to turn down.

A line of bubbles appears showing he's typing his reply. She checks her watch. She has precisely forty-five seconds before she needs to start the live with Tonka10. The reply from Hestheboy18 appears on the screen.

> I know who you are – Jessica.

Jess leaps off the bed and her laptop crashes to the floor.

23

Jess picks up her laptop and she types her reply.

> Who is this, and how do you know who I am?

She has approximately twenty seconds before her live begins, but she needs to sort this out. If her privacy has been breached, she won't be able to carry on with this work. She types out a quick message to her VIP client Tonkai0 saying she can't go ahead with the private show, a personal emergency has come up. While she's waiting for a confirmation of the cancellation, another message pops up from Hestheboy18.

> The only way for you to find out is to meet me.

> I can't do that.

Every inch of Jess is screaming at her to shut this down, block whoever this is, but the tiniest itch of curiosity won't let her. They know her name. It's possible they really do know who she is.

> I'm not playing games with you, Jessica. We need to meet.

And she needs to know who has found out her real identity. The only way to solve this is to go and meet them. Are they going to try and bribe her for their silence? If so, she's never going to put a stop to this.

Could it be someone who knows her well? But how have they found out? Every image and every reel she's put out there has been carefully curated so there are no personal objects or marks on her to distinguish who she is. She's always covered her face, even her ears, which can be recognised. She's made sure it's virtually impossible to identify her in any way. But this person knows her name. *How?* She wants to scream.

> Meet me at Roxton Park at 11.30 p.m. Come alone.

Jess shudders. This means they know where she lives. That's one of the places she regularly hangs out. It could be anyone on the internet who's managed to locate her, but it's more than likely someone local. So what choice does she have? It's not even about the money any more. She suspects that was just to reel her in. Maybe if she hangs around in the bushes first, she'll see who it is, then she can call the police and come straight home.

A text from Olly pops up saying he's so sorry he's not been in touch or answered her calls, but his nan had a fall and fractured her hip. He's been with her at the hospital. Jess feels bad now for cursing him when he didn't come back and help her deal with Fran and Sean.

> They're keeping her in overnight. I could really do with a hug right now. Can I see you?

She says how sorry she is to hear about his nan then explains about the VIP wanting to meet her alone and could he come to the park because she's nervous going on her own in the dark.

> I need to find out who knows it's me online

> Of course I'll be there

> But you need to stay hidden, they warned me to come alone

> I will. I'll get going now and see if I can spot them. Text me when you're nearby

> Will do, thank you! xxx

As she's changing into her joggers and sweatshirt, she gets a message from Tonka10.

> I was looking forward to that. Can we do it tomorrow, same time?

Jess sends a smiley face and goes offline. She neatly tidies away her outfit into the back of her wardrobe and ties the canopy back from the bed. She arranges the velvet cover in narrow folds across her dressing table chair.

It's already gone 11 p.m. If she leaves now, she'll be able to speak to Olly and find a good spot to hide and hopefully see who is threatening her. When she switches her bedroom light off, the streetlight outside her bedroom window shines in. Her curtains are still partially open. Why hadn't she noticed that before? She stands at the window in the dark and has a clear view of Colin's bedroom window across the road. Can he see right into her room when she has the light on? Could he have been spying on her with his binoculars? She's seen him a couple of times standing on the bank of the local Mere watching the birds on the water. He has a little notebook with a pencil attached that he jots things down with. What if he's been looking at more than wild birds? Could he know what she's been doing in the privacy of her bedroom? Is he the VIP demanding to meet her?

No. It's not possible. What is she thinking? She tosses her hair and shakes the thought away. She put her trust in him the night she was attacked, and she's got no reason to believe he'd betray her.

It's much more likely to be Sean, who has proven himself to be two-faced. She thought he liked her but after his behaviour with Fran today, she will never trust him again. If it's Sean who's arranged to meet her because he's found out what she does online, then she's going to be ready for him.

24

VICKI

My tablet screen lights up next to me on the sofa at 6 a.m. My eyes flick open at the bright light. I'm suddenly wide awake, anticipating a message from Lee to say where he is. Hopefully he's realised what he's done and promises to bring our children home.

But it's not from him, it's from Debbie. I didn't see her reply to the message I sent last night. The painkillers Marc gave me must have knocked me out. He's fast asleep on the recliner. I click open Debbie's first message.

> Hi Vicki, I've phoned Lee, he hasn't gone far, and he assures me they're staying at a mate's for the night, so hopefully he'll sleep on it and bring them back in the morning.

I scroll down and read her new message. My stomach tightens.

> I called him this morning, but he's already gone. Left about half an hour ago. How are you feeling? I'm on my way over to you now. Can you be ready to go in about twenty minutes?

My heart thuds. Shit. Where is he taking them? I thought he would have seen sense, especially after sleeping on it. I reply to her to say I'll be ready.

I try not to wake Marc as I struggle to sit up. He's still dressed and has kicked his boots off on the rug. My left knee and hip are sore and stiff and undoubtedly bruised from falling over, but my head feels clearer. Marc stirs and opens his eyes.

'Hey, let me help you,' he says and springs out of his seat. He takes both my hands and gently pulls me up to standing. 'Stupid question, but how are you feeling?'

'Much better, thanks. I just need the loo. You go back to sleep.'

He insists on helping me down the hallway to the downstairs toilet, then goes to the kitchen to make fresh coffee.

Just as I finish my breakfast, the doorbell rings and Marc gets up to answer it.

'Oh, it's you,' I hear him say and a moment later Debbie is standing in the living room doorway with her arms outstretched. I go straight to her, and she hugs me in her big warm arms. My knees soften with relief.

'It'll be alright. The kids will be safe with him,' she says.

'Will they though?' I pull back. 'Jess thought she smelt weed on him last night. He shouldn't have been driving in that state.'

'He would never put his children in danger,' Debbie says, holding my arms and looking me in the eyes. I nod and try to believe her.

'You didn't mention you'd called *his* sister,' Marc says, arms folded. He's only met Debbie once. After Lee had moved out, she arrived with her brother to collect some of his personal things I'd boxed up for him. He wouldn't hand over his keys so I could give one to Marc. Debbie backed him up; told me I shouldn't be shacking up with my boss or giving him a key to Lee's house. Said it was insulting especially after Marc had sacked him. I understood how upset they were, but I ended up having to change the locks. I couldn't have Lee turning up whenever he felt like it.

'You didn't want to help me, so what did you expect me to do?' I snap at him. 'I need to find them. I can't sit here any longer hoping the police will do it.'

'Well, I'm sorry, but I could have driven you if you'd asked,' he says.

'Don't bother. You're the one he blames for us splitting up, so you'd be the last person he'd want to see.'

'I could still drive you and keep a low profile when we find them.' Marc sounds hurt but I'm not sure I believe he wouldn't have something to say to Lee and make the whole situation worse.

'It's okay, Debbie's here now and she probably knows him better than both of us. So I need you to stay here in case he decides to bring them back.'

'But what about your fall, your bang to the head? You should get it checked out.'

'I feel much better after a few hours' sleep.'

'I'll be driving,' Debbie says. 'If she starts to feel ill, I'll take her straight to A&E, don't you worry.'

'Debbie's a trained nurse so I'm in safe hands.' I pick up my coat and bag and check my tablet is in it.

Marc shrugs. 'Okay, I'll wait here then, get the decorations down from the loft for you.'

'That would be helpful, thanks.' I hug him goodbye and follow Debbie out to her Toyota Surf.

'Right, any idea where we're heading?' She starts the car, and I sigh with relief that she's with me. Sometimes Marc seems to be deliberately obstructive.

I take my tablet out and check Alfie's location again on Find My. 'Alfie's phone is still switched off. Jess said Lee told the kids to take their swimming costumes, so I wonder if they could be heading for the seaside. The only place that makes sense to me is Blackpool.'

'Right, let's head for the M6 then,' Debbie says and puts her foot down.

I glance up at Jess's bedroom window as we drive away. She was so upset last night. I hope she's going to be okay.

25

DEBBIE

Debbie offers Vicki a piece of gum, but she shakes her head, so she stuffs it into her own mouth and concentrates on the road and chewing rather than the rage that is simmering inside her. It's a technique she learnt as a child to help her through a particularly difficult time. She still has to work hard to regulate her emotions, stop them overwhelming her and spilling over.

The roads are relatively clear before rush hour kicks in. She's used to being up this early on these dark winter mornings to feed the animals on the farm, but today she's feeling particularly tired. She didn't get much sleep after speaking to Lee last night. They agreed on one thing at least – Marc is a number one arsehole, and as much as she loves her sister-in-law, she cannot forgive her for dumping her brother for that piece of shit.

She only time she's seen him before today was at the house, after Lee and Vicki had split up. But from what she's heard about him, she's not sure how Lee could have worked for a man like that without losing his rag. She'd have given up on day one. Fortunately, she works for herself now, so she doesn't need to put up with an arrogant boss like that. She won't take any shit from anyone. Her and Rhona make the perfect team, and the farm gives her the life-style and space she needs to thrive. Rhona's nickname for her is Poppy, because she says she's vibrant and proud, rising up from the compost of life.

She checks the time. Lee has got a good fifty minutes' lead on them. When he called her last night, he sounded broken, and she wasn't sure what he was going to do next. Some of the things he was coming out with were insane. She tried to calm him, make him focus on his recovery so he can come to a sensible agreement with Vicki about seeing the kids. But he's just so angry. He talks about Marc with such venom, it's making him ill. She just hopes he knows what he's doing because Vicki is not in a forgiving mood. It doesn't help that Marc is still on Lee's case. In fact, they seem intent on destroying each other. She's not sure why they can't leave it and move on. For good or bad, Vicki's made her choice. It's not nice for Alfie and Bella to see this behaviour. She has a feeling there's something else bothering Lee, but she can't work out what it is yet. But she will.

She glances at Vicki who is staring out of the front windscreen in a trance. She wishes she could give her a big hug and tell her everything will be okay, but she can't.

26

VICKI

It's a slow run to the M6 heading north, but thankfully the main roads aren't flooded and there's not too much traffic around at this time of the morning. The constant thrum of the windscreen wipers on full reverberates through my body. The road ahead is a mass of grey cloaked by a heavy sheet of rain. It's a wonder Debbie can see anything at all.

I keep checking the tracking app on my tablet for Alfie's whereabouts, but his phone is still switched off. 'Do you think I should call the police again?'

'Why, do you think Lee's planning to do something stupid?' There's no indication in Debbie's demeanour that she's worried he will, but then there's not much that fazes her. She takes the gum from her mouth and presses it into the ashtray, then lights a cigarette from the dashboard lighter and opens the window a crack before blowing out the smoke. The sounds of heavy rain and wind are so much more violent without the glass as a shield. And the lingering smell of horse dung coming from the open boot finishes me off. I wonder how I'm going to get through this. She said she came straight from dropping off an early delivery nearby, which is why she arrived at my house so quickly.

'I'm worried about the frame of mind Lee's in; I mean, he's planned this, hasn't he? Waiting until I've gone out for the evening then taking my children away from me. How did he seem to you last night?'

She turns her head to me then back at the road again, her thick brown bob swinging. 'Not great. I think if Lee sees the police tailing him, he's more likely to make an impulsive move. Maybe he said he wasn't bringing them back because he just wants them to stay with him for a while, like a little holiday.'

'I think you're being overly optimistic because if that's the case, he should have spoken to me first or at least mentioned it to you. But I hope you're right, although I seriously think not.'

Debbie is quiet for a moment, drawing hard on her cigarette and blowing the smoke towards the window, which she quickly winds down wider and flicks the butt out. She shuts the window and lifts her right hand up high and bangs it down on the wheel. I jolt upright wondering what's wrong.

'If you'd just let him have some contact with them, he might not have felt so pushed into a corner like this,' she yells.

'Well, thanks for the support.' I fold my arms to hide the fact that I'm shaking all over.

'I thought you knew how I felt about you stopping him seeing them. When did you become so bloody selfish? I'm seriously pissed off with you, Vicki.'

She glares at me, and I stare open-mouthed at her.

'You used to bang on about supporting fathers' rights and how important it was that children maintained contact with both parents until *you* split up with Lee. Did you know that even if he was in prison, he'd have the right to see his kids, because he's still their dad? More importantly, they'd have the right to see him.'

'Alright, I know. Thanks for the lecture.' I turn away and stare out of the window, the darkness closing in on me. All I can see in the black reflection is my crumpled face.

'So tell me where this has come from then, because it's not like you. The Vicki I used to know would never have blocked her children from seeing their dad.'

'Maybe I'm not the same person any more,' I blurt out, and focus on the unlit stretch of road ahead. 'Anyway, you weren't here when things came to a head.'

'And don't I know it.' Debbie wobbles her head in that childish way she has, whenever she's being challenged. I don't mean to accuse her, but her being miles away in a Scottish island for all those months practically living like a monk while learning how to be an organic farmer meant that she wasn't here in the thick of everything we were going through as a couple.

'I couldn't let my children be around someone who was on drugs, not even their father. *Especially* their father. And I'm not going to apologise for that. I didn't want them to see him in that state. Some would say I was doing him a favour as well as them.'

'Look, I know it's been hard, and I'm sorry I wasn't here to help you, but Lee's not a bad person, is he? Obviously apart from the drugs, he's a great dad.'

'And not paying child support?'

'Yeah okay, there's that too. But he always tried to do his best for you and the kids. He's never stopped loving you all. You know that, don't you?'

'Which is why I'm not sending the police wading in, making this worse than it needs to be.'

'Fair enough. And I'm glad you want to give him a chance to explain. I just hope you've not left it too late.'

'What do you mean?' A chill runs through my body.

'I mean I hope he's not running away with your kids because he's reached the end of his rope.'

'Woah. You're not helping by saying that.'

'Okay, but I'm just being honest.'

I comb my hand through my hair. 'Why did you answer my call for help if you're just going to tell me off?'

'Because I care about you. I care about all of you. I'm just as worried as you are about Lee. I feel guilty for not being here for you all, especially for my brother.'

I glance across at Debbie and there's genuine anguish in her eyes. There isn't anyone I'd rather have with me right now, despite her telling me off.

'I'm scared, Vicki, if Lee is trying to pull off a *Fathers 4 Justice* stunt, they almost never end well.'

'I know. I must admit I've been thinking the same thing.' I grind my teeth. I'm tempted to try calling Lee again, but if he's driving his phone is probably still off. I don't want him getting irate with me while he's in charge of a moving vehicle with our kids in the back of it. If he's aware that we're on his tail, who knows what he will do.

27

DEBBIE

Barely twenty minutes into the journey and Debbie can't help losing her rag with Vicki. But she needs to be told. If she'd just continued to let Lee see Alfie and Bella regularly, even once a week, it would have made everything more bearable for him, and he'd never have gone into this downward spiral.

She partly blames herself for not being around when they first started having problems. It wasn't long after Vicki had started working as Marc's PA. Lee didn't tell her about how cosy they were getting. He says now that he thought he could handle it.

It's not like Vicki to be cruel. But ever since she's been with Marc, she's become cold and petty, almost a different person. Ruthless in the way she treats Lee. She gets that Vicki wants to put herself first occasionally, but she can't all the time when their kids are involved. Someone has to be truthful with her, and if that has to fall to Debbie, then so be it.

The way Lee was talking last night, she's worried he's going to do something stupid if things don't go his way today. Ideally once things are settled and he's seeing the children regularly again, he needs to get the help and support he needs. It's not a full-blown addiction yet, but it's going that way. Or is she kidding herself?

He admitted that he's been smoking every day, when for years it was only occasional. She was aware of him using it to cope with stress since he was about fourteen. A twinge of guilt accompanies the thought every time. He started because of what happened to her all those years ago. She knows it affected him badly too. They've all carried the pain around with them, and it's leached into their lives in different ways. Their parents turned to alcohol to block it all out, but what it did to them made it feel like she was being punished all over again. Even as a teenager she decided never to drink or touch drugs because she had a feeling that if she did, it would be the end of her.

She stubs her cigarette out in the ashtray and sighs, feeling a pang of disappointment that he's allowed the addiction to take hold, even though she gets that the break-up is devastating and difficult to cope with. But taking drugs is a slippery slope. And by giving in to the addiction, it means the monster who attacked her is winning.

And she can't have that, because she vowed never to let him ruin their lives.

28

VICKI

'Am I still heading for Blackpool?' Debbie asks.

'I don't know,' I say, trying to think what to do next. 'How about we stop at the next services too, and you call Lee. I think if you spoke to him, you'd be able to reason with him. He might give you a clue as to what he's planning to do and where he's going. But you can't let him know I'm with you.'

'And you think he's just going to tell me?' Debbie's eyes widen, still looking straight ahead.

'I do think he'll tell *you*. I need to know that Alfie and Bella are okay.'

'Alright but why don't we give it a bit longer. Like you said before, we don't want to panic him.'

'But if it's you, he won't get angry, and it'll be safer for him to speak while he's driving.'

Debbie doesn't answer. We continue up the motorway in silence. I wonder what she's thinking. Maybe she's regretting coming with me, going against her brother. Or perhaps she's weighing up what she thinks he's capable of in the worst-case scenario. Whichever it is, my chest feels hollowed out.

'The next services are a couple of miles up here.' Debbie nods once and doesn't take her eyes off the road.

I breathe a little easier and settle back in my seat. A text pops up on my tablet from Marc asking how we're getting on. I tell him we're halfway to Blackpool. My tablet rings. I answer and put it on loud speaker.

'I feel a bit useless sitting here,' Marc says. 'I wish you'd let me come with you.'

'Well, you're working and like I said, you'd be the last person Lee would want to see right now, and I really need to keep him onside. I've no idea what he's planning, but he must be desperate if he thinks he can take the kids without telling me.'

'Whereabouts are you?'

I tell him the location of the services we're going to stop at.

'I really think you should consider calling the police again,' he says. 'He's out of control and you're not equipped to deal with that. And what if he's armed? You don't know what he's capable of under the influence of drugs.'

Debbie's eyebrows rise.

'He has your children with him, and you don't even know where they are, you're just guessing.'

I think Marc has forgotten that Lee's sister is sitting right next to me. Or he doesn't know or care that she can hear what he's saying.

'Is there a chance Alfie's wearing those new trainers I gave him for his birthday?' Marc continues.

'I don't know, why?'

'Because I put an AirTag on them.'

My mouth drops open. 'What? You didn't tell me that.'

Debbie and I glance at each other.

'It's just so he doesn't lose them. They cost a lot.'

'Yes, I know and I'm sure he's grateful.'

'What I mean is, if he's wearing them I'll be able to track where they are, hang on a sec, I'll check the app.'

'They're an early birthday present,' I explain to her. 'Alfie wasn't supposed to wear them until the actual day, but maybe he put them on to show his dad.'

'Yeah, he's wearing them alright,' Marc says.

I press my hand to my forehead as relief floods through me.

'Thank God,' Debbie says, running a hand through her fringe.

'They're about forty minutes ahead of you. But the tag doesn't seem to be moving. My guess is they've stopped at the services after the next one.'

'Thanks, Marc. You're a lifesaver,' I say.

He laughs. 'Thank Alfie when you see him for not waiting until his birthday.'

'For once I won't mind that he's ignored what I say.' I laugh.

'By the way, I got the Christmas decorations down for you. Do you want me to put them up?'

'No, it's okay. It's something I normally do with the kids, so I'd rather wait until they're both home. I don't want to jinx it.'

'Okay. Look, I've got something to sort out at home, do you mind if I work from there?'

'No, but I'll need to text you for an update on their location.' I don't know how he can concentrate on work when we don't know if Alfie and Bella are safe.

'I'll keep my phone on next to me,' he says. 'And before you ask, I promise I won't forget to bring the bins round.'

'Thanks. I'm really grateful.' As I end the call, Debbie shoots me a look.

'He really doesn't like Lee, does he?' she says.

'Lee was never his biggest fan either.'

'Not easy for you though being in the middle, is it?'

I shake my head, glad she's acknowledging that. 'I just wish they could put their differences aside.'

'Do you think we should try and push on to the services after this one, so we can talk to Lee face to face?'

'I don't think we'll be able to catch up and he's not going to wait around; he's trying to get away. Anyway, he could be about to set off again, then we'll be talking to him while he's driving, which I didn't want to do. I'm really nervous about him being distracted, especially if he's been smoking and is still upset.'

'I don't mind phoning him, to see if he'll wait. I just hope he believes I'm on my own.'

'Thanks, but is he going to believe it's only you?'

'I don't know.' Debbie sighs.

'The next services are just up here. Could you call him first, see how he is then maybe he'll agree to hang on until we get there?' I point to the sign to turn off.

'Okay, let's try that,' she says.

29

Debbie pulls up at the services and we go in and order coffees. We find a quiet corner and Debbie calls Lee's number. I lean in to listen.

'Hey bro, how are you doing?'

'Hello Debs. I'm okay. Can I call you back? I'm kind of in the middle of something.'

'Oh right, are you okay? You sound a bit... stressed.'

'You could say that.'

'What's stressing you? A problem shared and all that.' She raises her eyebrows at me, and I lean in closer to hear him.

'Don't worry about it.'

'Hey. Is that the kids I can hear in the background?' Debbie suddenly says.

I'm not sure if she can really hear them but it's a good strategy to keep him on the line. Lee tries to butt in, but Debbie carries on speaking.

'Hey Alfie, Bella, how are you doing? Aunty Debs here.'

'Hello,' Bella replies half-heartedly. Her subdued tone makes my heart crumble. Alfie doesn't speak.

'Are you going somewhere nice?' Debbie asks in her over-exuberant voice, aimed at the children.

'We don't know, Dad won't tell us,' Alfie grumbles and swears.

'Enough of that. I've told them we're going to the seaside,' Lee says.

'Really, which one? Surely not in this weather. Raining like anything here.'

'Where's here?' Lee's voice is suddenly emotionless and dark.

'Oh, erm, at the stables.' Debbie's eyes widen at me.

'Right. So if my mobile dies I can call you back on the house phone, can I?'

'That's right, although I might not hear it from here.' She tries to say it in her same sing-song voice but the slight change in tone gives her away.

'You're not at home, are you? Sounds more like a service station. I can hear people talking and someone calling out a name to collect their food. Don't tell me, you're with Vicki.'

'Why do you say that?' Debbie's voice comes out too high, a sure sign of guilt.

'Because I knew she'd come after us. She's got her phone linked to Alfie's but I've switched it off, so she won't be able to follow us.'

I grab the phone from Debbie and speak clearly into it. 'What are you playing at taking the kids, Lee?'

'And there she is. Thought you could keep my children away from me, did you?' he snarls.

'Mum, Mum, I want to come home,' Bella shouts and Alfie shushes her.

'Where are you taking them?' I say slowly, emphasising each word.

He stays silent and for a second, I think he's cut the call.

'Please listen to me, Lee, they shouldn't be out in this treacherous weather, it's too dangerous, please take them somewhere safe.'

'Come on Lee, we can talk about this,' Debbie adds. 'Tell us where you are and we'll meet up with you.' She glances at me for my reaction. I nod, not wanting to reveal to him we know where he is. The last thing we want is to push him into doing something stupid. 'This is not good for the kids. They need their mum.'

'And you know they need *me*.' He emphasises the last word with such vehement emotion, my stomach clenches with pain.

'I want my mummy.' Bella's whimpering voice burrows under my skin; she sounds like she's three years old again.

The phone goes dead.

'No!' I shout, slamming my hand down on the table. A few people look over at us.

'Great. Now what?' Debbie says and finishes her coffee. I shake my head and bury my face in my hands.

30

DEBBIE

Debbie pays for snacks at the mini supermarket for their onward journey, while Vicki goes to the bathroom.

The call to Lee has left them both feeling despondent. What is he playing at snarling at her? She's trying her best to help him. It goes to show what pressure he's under. Or has he been smoking weed? She hopes he wouldn't be that reckless. She texts him as much, but he doesn't reply. She should tell him about the AirTags but decides not to. They need to know where he's heading and catch up with him as soon as possible.

Bella sounds genuinely distressed by his behaviour. He's not doing himself any favours upsetting her, and Alfie barely said a word. As for Marc, what the hell is his game suggesting Lee might have a weapon? If he said that to the police they'd send an armed response unit, and it could get Lee killed. Seems like Marc is doing everything he can to make sure Lee is out of the picture and win Alfie over giving him expensive trainers.

Before today, she'd only ever met Marc once, when she drove Lee back to his house to pick up the last of his clothes and personal items. He was there lurking in the background and wisely kept out of the way. Lee had moved out a few weeks earlier. Vicki tried to introduce him to her as he passed from one room to another, but she couldn't bring herself to look at him properly. He gave off a bad vibe and her rage about his part in Lee's marriage break-up was too raw at that point. She felt like going for him, which wouldn't have helped the situation. As it was, she made a comment about how he should be ashamed of himself moving in on another man's wife, which didn't seem to faze him one bit, but it upset Vicki. She told her that wasn't true, and Debbie shouldn't make allegations when she didn't know the full story. Debbie and Lee had made a quick exit after that.

She worries about her niece and nephew. She loves them and will do anything to protect them, and their dad. But this emotional upset in their early years will affect the rest of their lives. Alfie's already swearing and answering back. Who knows what he'll be like as an older teenager. He's in danger of copying his dad by experimenting with drugs.

On the walk back to the car, she opens a packet of stripy mints and offers Vicki one. She takes one and thanks her, dropping it in her mouth.

There was a time when she thought she'd have a family of her own one day. But that was when she was growing up, before the attack, and before she realised she didn't find men attractive in a romantic sense. In some ways it was a relief not to have to go through childbirth, but she often thinks it would have been nice to adopt. Rhona has two grown-up kids and a baby grandson and that's been so good for her. But has she focused a little too much on them instead of the problems her brother and sister-in-law were having?

She wonders if she should have been around for Lee and Vicki more when their marriage started falling apart. Maybe none of this would have happened if she'd stayed. Her decision to go to Scotland was hard, because it meant not seeing any of her family for a couple of months, but it's what she wanted.

Since the first lockdown, she's embraced the big outdoors. Rather than wallow at home she offered to help her elderly neighbours harvest their produce at the local allotments and was soon volunteering to help others. It got her interested in organic farming. She'd trained as a nurse after she left school, but found it hard to cope with emotionally, so she retrained as a chef and was working in a local restaurant when the pandemic hit. She was furloughed for months at a time. Helping others grow and harvest food changed her life overnight.

Back in the car, Debbie puts her seatbelt on and looks at Vicki who is reading something on her tablet. It's probably another message from Marc.

Debbie can't decide if he was wise to put an AirTag in Alfie's trainers or if it's because he's a control freak and wants to track wherever Alfie goes.

Either way, she doesn't like the way this man is influencing Vicki or making Lee's life a living nightmare.

31

VICKI

'I think we keep heading north for now,' Debbie says as we get back on the road.

'Hang on, Marc's just texted a map of the last AirTag location, it's near Preston, so they could well be on their way to Blackpool. That would make sense because we used to go there every year until we split up.' I look up the address.

'Don't you think he'll know you'll guess that and go somewhere else?'

'Possibly. But he'll be trying to get the kids onside, so I bet he'll give in to them wanting to go there, even in this weather. It's worth a try. We'll follow the AirTag tracker and see where it takes us. If I'm wrong, we'll have to rethink.'

'The satnav is saying we'll be in Blackpool in forty-five minutes,' Debbie says.

I shut my eyes, stifling a yawn. Just as I'm dozing off, my tablet rings. I sit up straight, hoping it's Lee, but it's Jess's mum, Cassie.

'Hi Vicki, we were wondering, are you out? It's just that we came back from London about ten past eleven last night but Jess wasn't at home. I assumed she was asleep as it was so quiet, but when I looked in on her, she wasn't there. I tried calling her but it kept going to voice mail, so Dom went straight out looking for her. He came back on his own, said the streets were deserted but there was a lot of debris from the storm, so wherever she went, she may have had problems getting home. I've just checked this morning, and she's not slept in her bed. I knocked on your door just now but there's no answer. You're not still in bed, are you? Sorry if you are and I've woken you up but we wondered if she mentioned to you where she was going?'

'I'm not at home but Marc could still be there. He said he's going to work from his house today but bring the recycle bins round before he left. Jess went home about 10 p.m. last night but she didn't mention to me she was planning on going out again.'

'Oh, that's strange. I wonder why she's not answering her phone. I've tried calling Olly too, but he's not picking up either.'

'Sounds like they could be together and don't want to be disturbed. I hope she's feeling okay. There's something I should tell you about some trouble at mine last night.' Vicki recounts everything that happened, the teenagers turning up and then Lee.

'Oh, I'm so sorry.'

'I'm not saying any of it is Jess's fault, but I did ask her why she didn't stop Lee, which is unfair I know, because how could she have? I'm out with Lee's sister now trying to work out where he's taking Alfie and Bella.'

'Christ. You don't think he's going to hurt them, do you? You hear these awful stories.'

'I bloody hope not, but when we called him, Bella sounded scared. He must be desperate to take them without telling me. I get that he's upset because he's not seen the children for a month, which I know is my fault, but the thing is, he's been smoking again, and I was trying to protect them from seeing him like that. He becomes so unreasonable and dangerous, not paying attention to what he's doing. I can only guess what mental state he's in. We're on our way to Blackpool right now, because we think that's where he's heading, but we could be completely wrong.' I trip over the words as a wave of panic overwhelms me wondering what he's going to do next.

'Jesus. Let me get Dom to call him. I don't think they've spoken for a few weeks, but they're still mates as far as I know. He might be able to get out of him where he's going and what he intends to do.'

'That would be so helpful, thank you.'

'I'm sure Jess is okay but I'm worried about what you've just said, so I'm going to try calling Olly's parents next, see if they're holed up round there. I'll get back to you when Dom's spoken to Lee.'

'Okay, thank you. I'll speak to you soon.'

I shut my eyes and try to nap, but everything is going round and round in my head. I don't know how I'm going to cope if Lee does anything to harm our children.

32

DEBBIE

Debbie can't help rolling her eyes when Cassie suggests Dom gives Lee a call. If he's such a good friend, where has he been all this time after the break-up? Yes, they were mates when they lived next door to each other, having a beer on the drive while one or other of them was fixing their car. But according to Lee, Dom hasn't contacted him once to see how he is after he moved out. And he barely said anything to him when he lost his job. Anyone would think Dom believed Marc's lies.

She's met their next-door neighbours several times at friends' and family gatherings. An odd couple was her first impression. He's all macho and muscles and into cars and sport, and she's a feisty petite small business owner who can't help being dominated by him. Their only child, Jess, is an intelligent girl. She noticed the intense way her dad watched her every move, probably because he didn't like the way the boys were eyeing her up.

Her most recent encounter with them was for Vicki's fortieth, only a couple of months before she split up with Lee as it turned out. Debbie had recently got back from Scotland and had a strong inkling they were having problems. She spoke to Lee, but he assured her they'd work it out. But she hadn't realised Marc was in the background cosying up to Vicki, pulling her strings.

Cassie and a few of Vicki's friends had organised the party at their local village hall. They got in a catering company she recommended to do a magnificent buffet and Dom insisted on being the DJ. He seemed to enjoy the attention, curating all Vicki's favourite tunes and chatting with the ladies who went up to ask him for special requests.

Jess was the belle of the ball in a strappy mini dress, but the whole look was spoilt by her sad face. Debbie asked Vicki if Jess was okay and she told her she'd had a row with her dad before the party about what she was wearing and him not letting her invite her boyfriend. Vicki said Cassie told her he was finding it hard to accept that his little girl was growing up. Jess ended up in tears and went home early. According to Vicki, Cassie tried to comfort her, but it was no good. She ended up putting on a brave face and staying with Dom to avoid a blow up in front of everyone. Vicki let slip about the many heated arguments she'd heard through the wall, including between Dom and Jess. What is it with some men needing to control women?

The road ahead is clear and the day is beginning to break in a bright red crack across the sky. Debbie drops another piece of chewing gum in her mouth and grips the steering wheel tighter. Vicki has dozed off, so she puts her foot down. Not long till they get to Blackpool now.

Her stomach balls into a knot at the thought of going near a beach again. She takes a few deep breaths to stay calm, because today isn't about her. But it doesn't stop her feeling anxious and riddled with guilt. Expecting Lee to keep her secret from Vicki all these years must have bled into their discontent and breakdown of trust. It was too much to ask of him. He never once complained, but now she wishes he had. Perhaps she should have been more open with Vicki, confided in her like she had with Rhona. But that's different, they're life-long partners, although she's only been able to hint that *something* happened to her. Christ, is Debbie the one who's pushed Lee to breaking point?

Without warning, her mind slides back to that sweltering afternoon on Hunstanton beach.

Mum had just finished applying sun lotion to Lee's back when the boy appeared. Lee was lying on his front on a beach towel, eyes closed. Debbie had tried to persuade him to join her for a dip in the sea, but he wouldn't. At nine years old he wouldn't admit it, but he was scared of the water. He hadn't learnt to swim yet and he was jealous that she could, although she'd only just received her confidence certificate at school. It was a huge achievement for her after the embarrassment of almost drowning in the previous term. Debbie's mum was lying on her front too, reading the latest Jackie Collins novel. Dad was dozing on a deck chair under his bucket hat, in the shade of their umbrella.

Debbie walked down the sand-dune slope on her own and started building a sandcastle nearer the water. A boy with dark hair and blue swimming trunks stopped by and asked if she needed any help. He'd screwed up one eye and shaded his face with his hand above his head to look at her properly. He was tanned and handsome. She nodded once, embarrassed at her cheeks flushing because a boy she didn't know had spoken to her, but flattered too because he was at least two years older. She was about to start secondary school in a few weeks, so she'd have to get used to being around older boys and stop being so childish.

He gently took the spade from her, dropped onto his knees and started digging a moat, flicking the sand behind him and stopping every so often to smile at her. When the next big wave came in, the water reached the narrow trench and flooded right round the castle. A buzz of exhilaration ran through her. She clapped her hands in delight, and he playfully dipped his hand in the water and splashed her legs, laughing. She shrieked and splashed him back, then he ran to the water's edge and she chased him.

For a second she'd glanced back at her family who were just as she'd left them. And despite her father's warning words about not going too far out ringing in her head, she'd trotted into the sea after him.

If only she'd heeded Dad's advice.

33

VICKI

I wake up at gone 8.30 a.m. I've been asleep a good half an hour. We're not far from Lytham St Annes on the outskirts of Blackpool. Debbie is humming along to George Michael on the radio, singing the line about how you've got to have faith.

'The storm isn't so bad up here,' I say to Debbie. She glances across at me and nods.

'Did the nap help?'

'Yeah, I feel a little better. Do you think it's worth calling Lee again? I could try FaceTime. I think I might be able to reason with him.'

'Possibly. Maybe text Marc first, find out where the AirTag is?'

'Yeah, good idea. Then I'll see if Dom managed to speak to Lee.' I check my tablet. There's a missed call from Cassie. I quickly text Marc for the AirTag's current location then I call her back.

'Hello Cass, any luck contacting Jess?' I ask first.

'No, nor Olly. And they're not at his house either according to his parents.'

'That's odd. Maybe they went to a party at a friend's house?'

'Possibly. I think I'll call a couple of her friends, see if they'll put a call out on their WhatsApp group. Jess will hate me for doing that, but I don't know what else to do. I need to make sure she's okay.'

'Let me know if you hear anything. Did Dom get through to Lee?'

'Yeah, that's why I tried to call you. Lee wouldn't tell him anything. Dom tried to persuade him to pull over at the services and he'd go up and meet with him this morning, but he wouldn't. Dom said Lee's too far gone, they were his exact words. He just couldn't get any sense out of him. He was rambling on about all sorts.'

'Shit.' Panic spikes through my heart. We need to get to him as soon as possible because my children could be in grave danger.

'Said it sounded like he was smoking while he was on the phone to him. He could hear Bella crying in the background. She was upset because she couldn't reach her bag to get her teddy according to Alfie, and Lee was refusing to stop the car.'

'Oh Jesus wept.' I press the pads of my fingers onto my forehead. 'What does he think he's doing?'

'It's crazy, isn't it?'

I tell her about the AirTag on Alfie's new trainers.

'At least you've got an idea where they are. Good luck with catching up with him. I hope everything is going to be okay. Call us if you need any help.'

'Same to you. Hopefully you'll find out where Jess is.'

'She's probably gone to meet Olly somewhere and forgotten to mention it. I guarantee they're not even bothered about us being worried.' She laughs.

We say goodbye and I check the reply from Marc. 'They're heading towards the South Pier, near Blackpool Tower,' I read to Debbie.

'We'll be there in approximately fifteen minutes,' Debbie says.

'I just hope they're okay. He shouldn't even be out with them in this weather.'

Debbie shakes her head and I can't even bring myself to speculate what he intends to do. Because whatever Lee is planning, I just hope that we're not too late.

34

DEBBIE

From what Debbie could hear of Vicki's conversation with Cassie, Dom has spoken to Lee, but it didn't sound good. Although she can't imagine that Dom had anything to say which would help her brother in a meaningful way. Writing him off as 'too far gone' is hardly a surprise coming from someone as self-centred as Dom.

Debbie prays Lee's only smoking straight cigarettes in front of the children, although that's bad enough. It's hard to defend his behaviour when he's upsetting his kids. Now she wishes she'd spoken to him at the services on her own, reminded him what they talked about. Maybe she should try and text him again, let him know about Marc putting AirTags in Alfie's new trainers, just as another example of him trying to take over Lee's family. It might put the fight back in him, because she senses he's losing the will to carry on.

But ironically, without the AirTags they wouldn't be able to track where Lee is taking them. Right now, it's more important than ever that they catch up with him and make sure the three of them are safe. If she told him they can track where he's going, she wouldn't put it past him to pull over and chuck the AirTags away. And they seem to be making good progress thanks to her driving like a bat out of hell whenever she can get away with it.

Vicki offers Debbie a small bottle of water. She thanks her and has a long drink then hands it back and offers Vicki a piece of gum, but she declines.

Debbie takes a couple of pieces herself and starts chewing hard, trying to suppress the fragments of memories coming at her of that day on the beach. But she can't stop them rushing back.

She'd been keen to show the boy how well she could swim, so she swam in the sea beside him. But before long he was moving into deeper waters, and she had to stop. Her toes could only just touch the ground, so she raised her hands and called to him that she was turning back, but he didn't seem to hear her. She thought she'd made it clear to him she wasn't allowed to go out of her depth, yet here he was leading her too far out. Or was she being unfair blaming him? She shouldn't have tried to show off by keeping up with him.

As she'd turned back to the shore, a big wave slapped into her and she lost her footing. Panic darted through her veins as her head went under. Water shot up her nostrils and into her mouth. She thought she was going to drown but she managed to bob back up to the surface again, coughing and spluttering. She tried to stand up, stretching her toes to find sand, there was nothing below her and she sank underwater again.

The boy swam over and lifted her up into his strong arms and kept hold of her. Relief flooded through her. He was her hero, and she'd tell her parents and everyone that when they were safely back on the shore. But he was swimming with her in the opposite direction, further out to sea. She pleaded with him to take her back, but he didn't answer. She could see her family and every person on the beach becoming smaller and smaller. The further out he swam with her the more petrified she became until she could barely catch her breath.

Soon, they were so far out she was sure that no one on the beach could see them. He turned on her then, dropping her out of his arms and gripping her wrists. His face changed from smiley to a dark menacing frown. He smirked as he grabbed her between her legs. She tried to protest but he pushed her head under the water, and when she came up gasping for air, he held her tight. She kicked and scratched him, but he wouldn't let go.

Then he swam off, leaving her to drown.

Thankfully a jet skier nearby had saved her and alerted the lifeguard on his radio and the boy was apprehended when he reached the shore.

She's relived every fragmented moment a thousand times since. Eventually she found her strength again, overcame her fear of water by training in a local swimming pool over several years with a patient and dedicated teacher. But she's never been near the sea again, or a beach.

Vicki is completely unaware of what happened to her, but maybe she should have allowed Lee to share her secret. She picks up a cigarette from the centre console and lights it, hoping Vicki doesn't notice the slight tremble in her hand.

35

VICKI

We park next to the pavement on South Promenade road at about 8.45 a.m. Sunrise was half an hour ago but it's so grey and rainy, it still feels like nighttime. The whole area is empty apart from the odd brave jogger and dog walker. The cold salty air fills my nostrils as we jump out. We both pull on big coats, woolly hats, gloves and boots from the back of the Surf, then stride onto Blackpool's South Pier.

'We need to hurry. Marc's message said the AirTag is located at the end of the pier. That means Lee and Bella are probably there too.'

'Where has he parked? I don't see his camper van. Marc couldn't have got it wrong, could he?'

'I don't see how.' We run down the pier, instinctively grabbing on to one another in an effort not to blow over. The old wooden frame creaks and the boards are slippery from so much rain. Dark choppy waves are visible through the gaps, reminding us of how close to danger we are. If a huge gust of wind were to catch us off balance, it could sweep us over the side into the deep treacherous sea below.

'Can you see them?' I shout but Debbie shakes her head. The further along the pier we go, the windier it becomes – this Victorian long-fingered structure sticking out across the sea.

Then I spot a dot of neon pink in the distance – the colour of Bella's rucksack – so we hurry towards it, trying not to be seen. As we get closer to the end of the pier, I can hear Lee shouting at Alfie to hurry up. He's practically dragging Bella along by the hand beneath the high stilts of the rollercoaster ride which reaches right to the edge of the railing. Bella's crying and complaining and doesn't let up, even when Lee begs her to.

'Hey, bro, what are you doing?' Debbie calls out, waving her arms at him in her olive wax coat and deerstalker hat. I hang back, hoping he doesn't see me straight away.

It takes a moment for Lee to register that someone has even spoken to him. When he swings round to face her and takes in who it is, his eyes widen, then he shrugs. I hide behind one of the comical photograph boards, where you put your face in the cutout and look like you're wearing a polka dot bikini next to an old man in his deck chair.

'What are you doing here?' he shouts into the wind.

'I wanted to see if you and the children were alright. You didn't sound so good on the phone,' Debbie yells back.

'How did you know where I was? Did *she* guess I'd come here?'

I step out from behind the board.

'Mum!' Bella cries out and lurches towards me, but Lee catches hold of the rucksack on her back and keeps her there. Alfie stands beside him but looks unsure what to do. He's like a little boy again, the bravado knocked out of him.

'Back off, Vicki,' Lee shouts and pulls Bella closer to him, holding them both against the perimeter railings. A metal post is missing next to them, the gap tied loosely with flimsy tape, blowing wildly in the wind.

'Be careful you don't slip!' I shout to them.

'I said back off or I'll jump and take them both with me,' Lee shouts. 'I mean it.'

'You're hurting me, Daddy,' Bella sobs and pulls back but her foot slides away from her under the railings, right over the edge of the pier. Lee grabs her, but her shoe gets stuck and slips off, flying into a gust of wind and down into the sea.

'Christ almighty, what are you doing?' I scream, tearing at my hair.

'Take it easy, Lee, why don't you let them come to me?' Debbie says in a steady voice.

'Please get them away from the edge,' I cry, holding my hands up. I step back so he doesn't feel threatened.

'You're not taking them away from me again.' Lee stands in front of them so they can't move. They are inches from the gap, wide enough for someone to fall through.

'Why are you doing this? They've not done anything wrong. Please let me take them home,' I scream into the wind.

'No chance. They're staying with me. I will not let that man step into my shoes. Into my life. *I'm* their dad, they should be with me,' he says, standing closer to the edge.

'He's not going to. That's not his style. What makes you even think that?' I ask.

Lee furrows his brow. 'Because he's taken everything else from me. You really think you know him, don't you?' It's more a mocking statement than a question.

'What do you mean?' I shout back, hoping he can hear me, but a huge gust of wind smacks Lee against the kids, squashing them against the railings, far too close to the gap. Both children cry out, their hands slipping from Lee's. He lets go of them briefly then grabs hold of their wrists even tighter.

'Please tell me what you mean?' I repeat, but Debbie interrupts us.

'Let the kids come to me,' she implores, but he ignores her, his eyes fixed on me as though he's deciding whether to tell me or not.

'Marc's the one who planted the drugs on me. He's the reason I got the sack,' Lee yells.

36

I shake my head. 'No... no, that's not right. You can't blame him just because he's with me now. You're the one who was found with drugs in your desk drawer.' I see the shock on Alfie's face and immediately wish I could take back my words. I didn't mean to say it out loud in front of them. I've been so careful not to give them specific reasons for their dad not working, then his absence from their lives. But maybe they *should* know about his addiction. It's time I stopped protecting him and them from reality.

'You don't understand. Marc is the one who set me up. He planted them there. I would never do drugs at work, and you know it.'

'Do I? I'm not sure I know you any more. And how exactly did you get to this conclusion? Because I'm certain he would never do that,' I shout back, hardly recognising the Lee I loved, but I have to admit his plea of innocence has a ring of truth about it. The pain of my rebuttal is all over his face.

'Yeah, you're right, he would never do his own dirty work. He got one of his minions to do it for him.'

'How do you know that?' I step closer, gripping onto the railing, not wanting to miss a word, but scared he'll see me as a threat.

'Because one of the boys who came to do work experience told me. Marc promised him a permanent job when he left school if he put a baggie in my drawer. Told him not to worry, it was just a prank between work colleagues, but when he heard I'd got the sack, he confessed to me that Marc had made him do it. Not surprising that he never did get a job offer after his two weeks were up. I should take Marc to a tribunal for unfair dismissal. If this boy tells them what he told me, Marc will be finished.'

'And who is this boy, do I know him?'

'I don't want to tell you and drop him in it, or for it to get back to Marc. The boy's a good lad. He didn't have to tell me what that scumbag did to me.'

'How do you know he's telling the truth?'

'How else would he know why I got sacked? I didn't tell anyone the reason except you. Unless you've been telling people?'

'No, I haven't told anyone.' I hate lying, but I can't tell him I told Cassie. She's the only person I mentioned it to as our families know each other well. Did she tell Dom or Jess? I can usually trust her not to gossip about my personal issues, even with her family. Or is it possible this boy made it up about Marc getting him to plant the drugs in Lee's desk. But why do that?

Another huge gust of wind wallops the side of the pier, sending Bella's teddy flying out of her hands and into the sea. She screams and this time manages to pull away from Lee, and with her head bowed, she charges towards me. I grab hold of her and pull her into my arms, kissing the top of her damp hair.

'It's okay, baby, it's okay,' I tell her.

'Lee, please let Alfie come to me. We can talk about this somewhere warm and dry.' Debbie steps towards him; her hat sweeps off her head and is carried away in the wind. Lee backs away, holding tightly onto Alfie's arm.

'So you're just going to let *him* take my children from me. He's already stolen my wife, lost me my job, and from what I've heard, he's practically living at my house. Why are you helping them do this to me, Debbie?'

'I'm not helping them do anything to you.' Debbie's voice is strained and raw, speaking loudly so she can be heard above the howling wind and rough sea. 'I'm just trying to look out for your children. You're putting them in danger behaving like this. Please let Alfie come to me.'

'*Please*, Lee,' I cry mournfully but my words are whipped away by the wind. 'I know you're upset that we're not together any more, but the drugs are making you paranoid and irrational. It doesn't have to be this way. I want you to get clean so we can move forward, be the good father that you are to our children. I want you to be a regular part of their lives.'

'Do you?' he shouts bitterly. 'Meanwhile you're moving on with *him* and our children. How long before they start calling him daddy?' He breaks down and cries into his hand.

'Lee, please,' Debbie pleads.

'What do you even see in him, apart from his money and status?' Lee continues, eyes focused on me. 'Is that what this is about, a smart move up the status ladder, because he can give you things I can't? I don't fit into that Instagram picture of a successful life, do I. And now you're just humouring me to get what you want.'

'No, I'm absolutely not. Just please stop with this self-pity. You had fifteen years with me. You had everything and threw it all away for a bit of weed. It's time you took responsibility for your own actions.'

'I know, I'm a failure.' Lee looks away.

'You're a great dad when you're clean. No one could ever replace you as their father, but they need safety and consistency, a strong and steady male role model in their lives, and right now, Marc is the right kind of influence they need.'

'He can't put a foot wrong in your eyes, can he? Everything he touches turns to money.'

'It's not about him. It's about you. I want to include you in every aspect of our children's upbringing, but not with you like this.' I point to his scruffy coat ripped at the pockets and dirty smears down the front. His hair and beard have grown too long and haven't been washed let alone combed in quite some time.

'But you still don't get it, do you?' He shouts, 'I'm in this state *because* of Marc. He doesn't want me around in any capacity. He's gone out of his way to destroy me. Take everything from me. Get me sacked, seduce my wife, steal my children, my house. What am I left with? Nothing. I have nothing. I'm living in a camper van, I have no job, no income and no family. What do you expect me to do?' For the first time I see the sheer desperation in his eyes, and something shifts in my chest.

'I'm so sorry. I should have been there for you more,' Debbie says, her voice breaking.

'You have got *nothing* to be sorry about, do you hear me?' He points at her.

I glance at Debbie. She's choked up. 'You desperately need help, Lee, and we will do everything we can to make that happen, I promise you,' I say and Debbie nods.

'It's no good, it's too late.' He shakes his head. 'I'm telling you now, he's going to stop you at every turn.'

'But why, what has he got against you?'

Lee shakes his head again, looking at the ground. 'I discovered something about him, and when I confronted him, he went crazy at me.'

'What was it? Tell me.' My throat is raw and croaky from shouting into the wind.

'It won't make any difference.'

'But I want to know what it is, please just tell me.'

'Ask him yourself. It's really not up to me to fill in the blanks for you.' He's straining so hard to be heard, he's red in the face. He bows his head and draws the back of his hand across his brow.

'Please, Lee, let Alfie come to me,' Debbie pleads.

Lee glances down at Alfie's distraught face and loosens his hold on his wrist. He says something to him and when he lets go, Alfie hesitates and rubs his skin, as though not wanting to leave his dad's side.

'Alfie, come on, please.' I wave to him and he runs into my open arms. Debbie steps towards Lee but a gust of wind pushes her back.

Lee's eyes widen and Debbie's mouth falls open. I glance behind me to see what they're looking at. A tall figure in a long, hooded raincoat is striding at pace in our direction.

37

DEBBIE

Debbie's nerves are in shreds. Lee threatening to jump with his kids is horrifying. She's shaking all over and tries not to show it, but she really thought this was it. Seeing him at rock bottom cuts deep. Even though he's an adult, Lee will always be her little brother. She knows how it feels to think there's a better alternative to living. It's so much harder witnessing it from someone you love.

If she could just understand what's going on in his head, she might be able to help him. He told her on the phone last night that he found out something about Marc but he wouldn't say what it was, only that he's struggling with it and that if Marc had genuine feelings for Vicki, he would be honest and tell her everything. She tried her hardest to persuade him to open up to her, but he started weeping down the phone. Hearing him hurting like that was so upsetting. For a minute she couldn't speak either. Now he's said the same to Vicki. Debbie needs to find out what it is because Lee is falling to pieces right in front of their eyes and it's scaring her. He was so close to the edge, but Alfie didn't seem to want to leave his dad at first, then he ran into Vicki's arms. It was such a relief.

But hang on, who's that marching towards them?

No, it can't be! What is he doing here?

38

VICKI

The man in the raincoat comes into clearer view.

'Not him!' Lee yells. 'Why is he here?'

I quickly hand Alfie and Bella over to Debbie, telling her to shelter under the rollercoaster behind them and instructing Alfie to stay there and look after his sister. Bella is still grizzling about her lost teddy bear, and Alfie holds her hand as Debbie ushers them to the area near the solid wooden stilts.

'Focus on me, Lee, talk to me,' I hear Debbie shout at him behind me as I hurry towards Marc to stop him coming any closer. I need to try to keep some distance between them, but my mind is scrabbling to find a reason why he's here when I specifically said he shouldn't come.

Marc's arms open wide as he strides towards me and when I reach him, he pulls me into a bear hug and tries to kiss me on the lips, but I pull away. This is not appropriate now, nor do we have time for this.

'What are you doing here?' I ask, not able to keep the irritation out of my voice. I twist round to check that Alfie and Bella are safely sheltered out of the storm.

'I couldn't concentrate on work while you're stuck out here in this weather. I needed to make sure you and the kids were okay. That's alright, isn't it? Aren't you pleased to see me?' He sounds mildly hurt and I frown at his question, which seems self-indulgent under the circumstances.

'Of course I am, but I need to get back to the kids.' I want to say back to Lee too, but don't want to poke Marc with that stick. I give him a quick hug back. 'You may as well wait for us in the car,' I try and say light-heartedly, all the time checking behind me to make sure Lee hasn't done anything to put himself or the children in any more danger.

'But what's going on over there, what's Lee up to taking off with the kids?' Marc lifts his chin and peers over my head at Lee standing on the edge of the pier, his coat flapping in the wind.

'I did say it was best if you didn't come,' I tell him firmly, my voice raspy at constantly speaking loudly above the howling wind and heavy rain beating on the wooden walkway.

'But did you find out why he ran off with them? They shouldn't be out in this bad weather. They should be safe at home.' He goes to take a step in Lee's direction, probably wanting to tell him exactly that, but I put a hand on his arm to keep him with me.

'I know, and you're right, it's not what I was expecting to be doing today, but you being here isn't going to help. He's in a bad way mentally right now and I just need to make sure he's okay.' I try and keep my voice steady, but I'm getting to the point of yelling at him to leave.

'Seriously, Vicki? Can't you see that he's got you running around to his tune? Always acting out like a real drama queen.'

'He's the father of my children.' I raise my voice to be heard above the escalating roar of the wind and constant boom of crashing waves below us.

'Yeah, and doesn't he like to play that card to get his own way? Honestly, Vicki, he's not going to stop playing up like a spoilt brat until he gets your full attention and sympathy.'

'That's not a fair or helpful thing to say right now. He's a good dad when he's not stoned. He's having a difficult time adjusting to not living with us any more, *and* he lost his job don't forget. It's a lot for anyone to cope with.' Moving forward a step to steady myself against the battering wind, I glance back at Lee and Debbie. She's still talking to him, keeping him calm. Alfie and Bella are huddled together under the rollercoaster.

'I know and I'm sorry, but the point is he's an addict and it won't help him in the long run if you pander to him; you'll end up becoming an enabler.'

'But I feel partly responsible because I've been so hard on him, not letting him see the kids, and right at this moment, he's struggling. I can't turn away and pretend it has nothing to do with me. Look, I need to go over and help

Debbie talk him down. So if you want to do anything to help, please look after the children under the rollercoaster over there, away from all this.' I swallow hard, my throat sore and dry.

'Of course. I'm here to do whatever I can. I only want to help you.' He holds his hands up and walks over to the shelter of the rollercoaster.

'Will someone tell me what the fuck he is doing here?' Lee screams at me.

'Please calm down.' I clench my teeth. 'Marc was concerned about me and the children, that's all. Please, just let us take you home.'

'Home? Ha! Where's that exactly? I don't have a home any more, do I? I've been living in my camper van since I got the sack because of that lowlife.'

'You told me you were renting a flat somewhere,' I say.

'Only because I knew you'd go on at me about not having somewhere suitable to take the children or let them sleep over.'

I stare at him, taking in the smudges of dirt on his clothes, the stitching that's come undone on the hem of his coat. His once clean nails are rimmed with dirt and bitten down. I should have noticed how far he'd let himself go.

'Come back to mine then,' Debbie says gently. 'There's loads of room at the farm, and I could do with another pair of hands.'

'I can't do that.' He shakes his head.

'Why not?'

'There's no point. Who's going to employ me after being sacked for bringing drugs to work? Doesn't look good on my CV. *He* made sure of that,' Lee jabs his finger in Marc's direction, a look of disgust on his face.

'That's not right, they should give you a chance,' I say.

'Did you read that in some wholesome women's magazine?' He sneers. 'I don't even get replies now when I apply for jobs. As soon as they've seen I've got a caution for possession, no one wants to know me. That goes for so-called friends too. If I can't get an interview, how am I ever going to be able to buy a place of my own? I can barely afford to eat.'

'We can sell the house. I've been thinking about it anyway. You'll have half the money from the sale,' I tell him.

'That won't be that much though will it, not since we remortgaged to do up the bathroom and kitchen. Anyway, what about you and the kids, how will you afford somewhere big enough?'

My eyes naturally slide sideways to Marc and the children standing with him.

'Oh of course, I get it, stupid me. You're moving into lover boy's mansion.' He nods and stares at the sea.

'No actually, but we're talking about selling up both houses and buying one together.'

'Right.' Lee tips his head up to the murky sky. 'I don't think I fit into this picture any more.'

'You do; the children need you.'

He shakes his head, eyes glistening. Then he twists away and steps into the gap, holding the horizontal metal poles either side. In one swift move he steps over the hazard tape, the toes of his trainers hanging over the edge of the pier as he sways in the wind.

Bella screams.

'What are you doing, Lee? Come back here,' I shout, holding my hand out to him.

'I told you, I don't fit into this cosy family picture any more.' He won't look at me and stares down at the waves crashing against the pier's ancient frame.

'Don't do this, Lee, the children need you.' I edge closer, sea spray on my skin, and reach out to him again.

'But what about you? *You* don't need me so what is there to live for?' He twists round, switching his hands from pole to pole so he's facing me.

'Think of the children. Please! Aren't they enough?'

'Daddy,' Bella sobs.

'Dad, please come back.' Alfie is crying and breaks free from Marc's hands. Debbie is holding Bella as tightly as she can. I dash over to stop Alfie running towards his dad and the gap in the railings.

Lee is leaning backwards, over the edge. Marc leaps forward and is across to him in moments. He grabs a fistful of Lee's jumper in his hand and pulls him towards him so their faces are only inches apart.

'Move back everyone, stand behind me,' Marc commands, waving his other hand like an oar.

'Get away from me,' I hear Lee hiss, followed by a string of expletives as he fights to push himself away from Marc.

'Don't be an idiot, Lee... be careful!' Marc cries out.

But Lee falls backwards, mouth open, arms flailing into the sea.

39

DEBBIE

Debbie's heart is in her throat. Marc stands on the edge of the pier looking down, slowly shaking his head. Why didn't he grab Lee with the other hand or do something to save him? He's useless. He was right there.

Bella is screaming at an ear-piercing pitch while Alfie runs to the railings and leans over to see if he can spot his dad in the water, but the sea is so rough and the waves are huge, it's impossible. Vicki calls frantically to Alfie to move back.

'Who's the strongest swimmer here, Marc?' Debbie shouts, expecting him to do the decent thing and jump in to save Lee, but his eyes widen with fear at her suggestion. He steps backwards, firmly shaking his head. After all his bravado and everything he's put Lee through, he's a coward.

Unless he doesn't want Lee to be saved.

Could he have pushed him? It's not inconceivable but it is hard to judge. Marc certainly made sure everyone was behind him, so no one had a clear view of him holding onto Lee. Vicki is trying to find out from him what happened. Now they're running across the other side of the pier trying to find Lee in the water, but it's impossible in this weather and we're running out of time.

There's only one thing for it, Debbie decides.

She'll have to go in.

40

VICKI

'Daddy!' Bella screams, high-pitched and deafening.

'Dad!' Alfie cries, yanking himself away from my grip.

'What have you done?' Debbie shouts.

Marc staggers backwards in a daze, holding up his hands.

I run over to Marc and tug at his coat sleeve. 'What the hell happened?'

'I don't know, it happened so quickly. He was trying to pull away from me and his jumper slipped clean out of my hand.' He stares at his open palm, shaking.

'Hurry, Mum, we need to help Dad,' Alfie cries, leaning over the railings, shouting Lee's name into the roar of the sea.

'Stay back,' I warn him.

'I can't see him, Mum, I can't see him anywhere.' Alfie is crying, nose streaming and Bella is still sobbing in Debbie's arms.

I peer over the side and search immediately below us, then as far away as it's possible to see, but there's no sign of Lee anywhere in the churning dark waves and seafoam.

'He could have drifted underneath us,' Marc says, and we all run to the opposite side of the pier to see if he's there. But he isn't. Should I dive in after him? I wish Marc would because I can't leave the children and I'm not a strong swimmer. We could both die out there. Is this it, has Lee gone forever? A stab of pain jabs my heart. I replay in my mind him dropping into the water, down deep and imagine him struggling to come up again. My heart quickens at the thought of him holding his breath, trying to reach the surface for air.

I pull Alfie away from the side just as another gust of wind presses into him and tries to tear him away from me. As I wrap him in my arms, there are tears in our eyes. How will I tell my son he may never see his dad again?

'What did he say to you before...? I couldn't hear him,' I say close to Alfie's ear.

'He said, *he's* already won,' Alfie sobs. My mouth opens at the bluntness of the words. He means Marc. But how could Lee give in and do *this*, right in front of the children?

'Stay with your mum and brother, Bella,' Debbie yells. 'Call the coast guard, Vicki, I'm going in.'

'What? You can't do that.' But she chucks me her keys and lets go of Bella. I reach out and snatch my daughter's hand tightly in mine, drawing her to me. I kiss the top of her sea-spray damp hair, then Alfie's.

Debbie kicks her ankle wellies off and steps over the tape.

'Are you sure about this?' I ask her, not knowing if I should try and stop her or offer to do it myself. But I can't do either. Does this mean I'm a coward? They say you don't really know who you are until you're put in a life-or-death situation. All I know in my heart is that I need to stay and protect my children but if one of them had gone in, I wouldn't hesitate to save them. I glance at Marc to see if he'll change his mind and go in, but he just shrugs. I can guess what he's thinking: it's her brother. And in a way he's right; what closer bond is there than blood?

Debbie nods to me then she launches herself off the edge of the pier, dropping down into the sea with the smallest splash. Both children start screaming and crying again, and I huddle them to me trying to reassure them that their aunty is a brave and strong swimmer and she's going to try her best to save Daddy.

I'm in a daze as I lead them under the shelter of the rollercoaster where Marc is hunched over his phone. I don't know how he can focus on anything after what's happened to Lee. Perhaps it's his way of blocking out reality. I stay with the children and use Marc's phone to dial 999 to alert the coast guard.

When I get through, I describe where we are and what's happened and go and peer back over the edge as I speak, searching for any sign of Lee or Debbie in the wildly choppy water below. But I can't see either of them anywhere and my mind skips ahead to me having to explain to Alfie and Bella that their dad and aunty have drowned. I shake away the thought, and pray that's not going to happen, instead they're going to be rescued alive.

Within minutes of my call, I spot a speed lifeboat being launched from a jetty further up the beach. Then I spot what looks like two tiny heads bobbing up and down in the waves. Debbie appears to be supporting her brother in the crook of her arm, desperately trying to keep his face above water as the speed-boat careens towards them at high speed. Thank God they're both alive.

I escort the children back to the safety of Debbie's car with Marc following close behind. His car is parked nearby but he gets in the passenger seat next to me. We watch as the lifeboat comes into land. An ambulance is waiting for them, and four paramedics lift two people on board in stretchers under shiny metallic blankets. Marc draws me into his chest, and I cry into my hands with relief.

41

Marc goes off in his car to find us a hotel for the night and I follow the ambulance to the local hospital, trying not to break the speed limit.

In Accident and Emergency, I ask about Lee and Debbie but all the receptionist can tell me is that the two people who were rescued from the sea are being treated.

Once I've settled the children in the busy waiting room with a hot chocolate each and a lunchbox of sandwiches from the cool bag in Debbie's car, I check my phone. Nothing yet from Marc. It's not exactly high season so he shouldn't have any problem finding vacancies. I think back to what Lee said about him. Could Marc really have gone out of his way to get him sacked, or was Lee trying to frame him? Marc's always been so professional, I can't imagine a spiteful side to him.

There's a text from Cassie saying they've still not heard from Jess. I wonder why she's gone off without telling her mum. I hope she's okay.

'Is Daddy going to die?' Bella asks. Alfie takes a small doll out of her rucksack and hands it to her. He tells her people can be saved, he learnt about it at school, and he shows her how to press its chest with her fingers to give it CPR.

'Sweetheart, I don't know the answer to that, but if they don't come and tell us how he is soon, I'll go and ask a nurse, I promise.' I'm not ready to acknowledge that Lee deliberately pushed himself away from Marc and fell into the sea, wanting to end his life.

She nods. 'Do you think the rescue people found my teddy too?' Bella asks.

'I'm sorry but I doubt that very much.' I stroke her hair.

Bella starts to cry so I hug her to my chest, and we rock together gently until she's quiet again.

When Bella is finally engrossed in a puzzle game in the kids' play corner and Alfie is reading something on his tablet, I take a moment to stand outside the building near the smokers and sip my coffee. I lean the side of my head against the window so I can keep an eye on the children and see if anyone comes to give us an update on Lee and Debbie.

I take in a long deep breath and let it out slowly. It's been twenty years since I last smoked a cigarette but the ritual of hanging around other smokers, taking a few moments out of a hectic day, never quite leaves you. I read somewhere that taking in a lungful of fresh air then blowing it out is the equivalent to drawing on a cigarette. It's certainly a healthier, more mindful option.

I can't help wishing Marc hadn't come. Especially without telling me. I'm sure Debbie and I could have persuaded Lee down if he wasn't there.

Could there be any truth in anything Lee insinuated about Marc, or is he just bitter and paranoid? He said I didn't really know him. What did Lee find out about him for him to think that? I can't get it out of my mind. It's hard to believe Marc would have asked someone to plant drugs in Lee's desk deliberately. And all because Lee confronted him with something about his past? Seems unlikely. Would Lee really lie about it just to make Marc look bad? Probably. It's the sort of thing he might do to try and put me off him. But if it is true, what kind of secret would provoke such an extreme response from Marc? The thought of him not being able to share it with me is a worry. It must be something bad for him to ruin Lee's career, and not want me to know about it. But then am I any better? I've kept my secret from him. If we can't be honest with each other at this stage in our relationship, where does that leave us? The truth is, I'm not prepared to share my secret with either Marc or Lee. How can I when I know they'd both be heartbroken? I take in another deep breath and just hope Lee makes a full recovery, not just for the children's sake, but so I can quiz him about this secret he's found out about Marc, because it seems to be the reason they despise each other.

Alfie has moved onto a child's chair in the play area so he's next to Bella. I couldn't bear it if they lost their dad, no matter how mad he makes me sometimes.

I push the heavy door and go back inside and sit with them. A few minutes later a nurse comes into the waiting room and makes a beeline for me.

'Are you Lee Kendle's wife?'

I nod, not wanting to correct her because I need to know right now how he is without wasting time explaining we're separated.

'Both Lee and his sister Debbie are in intensive care and are stable. Lee has hypothermia but he's responding well to treatment. Do you know if he spent the longest in the water?'

'Yes, by several minutes.'

'That would explain it. There's a policeman outside who would like to ask you a few questions about what happened. They'd like to take a statement from you and anyone else who was a witness.'

I nod. 'But are they both going to be okay?'

'Lee still has some water in his lungs, but he should make a full recovery in a few days. Debbie fared much better. She's exhausted but doing well. She saved her brother's life.'

I thank her and hug the children, tears streaming down my face.

'There's nothing else you can do right now, so you may as well come back in the morning.' She gives a brief smile and leaves the waiting room.

Marc has texted me the address of a hotel he's found for tonight. He will have to go back to work in the morning. I can't have him with us when we're visiting Lee.

When we get outside, I speak to the policewoman and tell her briefly what happened. I agree to go into the station, and send Marc too, so we can both give our statements.

As we're walking back to the car, my tablet rings. It's Cassie.

'Is everything okay?' I ask her, helping the children climb in Debbie's car, then shut the door.

'No... no it's not, something terrible has happened,' Cassie says, her tone desperate, distraught. I stand still.

'Oh God. What is it?' I bring my tablet closer to my face.

'It's Olly, Jess's boyfriend. He's been found dead.'

42

VICKI

'What? Are you sure?' I ask, leaning against Debbie's car, hoping the children can't hear my conversation.

'He was found in the park near our house. His body was discovered by a dog walker about an hour ago. I can't stop shaking.'

'Oh my God, is Dom with you?'

'Yes, he's right here. The police turned up at the door. I thought they'd found Jess.' She breaks down crying uncontrollably.

'Jesus, Cassie. Do they know what happened to him?'

'It looks like he was struck from behind and the side of his head hit a rock. The police think it could be a mugging gone wrong because his phone is missing.'

'That's awful. Who the hell kills someone for their phone? I assume Jess was with him; is she okay?'

'That's the thing, she wasn't.'

'But she's back home now, right?'

'No, she's not.'

'So where do you think she's gone?' I ask and get in the car.

'We don't know, her phone is still switched off.'

'Do you think she had an argument with Olly?'

'What are you saying?' Cassie asks.

I can't even begin to imagine what's going through Cassie's mind, but Jess hurting her boyfriend and running off probably isn't one of them.

'There's no way this is anything to do with Jess. She loved Olly.'

I open my mouth to speak then shut it again. It's not my secret to tell. I'm glad we're not on FaceTime so she can't see my expression. I thought Jess would have confided in her mum about sleeping with another boy. She told me she was drunk, and it was a terrible mistake and how she felt bad about it, because she hadn't even slept with Olly yet.

'Do the police have any idea where she could have gone?' I ask.

'None. Like I said, her phone is switched off so there's no way of knowing. We've tried contacting all her friends, but no one has seen her.'

'Hang on, I'm sure she said she has the "phone findable after power off" function enabled on her mobile, because we talked about it after she lost her phone at our house one time. I found it under our sofa. So you should still be able to find out the last location of her mobile before it was turned off. It might help.'

'Thanks, I'll check her tablet.'

'Can you think of anyone who would want to hurt Olly? Or are the police convinced it was a random attack?' I rub my forehead, still trying to take in the shocking news.

'I'm not sure yet. He lived with his gran. She'll be devastated.' Cassie can barely get the words out, like she's going to cry again.

'Oh no, that's awful. Can you think where Jess could be? Do you think she saw something?'

'I don't know. I just wish she'd contact us, let us know she's okay. We're going out of our minds here.'

'I wish there was something I could do.' What if Jess has been hurt too? But I don't say it aloud.

'You don't think it's anything to do with those kids who turned up at your house do you?' Cassie sounds hopeful that I might know more than I'm saying, but I'm not sure that I do.

'Possibly. Lee chased them out of the house, but what if they came back and followed Jess and Olly to the park?' I imagine they were pretty angry at being made to leave.

'Oh Jesus. Maybe they attacked Olly and Jess ran off scared?'

'Jess told me that Fran made her do some awful things and posted the videos online. She's the same girl who's been bullying Jess at school.'

Cassie is silent on the line. I've put my foot in it.

'Cassie, are you there? Didn't she tell you about it?'

'No, she did not,' comes the curt reply. 'How do you know about this and not me?'

'I don't know. Maybe it was easier for her to tell someone outside the family?'

Another silence.

'Do you know if Jess had another argument with her dad, and has gone off to cool down?' I have to ask although she'll hate me for it. We both know Dom has a hot temper. Jess was probably too scared to say anything to them about the bullies in case he went round mouthing off to Fran's parents. But Cassie did say Dom went out looking for Jess after they got back from the theatre. What if he found Jess and Olly together at the park and they had a massive argument?

'I don't know what you're trying to imply, but we did not argue,' comes the frosty reply from Dom. Shit. I'd forgotten he was there.

'Sorry Dom, I didn't mean anything by it,' I lie. 'Just trying to come up with reasons for her disappearing without telling you.'

'I'll contact the school, see what they have to say about the bullying. So what else isn't my daughter telling me that you know about?' Cassie tone is now as stoney as Dom's.

'Cassie, please. We chat a bit when she's here babysitting, that's all. My mum was always the last to know about anything I was up to, I made sure of it. Weren't you like that at her age too?'

'I suppose so.' She pauses before changing the subject and asks if I caught up with Lee and the kids. I tell her what happened and where I am.

'Oh Vicki, I'm sorry to hear that. Are Lee and Debbie going to be okay?'

'I think so, but Lee's in intensive care.'

'I'll go up and see him, cheer him up,' Dom says.

'He'd like that,' I say. 'Marc turned up, which made things so much worse.'

'He probably only wanted to help,' Cassie says.

'Yes, I suppose so.' Now is not the right time to tell them that Lee accused Marc of getting him sacked.

'I'd better let you go, you've probably got loads of people you need to call, and I need to go and see to the kids. Let me know if you hear any more about Olly's attack and when Jess is found, okay?'

'Will do. And I hope Lee and his sister make a full recovery,' Cassie says.

'Ditto,' Dom adds.

I end the call and gaze up at the sky. Poor Olly. I only met him a couple of times and he seemed such a kind boy.

Where are you, Jess?

I hope she's okay. I'm selfishly grateful Cassie doesn't appear to know about my secret visit to the clinic, otherwise she would have come straight out asking me all sorts of questions. Jess has been holding back quite a lot herself, especially from her parents. I wish I knew another way of contacting her. My guess is she was with Olly when he was attacked but managed to run off. She could be scared they'd come after her if she says anything. Unless... No. I'm pretty sure the Jess I know wouldn't be capable of hurting anyone.

Except you never really know what people are capable of, do you?

43

Marc is waiting for us in the hotel car park along the seafront. We dump our bags in our room, freshen up, then go out for a wander around the town and find somewhere to eat. I'm still in shock so barely have anything.

It's evening by the time we get back. I ring the hospital for an update, and the nurse tells me that Lee is due to come out of intensive care in a few hours, so we should be able to visit him in the morning, and Debbie will be discharged, all being well. It's a relief to know they are both on the mend.

When we get back to the hotel, Marc helps by carrying a sleeping Bella up to our room. Once I've settled them both down for the night, I turn the main lights off and we have a long hug. Then we sit on the bed with a dim wall lamp on and drink a couple of small bottles of wine from the mini bar.

'What happened to Lee... I can't get it out of my head,' he says, blinking hard. 'I tried to save him, but I don't know what else I could have done. He was leaning back so far and his jumper just slipped out of my hand.' He holds his hand out in front of him, reliving the moment.

'I think he wanted to fall, to get away from you, from all of us, and life in general.'

'Weed is notorious for making people paranoid and seeing me must have triggered him. I'm so sorry. You were right as usual. I should have stayed away, but I thought I was helping.'

I nod. It's too late for sorry.

'And what he said, you know I had no choice but to sack him, don't you? If I hadn't, I'd have been breaching a company rule.'

'Rules you presumably made. So I'm guessing you could have made an exception? Launched an investigation at least.' I purse my lips, trying to control my annoyance. I suspect he's only saying this because it's Lee.

'I really can't be seen to change the rules when it suits me. Anyway, there wouldn't have been any point. The evidence was right there for everyone to see. We only investigate if there's any doubt.'

'And there is doubt. He thinks he was set up, by you or someone else.'

Marc shakes his head slowly, eyebrows raised. 'I think he's doing everything he can to shift the blame. And I get it, I do. He's a desperate man.'

'Where's the evidence that Lee brought the drugs in and put them there himself? I mean it's an unlocked drawer, so anyone could have slipped them in.' The more she considers this possibility, the more she's inclined to question whether Lee is guilty.

'It seems unlikely. It was his desk. No one else ever sat there, so who would do that?'

'Anyone who wanted to get him into trouble?' I raise an eyebrow, but his expression doesn't change.

'He was one of our most popular and hard-working employees. A huge loss to the business, as you know. I can't think of anyone who wanted him sacked.'

'You're the owner. You could have given him the benefit of the doubt.'

Marc shakes his head and finishes his glass of wine. 'Like I said, I really couldn't make an exception for anyone, not even if you asked me. I'm sorry. I didn't know you felt so strongly about it.'

'Well to be honest I didn't until Lee said today that he thought he'd been framed.'

'Drugs make people blame everyone around them except themselves. It's part of being under the control of the substance. Addicts come up with all sorts of excuses and reasons for their behaviour and will defend the drug to the bitter end.'

I nod. He sounds convincing, but I'd like to hear more of Lee's side of this. What was this secret that set them at loggerheads in the first place?

'Lee mentioned he'd found out something about you, said you threatened him to keep quiet and that's why you set him up.'

Marc's eyes widen, then he shakes his head. 'I don't know why I'm so surprised. He'll come up with anything to explain his behaviour. Did he tell you what it was?' He unties his shoe laces, head bowed.

'No. He wouldn't. Told me to ask you.'

'He's playing games with you, Vicki. It's actually quite sad how far he's fallen in such a short space of time. I hope he gets the help he needs.' He tops up our glasses and I update him briefly on what happened at the hospital and about Olly being found dead, and that Jess is still missing.

'Blimey, now that is shocking. What is up with this generation?' He finishes his second drink in one go.

'They think it could have been a random mugging, but it's more likely to be teenagers they know, isn't it? What if it's something to do with the ones who barged into my house? Maybe Olly had a disagreement with one of them. If only Jess would get in touch. I hope nothing has happened to her as well.' I look down at my tablet and dial her number but her phone is still coming up as switched off.

'You go home in the morning. I'm going to go back to the hospital, hopefully take the kids to see their dad if he's well enough, leave Debbie's car for her as well. The hospital said she'll be well enough to be discharged, then we'll probably get the train home.'

'I can wait and give you a lift if you like?' he offers, pouring water into his empty glass. He glugs it down.

'But don't you have to get to work?'

'I can go in a bit later if you need me.'

'No, it's okay, you go. I need to see how they are.'

'Fair enough. I think I'll have a quick shower before bed,' he says, going off to the en-suite. As soon as he locks the bathroom door, I relax properly – at last, allowing myself to stretch out on top of the duvet. I'm surprised at how good it feels. The truth is, I wish I was alone right now, apart from the children who are fast asleep. I should have insisted on separate rooms. I sigh. Marc is supposed to be moving in soon, but now I feel unsure about what to do, especially after everything Lee accused him of. It's not like him to be so vehement. I hope he's well enough for me to visit him in the morning so I can ask him again what this secret is, especially as Marc insists there isn't anything. If he is keeping something from me, I ought to know before I commit myself to selling my house and buying one with him. Maybe I'll say it's best to wait a while before he moves in too. Tell him I'm not ready for such a big commitment, especially after everything that's happened. He's been staying over three or four times a week for over a month, and I've enjoyed having him round but sometimes it does feel claustrophobic and lately I'm always a little bit relieved when he goes home. That can't be good, can it? But it's probably because I've become so used to my own space.

I hear the toilet flush and the shower switch on. I pick up my tablet, hoping for an update from Cassie, but instead I'm astonished to find a message from Jess.

44

I read Jess's message twice.

> I've gone away for a while, so please don't try to look for me

I frantically reply, hoping she's still there.

> Where are you? Your mum is worried sick!

A few seconds tick by then a reply pops up.

> You can't tell her I contacted you. Promise me

> Are you okay? Please tell me where you are

No answer. I start typing.

> Please Jess! Everyone is so worried about you

Nothing. I type again.

> If you know anything about Olly's death, please tell me. I can help you

There's no reply. I press the call button but after half a ring it cuts off.

I have to tell Cassie that her daughter has contacted me. Jess can't really expect me not to. If I do nothing and something happens to her, it's on me and I'd never forgive myself.

Marc comes out of the bathroom and climbs into bed. I check the children are still asleep as I tiptoe past them, tablet in my hand, and quietly shut the bathroom door behind me.

> Do you know who killed Olly?

I text again, but there's no reply. It's not even registering as delivered so she must have switched her phone off. I've spooked her. She's confided in me, but this is too important to stay quiet. Her boyfriend is dead and now she is missing. She could be in danger. What if she has been coerced into whatever's going on, been told not to tell anyone?

What a day. I lean across the sink and peer into the mirror. There are dark rings under my eyes, and my skin is waxy pale.

I wash my face staring down into the plug hole, then pat it dry with a fresh towel from the rack above the bath. I could show Jess's messages to the police in the morning. I *can't* do nothing. If she were my daughter, I'd be worried sick about where she was. I can't let Cassie down. If our roles were reversed, I'd be devastated if she kept something like this from me. If Jess ends up hating me and tells everyone my secret, then so be it, I'll have to live with that. I have to take that chance.

I tap open my tablet and text Cassie that I've heard from Jess, then I forward the messages to her. We can talk about it in the morning if she wants to, I'm exhausted right now and it's up to her and Dom to decide whether to go to the police about them. Hopefully she will and they'll be able to find a clue as to where she is. My tablet pings a couple of minutes later. A reply from Cassie.

> Thanks for these. I've sent them straight over to the police to see if they can pinpoint where they're sent from. I've tried texting and calling Jess, but her phone is off.

I tap out a reply.

> Give her time. I'm sure she'll be in touch with you soon. I'll try her again tomorrow.

Thank you. The sooner we can find out where that message was sent from, the sooner the police will be able to find her. Olly's death and her disappearance are all over the local Facebook page and her best friend Tori is helping me contact as many people who know Jess as possible, to find out if anyone has seen or heard from her or know anything else of importance. No one seems to know if she was with Olly when he was attacked.

> I'm glad you've got Tori's help. Keep me posted, won't you?

Will do.

I switch my tablet off then brush my teeth with the basic toothbrush from the kits we bought at the reception desk. After I've checked on Alfie and Bella, I climb into bed. Marc is already asleep.

I switch the light off and lie under the duvet, but my mind starts going through everything that's happened, all that was said on the pier playing over and over in my mind, and the image of the moment Lee fell backwards. I could have prevented it at various times, starting with letting him see his children a month ago.

I stare at the ceiling. Why did I have to be so high and mighty telling Lee he couldn't see them? I could have insisted I stayed while he visited, but to not let him see them at all? I wince, imagining how that's affected the children let alone Lee.

It was Marc who suggested I stand up to him, not be weak and give in to his demands to see the children when he wanted to, especially if he wasn't prepared to stop doing drugs. I shouldn't have listened to him. I went against my instinct that no matter what a father has done wrong he should still be allowed contact with his children. And more than that, *they* needed to see their dad. Alfie and Bella need to know none of Mum and Dad splitting up or Dad moving out was their fault and they are loved by both of us.

But I thought it was right at the time. I was convinced that if I stopped Lee seeing them for a few weeks, it would give him a big enough reason to make him want to get clean once and for all. The sense of a heavy weight pressing down on the top of my head is unbearable.

I shut my eyes and once again relive the awful moment of him falling in slow motion. Lee's look of astonishment, grasping at the air with empty hands as he dropped backwards from the pier.

My eyes flick open. I don't think he let go deliberately, because as he fell, the look of surprise on his face changed to fear.

45

I sit up slowly and gaze at Marc breathing softly next to me. The dark stubble on his chin suits him, makes him look even more handsome. Did Lee's jumper slip from his fingers by accident, or could he have let go? Why did he really turn up today? Is it possible that Lee was telling the truth and Marc got someone to plant drugs in his drawer, just to get him sacked? But if he did, what was the reason? It can't be so he could get closer to me because we were already seeing each other. I thought we had a natural chemistry from the moment we first met, and that our relationship grew organically. Lee and I already had marital problems by the time I started working at the company, so he didn't split us up as Lee claims.

Lots of women at work liked Marc. Single women younger than me and older ones too. Why was he interested in me, a married woman? I've been asking myself that question from the first time he asked me out for a coffee one lunchtime. The looks of surprise I got as we walked back into the building, the new girl with the founder was apparently something to behold. I admit I secretly enjoyed all the attention. I felt special for being picked out to spend time with him. I soon became his right-hand woman, and it was common knowledge that we were an item outside of work too. Lee had lost his job and moved out by then and I had begun divorce proceedings, so there was nothing to be ashamed of.

Until I fell pregnant that is. It was a shock when I took the test because I'd always been so careful. But as the days went by, I found it harder to tell Marc about it because I knew he'd be over the moon and I just wasn't. I couldn't face being pregnant again and everything that comes with that, so I had to make the difficult decision to have an abortion but not tell him. It's the only thing I've kept from him. I couldn't deal with bringing up another child when I'd got past that stage of my life and was finally making time for me, building my career, my new relationship and spending time with my children, who I cherish.

Marc would have wanted me to keep the baby, and I didn't want him to have that power over me. Make me feel guilty or selfish for not wanting it. Possibly guilt-trip me into going ahead with the pregnancy just for him, because he'd always wanted a child of his own. Why should that be my responsibility? No. I needed it to be my choice. It's my life. I'd be the one having to start over again with night feeds, changing nappies. And a career break in my forties? I couldn't do it.

But what I didn't realise when I had the termination procedure was the guilt I would carry around with me every time I saw him, reminding me of this secret, which would gradually gnaw its way between us. I hoped it would fade, and we'd move into his luxury house and have the perfect life I've always dreamed of. But that's not the plan. He wants to sell up and move in with me until we can buy a place of our own together, but now I don't know if I can do it. That's his idea, his decision, not mine, although I agreed to it thinking it could work. I don't know if I can give up my space. Is it what I really want? If I sell up and buy somewhere with him, I'll be giving up the independence I've worked so hard for.

I lie back down and stare at the ceiling again. Lee almost died today, and Debbie could have died too. Am I the one who's caused all this? If Lee doesn't recover, I'll never be able to forgive myself.

I need to find out the truth about why Lee fell and who put the drugs in his drawer, because if it was down to Marc, I'm seriously not sure I can be with him any more.

I shut my eyes and a swirl of sleep washes over me. Under the covers, Marc's hand closes firmly over mine. My eyes flick open and a tiny part of me is scared that he can read my thoughts.

46

I wake up at 7 a.m. and look across at the children who are still asleep in their bunkbeds. As I turn over onto my back, I notice Marc isn't next to me.

'Morning,' he says, coming out of the bathroom, showered and dressed in his underwear. 'How are you?' His voice is bright and cheerful as though we're on holiday, and not as if we're waiting to see how two people are after almost drowning in the cold rough sea.

'Shattered. I didn't sleep well, worrying about everything. How about you?' I sit up and rub my eyes. I could quite happily go back to sleep for another twenty minutes at least, but the need to see Lee, see how he is and hopefully gets some answers, is far greater.

'You know me, I sleep like a log whatever's going on.' He laughs and pulls on his trousers and shirt, then buttons them up. 'I'm going to get off. I forgot I do need to be in the office this morning. One of our biggest clients is coming in to discuss a block of flats they're building. Don't worry, I'll let HR know you'll be taking today as leave.' He shoulders his coat on and picks up his laptop case.

I don't remember him mentioning it, but then I wouldn't necessarily know about all his appointments, especially as I'm not going in. 'Yeah, course. You go. We're going back to the hospital.' He nods once to acknowledge what I've said but his pursed lips tell me he still doesn't agree with me going to see Lee. He turns to go.

'And Marc, I've been thinking...' I wait for him to look at me. 'With all this going on, I think it would be best if we leave it for a few days... you know, you moving in.'

He scans the floor, then looks up at me with a smile. I wish I knew what he was thinking.

'Yeah, you know, you're probably right.'

'We can talk about it tonight, if you like.'

'Yeah.' He nods.

I keep my lips firmly shut before I say anything else and end up talking myself out of it, which is what I usually do. My tablet rings on the bedside table. It's the hospital. I hold up a hand for Marc to wait. When I end the call, I pinch my lips together and swallow as last night's events hit me hard.

'Debbie is well enough to come home, and Lee is out of intensive care, and has been moved to a general ward.'

'And he's in the best place. There's not much else you can do to help. Why don't you come back with me?'

'No, it's okay, you need to go and we're nowhere near ready. Anyway, I promised the children I'd take them in to see him.' It's not a lie; I did promise them, especially as it's Alfie's birthday tomorrow, but I'm also keen to ask Lee what proof he has about Marc being the reason he lost his job, and what he has to say about falling off the pier. Did he want to end his life? Or maybe he wanted to make it look like it was Marc's fault for not holding on to him firmly enough. Right now, I can't entertain the third possibility, that Marc is fully responsible.

'I'll see you later.' Marc stalks across to me, bends over the bed, and kisses my lips, leaving a cold, wet minty-smelling smear. As he walks out of the door, I can't help wiping my mouth with the back of my hand.

47

DEBBIE

The nurses let Debbie go in to see Lee as soon as she's been discharged. He's sitting up in bed, still drowsy but she's so ecstatic he's alive and doing well. She gives him the biggest hug but can't stop the tears rolling down her face.

'It's good to see you too, sis,' he says.

She wipes her eyes before she can speak. 'I'm so glad you're okay.'

'You saved my life.' His eyebrows rise and he examines her face. 'You're a bloody hero, do you know that?'

'Just returning the favour.' She smiles and tilts her head.

'Come on, I didn't save you.'

'Maybe not that time but you've saved me a thousand times since, and you know it.' She prods his arm playfully.

He shrugs in a modest acknowledgement of all the times he's kept her going since that day on the beach and after their parents died. He gave her all the reasons and support to help her go on living.

'So what happened up there? Did you mean to fall? You were in a hell of a dark state of mind.' She frowns and tears fall from her eyes. 'I thought I'd lost you.'

'I would never have done that, to you or in front of my kids, give me some credit.'

She nods and blows her nose. 'So what then?'

'That bastard dropped me.'

'Are you being serious? Marc tried to kill you?'

'Yeah. A hundred per cent. Looked me right in the eye as he did it.'

'But why?'

He shrugs again and looks down at the neatly folded sheet.

'You need to report it to the police.'

'Where's the proof? It's my word against his.'

'Maybe, but you have to tell Vicki. She shouldn't be with someone like that.'

'I know. And he's not the man Vicki believes he is, and I don't know how to tell her.'

'Then tell me and I will. Come on, who is he?'

Lee reaches for her hands and holds them in his, looks her directly in the eyes.

'His real name is Kevin Young.'

48

VICKI

The children and I are dressed and eating breakfast in the hotel diner. Thankfully it's a bright sunny day, a complete contrast to yesterday. I finish the full English and sip my second cup of coffee. My tablet pings a text from Cassie.

> Is it okay to call? I really need to speak to you.

I tell the children I'm just going into the foyer to call Jess's mum while they finish their breakfast. I stride out of the dining room and dial her number.

'Have you seen this video?' Cassie cries without even a good morning.

'No, I've not had a chance.'

'The headmistress at Jess's school phoned me about a disgusting video on TikTok, posted by Fran, the girl you said has been bullying Jess. Some of the children in their year were looking at it at break time this morning and one of the teachers asked what they were watching. She had a look and was shocked. This Fran girl has not been in school since last week. And now a few of her gang are absent too.'

'I'm sorry, I haven't seen any yet. I hope they expel them. Jess told me some of the nasty things they made her do. They threatened to do those things to Alfie and Bella first, and Jess bravely stepped in.'

'No, I'm not talking about those. There's a new one.' Cassie takes in a gulp of air. 'It's so much worse.' It sounds like she's having a mild panic attack.

'Cassie, just slow down a sec. Breathe through your nose and out of your mouth, that's it. What do you mean a new one?'

It's another few seconds before she speaks again.

'A new video of Jess, but this time she's tied up in what looks like a derelict building, and she's blindfolded, on her knees...' Cassie pauses again, struggling for breath.

'Shit, Cassie! And is it the same girl, Fran, doing this?' A wave of light-headedness crashes over me.

'Yes, and a boy the school said is called Sean is filming it. He looks into the camera demanding a ransom otherwise they're going to execute Jess, then he pans round to Jess kneeling on the floor of this dirty room with plants growing up the walls, and oh God this girl, she... she's holding up a knife, a machete right next to Jess's head, which they've covered in a black bag. I can't bear to think of what they might do to her. The bastards look so bloody pleased with themselves. They're animals! Honestly, I could scream.'

'Oh my God, have you told the police?'

'The school called them straight away. We've just been up there. They're looking for them right now, trying to track their phones to see if they will lead them to Jess. They are utterly vile. Knowing children have watched these videos thousands of times already makes it worse and so much more real. Dom is going out of his mind. I swear he's going to kill them if he gets hold of these scumbags.'

'Shit. And do the police think these two could have killed Olly and taken Jess?'

'They didn't say but it would add up, wouldn't it? Perhaps Olly and Jess were out at the park together, and this Fran and Sean attacked them. Knowing Olly, he would have tried to defend Jess and that's when they hit him over the head. They left him for dead and kidnapped her.'

I try and let this sink in and imagine how frightened Jess must be, wherever they're keeping her.

'So do the police think it was her texting me last night? Or was it one of them using her phone, trying to make us think she's just gone off and wants to be left alone?'

'They don't know for sure, but they're going to trace her mobile signal as a matter of urgency.' Cassie's voice is barely audible over her crying. 'I just hope she's still alive.'

I'm in a daze by the time we arrive at the hospital. Cassie promised to call me as soon as she hears any updates.

I book the parking on the app and follow Alfie and Bella up the steps to the main entrance. Before we go in, I take my tablet out of my bag to make sure it's not on silent in case Cassie tries to call me. To my surprise, it starts ringing in my hand. I answer the call.

'You need to hurry.' Debbie's voice is breathless and distraught.

'What's happened? We're just coming in the main doors of the hospital.'

'They think Lee's had a heart attack.'

49

Debbie gives me directions to ward B, and we take a lift up to the third floor. My mind is racing. How much should I tell the kids? What if Lee doesn't pull through? Do I really want them to see their father in a state after everything they went through yesterday?

When the lift doors open, we're met by Debbie who's in floods of tears. I open my arms and hug her.

She pulls the kids in for a hug too, but Alfie pulls away. 'Where's my dad?' he pleads.

'How are you, and how is Lee?' I ask, rubbing Debbie's arm as she looks at me forlornly. She's always been there for her baby brother.

'I'm okay, but he's not great.'

I barely know what to say to her. I'm desperate to find out what happened but not in front of the children.

'I want my daddy,' Bella cries loudly. I pull back and kiss her forehead.

Debbie leads us towards the double doors.

'We have to hope he can pull through.' She attempts to wipe away her tears with her fingers and turns to the children. 'They're doing everything they can to help your daddy, I promise you.'

'What would have triggered a heart attack, do they know?'

'If they do, they haven't told me anything yet.' She sniffs and wipes her nose with a tissue and leads us to the seating area in the waiting room.

'It sounded like he was doing so well.' I flop down into a seat, and Debbie and the children do the same.

Debbie lets out a long sigh. 'He was. I thought he'd turned a corner this morning. They moved him to his own room on the ward and let me sit by his bed for a while. I held his hand and told him you and the kids were coming to visit and how much we all loved him and wanted him to get better.'

'Alfie why don't you take your sister to the play area over there so Aunty Debbie and I can have a chat.'

'Do I have to?' Alfie kicks a sweet wrapper on the ground.

'Please. Just for a little while.'

I kiss Bella on the cheek and gently tap Alfie's arm. They reluctantly get up and mooch over to the brightly coloured corner full of books and wooden toys, which is probably the last thing they want to do right now, but I don't want them hearing the details of what happened to their dad.

'What happened after you spoke to Lee this morning?'

'He was fine. In fairly good spirits. At least I thought he was.'

'What were you talking about? Was he getting himself worked up again?'

'He told me something that upset me actually.'

'What was that?'

She stares at me then blinks and looks away. 'I can't really say.'

'Why not?' I try and catch her eye.

'It's something private between me and my brother.'

'Fair enough, but were you with him when it happened?'

'I'd just gone to the bathroom. I was only a few minutes, but when I came back he was clutching his chest.'

'So what did you do?'

'I called the nurses and they swooped straight in and I was ushered away.' She wipes fresh tears from her eyes. 'I don't understand it. He was perfectly stable; they were talking about him coming home in a day or two.'

'That must have been terrifying.' I cover my mouth with my hand.

'It was so frightening.'

'But are you saying he was upset about something?'

'We both were, but it wasn't my fault.'

'I'm not blaming you, I'm just trying to find out what caused it, if anything.'

'After everything he went through yesterday, I couldn't believe it. I'm really struggling to cope with all this.' Her skin is pale and drawn. Out of all of us,

Debbie's normally the strongest. When Lee's mum died a couple of years ago, she was the one who organised everything and kept the family together. Lee was in pieces. He'd always struggled to some degree with addiction and depression, but us splitting up was the start of it getting worse.

I twist my hands together and lean towards Debbie sitting in the chair opposite me. 'Have the doctors told you anything at all about how he is?' I daren't ask if he's expected to pull through. I'm not sure I'm ready for the answer.

'Not yet. I'm hoping they'll let me in to see him soon.'

'I'm sorry, it's too much to take in all at once, isn't it?' I reach out and take her hand in both of mine and we sit quietly for a few minutes. 'You've been through quite an ordeal in the last twelve hours. Are you okay?'

'I thought I was fine, but perhaps it's delayed shock.'

Alfie glances over at us from where he's stacking Jenga bricks on a low table with Bella. He's barely said a word, but he's bound to have lots of questions. He's desperate to see his dad. I thought he'd be pestering about his birthday tomorrow, but instead he's watching his sister for me without any complaint.

'So where's Marc,' Debbie asks after a while, breaking the silence. 'I thought he was with you?'

'Oh no, he had to go back to work. He shouldn't have even come yesterday. I'm sorry about that. I was annoyed with him, especially when Lee got so worked up when he saw him.'

'That's strange because... I could have sworn I saw him in the corridor earlier.' Debbie blinks rapidly and looks towards the door.

I shake my head. 'It can't have been him. He left the hotel about forty minutes before we did and went straight back to work. It's the opposite direction, so he wouldn't have been able to call in on the way even if he'd wanted to.'

'Oh, sorry. Ignore me. My head's all over the place, I've hardly slept. It must have been someone who looked a bit like him.' She drags her fingers over her eyelids.

'Are you sure you're okay?'

'I'm still tired even though they've discharged me. I was so exhausted when they pulled us out of the water. It's going to take me a good few days to process this and feel normal again. I'm still trying to get my head around what happened.'

'Me too. I can't believe it. You're both so lucky to be alive.'

I just hope that Lee pulls through.

50

DEBBIE

Debbie is still reeling from what Lee told her, and now this, a possible heart attack? She'd gone to the toilet to be sick and can't have been more than a few minutes. Did she cause his stress by her violent reaction? Or was it from him holding in this secret, knowing how badly it would affect her?

She can barely look Vicki in the eye. And some of the things Vicki says make her question everything. Debbie swears on her niece's life that she saw Marc in the corridor earlier, yet Vicki flatly denies he could have been here. Could Vicki be savvier about this whole situation than she's letting on? Maybe it was someone who happened to look like him. Or is Debbie going mad? Normal life feels strange after nearly drowning last night, almost like she's play-acting reality.

The sea was so choppy when Debbie jumped in. She didn't think she was going to make it out alive or find Lee. The waves swallowed her up several times and she thought she would come across his lifeless body. But when she found him, he'd managed to keep his head above water. Although he was limp and out of energy, ready to sink like a dead weight, he still had enough fight in him of someone who wanted to live.

Debbie supported his head out of the water, and they were picked up by the coast guard soon after.

There's simply no way that Lee intended to jump.

51

VICKI

I scan Debbie's face to check she's okay before I question her. 'I wanted to ask you about when you were up on the pier trying to talk Lee down. Did he say anything to you that could help me understand exactly what this is all about, and why he took the kids and threatened to jump with them?'

Debbie's eyes flick up and down at me. 'Apart from not being able to see his own children you mean? Only that his old boss has it in for him.'

I cringe inwardly at her words. Her tone has changed now, no longer the supportive sister-in-law.

'You mean Marc?' I ask.

'Yeah.' She sweeps her gaze away from me.

'There must be more to it. Please, you have to tell me.' I try to meet her eyes but she's staring at the floor. 'Debbie, come on. Lee threatened to jump off that pier *with* our children. What drove him to even think of doing that? Don't I deserve to know what's going on with him and Marc?'

'He would never have hurt his children, Vicki. He was only trying to get through to you.'

'About what?' As my voice rises, a couple of people behind us tut at me. I scan around us and add in a whisper, 'Look, this is not the best place for this conversation, shall we go outside?'

'Sure.' She stands up and waits by the door while I go over and tell Alfie that we'll just be outside, and they can see us through the window. I kiss both him and Bella on the tops of their heads and follow Debbie out of the door.

She folds her arms and leans against the full-length window waiting for me to speak.

'If you know what Lee was trying to make me understand, please tell me.'

She sighs. 'I promised him I wouldn't say anything, especially to you.'

'But he could die in there. I need to understand what was going through his head, what's been going on.'

She sighs again. 'Okay, I'll tell you what I can, but it's not the full picture and it's only because you're right, he might not pull through.' She swallows hard and presses her fingers to her lips. 'You already know how adamant he was that it was Marc who framed him at work with the drugs?'

I nod.

'Well, he's certain it was so Marc could get him out of the way.'

'But why?'

'So he could be with you – or so he thought to begin with – but there's a lot more to it. Lee says he found out something unsavoury that Marc did in the past.'

'What sort of thing?' I screw up my eyes. None of this sounds plausible but I want to hear what she has to say.

'He wouldn't say precisely, but it was to do with when he was a teenager and someone he met while on holiday with his mum. Has he told you anything about that?' She studies my face, possibly hoping I know more about it than she does.

I shake my head. 'Marc's not great at sharing his feelings or much about his past, like most of the men I've known to be honest. All he's told me was that his dad left his mum when he was fourteen, and he left the family home soon after. His mum gave his dog away while he was at school one day. Came home and couldn't find her. A bag with the dog's bed and bowl were in the rubbish bin. He was distraught, but she insisted they couldn't afford to feed it any more, so Marc ran away from home that night and never went back.'

Debbie nods sagely. 'And you believed him?'

'Why wouldn't I?' I fold my arms. She doesn't seem prepared to hear Marc's side of things. 'He seemed genuinely upset by it, even now.'

'Lee told me he confronted Marc and threatened to tell everyone at work what he'd found out – if he didn't stop flirting with you – but Marc said he had no proof, so Lee went away and did some more digging.' Debbie's eyes fix on me. 'He found out Marc was in trouble with the law.'

'No, that can't be right, he's never mentioned anything like that. Lee must have got it wrong. As far as I know, Marc has never been in trouble with the police. I'm sorry but I think Lee will do whatever he can to get back at Marc because I'm with him now, and he's still finding it hard to accept.'

'But Lee says he confronted him about it a second time, hoped his threat to share the information at work would be enough to make him back off from you, but instead Marc must have asked someone to plant the drugs in Lee's drawer and got him sacked.'

'So if all that's true, why didn't Lee tell me about it at the time? He should have said something to me.'

'Lee didn't think you'd believe him, or at least he knew Marc would deny it and twist it round to make it look like Lee was trying to frame him. Marc had already threatened him with the sack if he said a word about it to anyone, especially you. He thinks Marc has you under his spell. You believe every word he says and don't listen to him any more. He said Marc has stolen his life, but he won't let him have his children too. We decided the best he could do was damage control, get the children as far away from Marc as he could, so that's why he took them away.'

'So *you* were in on this?'

'I was only trying to help my brother.'

'And threatening to kill himself *and* the children, was part of your master plan too?' I blink at her, trying to understand how she could do this. I thought I could trust her.

'No, is the short answer. He went too far,' she says quietly.

Debbie's always been a kind and honest person, and her loyalty is understandably with her brother, but to do this? What she says doesn't match up with the Marc I know, whereas Lee has had a big problem with Marc from the moment I started working at Venture Properties.

'I just wish Lee could accept that Marc and I are a couple now, so we can all move on, focus on co-parenting our children.'

'I know, but it's not that simple. What Lee did was an extreme thing to do but I promise you, he never meant to harm the children or himself.'

'You don't know that for certain though, do you?'

Her silence and pained expression say it all.

'You've not told me what actually happened when you jumped in the sea,' I say.

Debbie takes in a deep breath before speaking again.

'Lee had drifted right under the pier and was struggling to stay afloat. I managed to catch up with him. He was fighting to stay alive, which proves to me he didn't want to end his life only moments before. I held his head above water and reassured him the lifeboat was on its way.'

'Was he able to communicate anything to you about how he fell?'

'He was struggling to speak but managed to gasp four words.'

'What were they?'

'He – let – me – go.'

52

'I don't believe you,' I snap, without stopping to think how me defending Marc will sound to Debbie, but still, I'm not convinced a half-drowning man is capable of speaking.

Debbie's brows rise. 'Lee's jumper did *not* just slip out of Marc's hand by accident.'

I stand up straighter. 'You're accusing Marc of deliberately letting Lee drop into the rough sea during a storm, right in front of us?'

Debbie blinks at me stoney-faced.

'Are you actually serious? He was trying to save him.' I'm shaken that she is saying the same thing I've been questioning myself.

'Made sure we were all behind him so we couldn't see it clearly though, didn't he?'

My mouth opens but I'm lost for words. 'Hang on, is this some sort of conspiracy theory you have with Lee? Because this character assassination of Marc is unforgivable.'

Debbie's expression is defiant.

'So you agreed to drive me to Blackpool, because you and Lee planned it between you?'

Debbie stays silent.

'Hang on, so you really knew he was planning to take my children, didn't you?' I wave my finger at her.

'Not until a short while before.'

'I can't believe it.'

'They're his children too don't forget, and you wouldn't let him see them.' Her eyes narrow at me. 'What kind of mother does that?'

Alfie is staring at us through the window. I automatically smile and give him a little finger wave. He tentatively waves back and returns to what he was doing. I step aside to the edge of the pavement for a family of three to walk past us. As soon as they're out of earshot, I carry on speaking, lowering my voice.

'I was trying to help Lee see what he would lose if he didn't give up the weed. I thought you understood that.'

'I did to start with, but then I realised how convenient it was for you and your new boyfriend not to have Lee around, getting in the way of your plans or questioning the choices you were making for his children. He told me all about the babysitter, still a child herself and unable to stop a crowd of sweary teenagers invading the house, drinking alcohol, making rude videos and frightening the life out of Alfie and Bella, unable to do a proper job of keeping them safe. If Lee hadn't turned up when he did and got rid of them all, who knows how it would have ended.'

'That is so unfair,' I yell at her.

She folds her arms. 'Really? And the way you've behaved towards my brother isn't? Lee needs understanding and co-operation so he can get the help he needs. Don't you see that banning him from being with his children has only made his addiction worse? He's been distraught not seeing them. You have no idea. All he wants is to get clean and be with them. And on top of it all, you're with the man who caused the break-up of his marriage. Have you stopped for one second and thought about how Lee feels?'

'Of course I have,' I say quietly, tears building in my eyes. 'I thought you were my friend.'

'I am, but I'm Lee's sister first and I've kept my mouth shut for far too long.'

I stare down at the pavement. I should have expected this, but she always led me to believe she was on my side when it came to parenting. Her comment about it being easier not to have to run things past Lee first cuts deep, because it's true. I suppose on the days Marc stayed over, we'd been playing happy families with the children. I'm too ashamed to admit it's been a relief not handing them over to their dad on Saturdays or Sundays, because it's often accompanied by an argument about what time he should bring them home or some petty detail about their clothes or behaviour. Every weekend I found it more and more unbearable, painful even, being separated from them for a whole day at a time, wondering where Lee had taken them, if he was feeding them properly and making sure they were safe. I even worried in case he was getting stoned in front of them.

A nurse with shoulder-length black hair hurries into the waiting area, one hand in her pocket, scanning the room. I lipread Lee's name on her lips and without saying a word to Debbie, I dash to the main doors. When I reach the waiting room, the nurse is turning away and I shout, 'Wait!'

She pivots on her heel and studies me with small dark eyes. I glance across at Alfie who is standing in the wreckage of a pile of bricks, holding his sister's hand.

'Are you looking for me?' I say to the nurse, slightly breathless.

'Mrs Kendle?'

'Yes, that's me.' I squint at my automatic response to my married name.

'Actually, I'm his next of kin,' Debbie says loudly, striding forward. I could knock her down for being so rude. The nurse turns to her. 'I'm his sister, Debbie Kendle. *She* is separated from him.'

'Can you both follow me please,' the nurse says and turns on her heel. She scans in her card at the door and leads us through to a network of corridors, at the end of which she opens another door to the right and ushers us in. It's a space not much bigger than a cupboard. Debbie is too close to me, breathing heavily, her skin sallow.

'I'm sorry to have to tell you this, but Mr Kendle was attacked in his bed possibly while he was sleeping. It appears someone tried to smother him with a pillow. Thankfully they were disturbed and ran off. This is the probable cause of Mr Kendle's panic attack, thankfully not a heart attack as we first thought.'

Debbie and I stare at each other, wide-eyed.

'Do they know who did it?' I ask. 'Can the hospital find out?'

'Is he okay?' Debbie's face crumples.

'The hospital will of course be investigating the incident, and the police will be checking through the CCTV to see who went in and out of Mr Kendle's room.'

Debbie's mouth has dropped open. 'I know who did it. I saw him. I saw Marc, here in the hospital. I knew I had. He's tried to silence Lee again.'

'You can't say that, Debbie. And you did not see him. I told you before, he left the hotel early and headed south for an important meeting.' My voice is unnaturally shrill. Could Marc really have come to the hospital first to hurt Lee? I don't want to believe it's possible.

Debbie ignores me and speaks to the nurse, who looks baffled. 'We'll see what the police find, won't we?'

I steal a side glance at her. She was probably going in and out of his room more than anyone.

'How is my brother, is he going to be okay?'

'Mr Kendle is recovering and has been given something to sedate him. Thankfully there doesn't appear to be any lasting damage apart from the obvious trauma of the attack. It would be advisable for you all to come back later.'

'I really must insist on seeing him now, just for a few moments.' Debbie wrings her hands together. 'I'm the one who saved him from drowning.'

The nurse squints at Debbie with her tiny eyes. 'Okay. Just for a minute or two until he falls asleep. Only you though.'

Debbie's face softens and rage rises in my chest at her deliberate moves to undermine me at every turn.

'What about his children?' I ask. 'They've been waiting to see him.'

'They'd be better to come back this afternoon.' The nurse shows us out through the security door then Debbie follows her down the corridor, into the main hospital.

In the waiting room, I wrap my arms around Alfie and Bella. What is Debbie playing at trying to frame Marc at every opportunity when she's got no evidence whatsoever? Now she's planted that grain of doubt in my head, I need to know if there's any truth in whether Marc let go of Lee deliberately or not.

'Is Dad going to be okay?' Alfie asks.

'Yes, I think so.'

'When can I see Daddy?' Bella says in a weary voice.

'We'll have to wait and hope he's well enough this afternoon.'

Only then can I insist he tells me what he knows about Marc.

53

It's stopped raining and the wind has died down since yesterday, although it's still quite blowy. I take the children to the beach. It's mostly deserted apart from the odd dog walker and jogger.

I sit on a dry patch of sand and text Marc to see if he's okay. Maybe I was too harsh telling him not to move in yet. But I honestly can't face it right now with so much upset. And if he did have anything to do with Lee being sacked, I'm not sure I can continue seeing him.

I check my messages. Cassie's not contacted me yet. Maybe she's heard from the police about Jess's whereabouts by now. I find her number and tap the screen.

She picks up straight away.

'Any news about Jess?' I ask.

'Nothing.' Her voice is strung out. 'Has she tried to contact you again?'

'I wish she had so I could put you out of your misery.'

'I'm running out of options. Where can they have taken her, Vicki? All I can think about is those monsters hurting my girl.'

'I watched the video on TikTok. The place where they filmed it makes me think of that derelict house set back from the old road near town. Part of the roof looks missing or half demolished. When I drive past, I often think it's the sort of place squatters would hang out so no one could find them. I wonder if the police have looked there.'

'I'll mention it to them. We drove past it yesterday, but there was no sign of anyone. I can't bear this waiting and not knowing. I just want her back home safe.'

'I'm so sorry this is happening. I wish I could do more to help.'

'I've got this nausea stuck in my throat all the time, and I'm just so exhausted...' Cassie is quiet for a moment or two. 'Hang on, Vicki, the police are trying to get through. I'll call you straight back.'

The line goes dead, and I clutch my tablet to my chest with both hands, hoping the police have some good news for Cassie and Dom to grasp onto. Hopefully they've located Jess. I pray nothing bad has happened to her.

I stand up and head towards the children who've wandered near the shore. They're running into the wind with their arms out by their sides like airplanes, zooming this way and that, hair blowing in all directions. A surge of joy rises in my chest that they're here with me, safe and well. The thought of what Lee might have done to them chills me to the core. I'm not sure I can trust him after this.

A text from Marc appears on my tablet. I slide the screen open and read – it's a reply to my earlier message.

> I'm okay thanks. How's it going with you? Taken the kids to see Lee yet? Everyone at work sends you their best wishes. They can't believe Lee is still causing you so much grief.

> Hoping to take them to see him this afternoon.

I stab my reply and hit send. One of his worst traits is criticising my ex. When he did it at the beginning of our relationship, I didn't mind so much because it felt like he was fully taking my side. But now it's becoming difficult to navigate these two men in my life, butting horns every chance they get.

> All I'm saying is he doesn't deserve your concern after his histrionics yesterday.

I ignore him but he texts again.

> Is there anything else we need for Alfie's birthday celebrations tomorrow?

> I don't think so.

> Will I see you later?

> Might be getting a train back tonight. Not sure what time.

I hesitate before adding:

> I've fallen out with Debbie. Will explain it all later over a glass of red.

He replies but I ignore it because Cassie's number pops up on the screen at the same time. I imagine it's his usual thumbs up emoji. I answer Cassie's call, desperate to know what the police had to say.

Cassie catches her breath before she speaks.

'Hello?' she croaks.

'Are you okay, Cass? Have they found her?' I keep my voice quiet, not wanting to overwhelm her because I can tell she's been crying.

'The police have traced Jess's phone signal from the texts she sent you last night. They confirmed it was the last time her phone was switched on.'

'That... that's good.' It's hard to think of the right thing to say without knowing more. If it is good, why is she crying, because they don't sound like happy tears. I'm desperate to ask more questions, but this isn't about me. I'm sure Cassie will tell me when she's ready.

'They do think it's possible that someone is keeping her locked up against her will. They're sending officers out to search the area for her.' Cassie's voice is monotone, like she's gone into shock.

'Okay well I can post a call out on the town's Facebook page, gather as many of our friends and local people as we can, so we can search for her together.'

'I don't know how many would be prepared to travel that far,' she says.

'What do you mean travel? They wouldn't have far to go.'

'Sorry, didn't I say? The nearest mast her mobile pinged to isn't around here, it's up where you are, in Blackpool.'

54

'What's Jess doing up here in Blackpool?' I pause to let it sink in. 'I thought she went missing near home?'

'That's what the police assumed too. We all did. They're as surprised as we are.'

'Maybe this girl, Fran, thought no one would ever look for her this far away. At least not so soon,' I say.

'But why let Jess text you? They must have known her phone signal would be traceable,' Cassie says.

'To make it look like she's run away? But then why post on TikTok showing what they're doing to her? I don't know. I've tried to call her again, but her phone is switched off.'

'I just hope she's okay. I'll keep trying to call her too, see if I can get through and at least it will give the police an update on her current location.'

'I'm glad the police have something to go on now,' I say, 'and hopefully she'll be found soon.'

'So do I. They're coming to search her room and take her laptop. I'm contacting as many people as I can from her contacts on social media, although I'm not on any of those apps – TikTok, Snapchat or Discord. Anyway, how's Lee? Have you been to see him yet?'

I explain to her what the nurse said about someone attacking him.

'That's awful. Who would do that?'

'I'm not sure, but Debbie got quite aggressive with me. She seems convinced it was Marc even though I told her he drove back to the office early this morning. She also thinks he deliberately let go of Lee's jumper so he'd fall into the sea. Then she had quite a go at me about not letting Lee see the kids.' It's more likely to have been one of Lee's druggie mates attacking him for an unpaid debt, but I doubt if Debbie wants to admit that. I'm not sure how they'd know he was in hospital in Blackpool though. Unless they followed him. Perhaps this was just a warning shot, and they intend to come back and finish the job if he doesn't pay up.

'What? She's out of order and has no reason to blame Marc and then take it out on you, although I can understand her defending her brother.'

'She really seems to have it in for Marc, but he can't possibly have gone to the hospital and done this. He has no reason to want to hurt Lee.' Even as I say it, I wonder about the secret Lee found out about him. What if Marc did have a reason to set Lee up at work to get him sacked? But could he really have dropped him in the sea and gone to the hospital to suffocate him? That's tantamount to attempted murder, isn't it?

'And I take it you've told Debbie that Marc can't have done it?' Cassie says.

'Yes, but it's impossible to reason with her. I'm hoping to take the kids to visit their dad this afternoon, but it looks like we'll be getting a train home, because I doubt if we'll be offered a lift, not that I fancy a long car drive in silence. Unless you want me to join in the search around here before I go?'

'It's okay. Get the kids home. You must have plans for Alfie's birthday tomorrow.'

'There's nothing that can't be changed. I can stay another day and help?'

'No, it's fine. You and the kids have had enough to cope with. Dom and some of his mates have gone up there to help the police search. To be honest, I'd really appreciate your support back here, in case Jess does manage to escape wherever she is and come home. Oh God. The police want me to go through her room to see if I can find any clues about where she's been taken and a reason for it, aside from being bullied by Fran. Could you help me do that, if you don't mind? They've already taken her laptop to check her internet history and messages.'

'I'm more than happy to come back and help you as soon as I'm done here.'

'Thanks, Vic. I really appreciate it.'

'I'd better get back to the kids and see if Lee is well enough for visitors this afternoon. Speak to you soon.'

* * *

After lunch, I take the kids into a side room to see Lee, who is propped up on several pillows. Alfie and Bella run towards the bed, and he puts out his hands to them.

'Are you looking forward to your birthday?' Lee gives Alfie a hug. Alfie nods but can't speak, tears running down his face.

'We've missed you so much, Daddy.' Bella kisses his cheek and smooths back his hair, just like I do to her when she's ill in bed.

'How are you feeling?' I ask, standing over them.

'Doctor said I'm good at cheating death,' Lee half jokes.

'Why did you have to jump off the pier?' Alfie swipes tears from his eyes with his fingers. 'We thought you were dead.'

Lee glares at me. I'm waiting for the answer to that too. Now is the perfect time to speak to him without Debbie interfering, but it's going to be tricky with the children listening. I'm tempted to ask him where Debbie is but decide it's best not to bring her up.

'Why don't you sit down?' He looks at me, patting the bed. Alfie and Bella stand either side of him.

'Thanks,' I say and sit on the high-backed chair next to him.

'So did you mean to fall?' I ask.

'No, I didn't, that's the thing.' He looks at Alfie and covers his hand with his. 'It was an accident. I'm sorry for scaring you.'

'But you told Mum you were going to jump in with *us*,' he sniffles.

'I know and I'm sorry, I was upset with her. But I would never have done that. I'd never hurt either of you, do you hear me?' He turns his head to look at Bella then back at Alfie, waiting for each of them to nod and show they've understood.

'I only want what's best for you both, and now your mum is with another man I thought you might want to start calling him Dad, and it tears me up inside.'

'We'd never call him Daddy,' Bella says, indignant at the suggestion.

Alfie sniffs. I reach in my back pocket for a tissue and hand it to him.

The door squeaks open and Debbie walks in with a brown paper bag of what I'm guessing are sweets, and a copy of *the Mirror*.

'Ah, you're here already,' she says to me.

I don't reply.

'All ready for your birthday, Alfie? Your last day of being twelve, wow.' She takes out a rhubarb and custard and stuffs it in her mouth then offers the bag to the kids. They each take an oblong red and yellow sweet.

'Why don't you two go with Aunty Debbie to the café and have a hot chocolate and a cake?' Lee says, indicating to her with his eyes that he and I need to have a private chat.

'Do we have to?' Bella asks.

'We've only just got here,' Alfie whines.

'Come along, children. I think they've got cookie ice-cream.'

'We've already had an ice-cream. At the seaside,' Bella says in a flat voice.

'Bit cold for the beach, isn't it?' One of Debbie's eyebrows rises.

'And it's too cold for ice-cream,' Alfie shoots back. 'I want a Monster drink.'

'You're not having one of those. A hot chocolate would be nice though, wouldn't it?' I say to him gently, coaxing him to go with Debbie. 'You'll only be gone for a few minutes. Daddy and I would like to have a little talk about yesterday, on our own.'

'Hot chocolate's for girls,' Alfie says, and I squeeze his hand as he passes me.

As soon as the door has closed, Lee's smile drops.

'Did you see who attacked you?' I ask.

'No, I'd dozed off and woke up to a cushion over my face.'

'Christ, Lee.'

'Fortunately, the nurse had left the buzzer by my right hand so I managed to press it. Whoever it was must have been alerted to the light that comes on above the bed, because they scarpered pretty quickly. By the time I'd pushed the pillow off my face, they'd gone.'

'My God, who would do that do you?' But from the deep sigh and the way he's looking at me, I can guess what he's going to say.

'If you want to know the truth, Vicki, I think it was Marc.'

55

'Seriously? You've got to stop accusing him, Lee.' I point a finger. 'Marc was at work.'

'Debbie is sure she saw him in the corridor.'

'She is just winding you up, fanning the flames.'

'Who else would it be? When I was on the edge of the pier and Marc had hold of my jumper, he looked me straight in the eye as he opened his hand and deliberately let go of me. He even had a little smirk on his face.'

'I don't believe you. He would never do that.' I stand, ready to walk straight back out, but the sliver of doubt growing in me keeps me there. 'You're saying all this to try and split us up.'

'I knew you'd think that. Where's the Vicki I used to know and love? Replaced by this cold selfish woman in front of me?'

'Get lost.' I stand behind the chair, both hands on it. 'Your sister told me all about your plan to run off with the children behind my back, and how she was in on it, offering to drive me up here, making out she was helping me, while all the time she knew you intended to use our children as a weapon to get your own way. Not a thought to how it would affect them emotionally, let alone me.' I can't help raising my voice. 'And now you're accusing Marc of attempting to kill you. Do you know how ridiculous you sound?'

'I knew Marc would do something else to try and get rid of me. Although I didn't think he actually wanted to kill me. Getting me sacked obviously wasn't enough for him.'

'He did not! And you can't prove otherwise. Anyway, it's *you* who's tried to set him up with your madcap plan and it's backfired. Is this all because you lost your job?'

'I was unfairly sacked. He framed me. But I don't suppose I can prove it to you. It comes down to trust, doesn't it? And you don't trust me any more.'

'I might trust you more if you told me what you found out about him. Debbie says you've been digging, and you hinted to me about it yesterday. Or were you making that up as well?'

'Just leave it.' He sighs and turns his head away.

'Tell me what it is. If there's any truth in it, if you want me to trust you again, you need to tell me what you know.'

'It was nothing, really.'

'How can it be nothing if you say it was enough to get you fired?'

'You should probably ask him yourself.'

'I want to hear it from you.' I pace up and down the room, unable to contain my agitation.

'It's not for me to say.' Lee sighs. '*He* should be telling you this.'

'Why? I want you to tell me as you're the great detective. Why are you and Debbie so determined to turn me against him?'

'Look, I'm tired of fighting, Vicki. Maybe you and Marc are a perfect match after all. He probably doesn't even think you should be here. But if you truly trusted him, you'd be able to ask him about his past and get a straight answer. I just want to see my kids every day or at least every week, that's all.'

'Tell me how you found out whatever it is you won't tell me.' I stop pacing and point at him.

He lets out another long sigh. 'Alright, alright. It was before you started working at Venture, and coming up to Mother's Day. Some of the women in the office were chatting about what they were going to buy their mothers, whether they were going to take them out for lunch etc. One of them casually asked Marc what he normally did to celebrate his mum, and he piped up that he didn't believe in Mother's Day because it was created by card companies to make money, so he'd never sent her a card or anything. They were all shocked into silence, then one of them, Mimi, who left soon after, made the mistake of asking if his mum was okay with that. He went ballistic at her. Said he didn't give a shit what she thought because he hadn't spoken to his mother in thirty years and didn't intend to start now, then he stormed out.'

'Jesus, are you serious? That's quite a reaction.'

'Just a bit. It got me wondering about his background, but I didn't do anything about it straight away. Then when you joined the company and he started sniffing around you, I felt I needed to find out more about him to try and make him back off.'

'He hasn't told me much about his childhood, only that he doesn't have a relationship with his mother after an incident where she gave away his dog, and he couldn't forgive her. It's clearly affected him deeply. He doesn't like talking about his life when he was growing up. The only other thing he mentioned was that he left home because of it, when he was about fifteen.'

'Left home, is that what he told you?' Lee nods.

'Debbie said you found out something that happened when he was on holiday with his mum, when he was a teenager?'

For a second Lee's face is blank as though he's not really here. 'Yeah, okay, well I found out he hurt someone.'

'Are you sure? Could you have got him mixed up with some other boy? Marc has never been in trouble with the police.'

'There's no mix up. I found out his mother is called Sheila, and dad Keith.'

'But *how* do you know all this?'

'I stayed late at the office one night and had a nosey through his HR file. I found a photocopy of his passport and some other papers, so I took a note of his date and place of birth. He was born in a small Cambridgeshire village, so I went there one weekend and spoke to a few of the locals who remember him and his family, and when he got in trouble with the police.'

'You went to a lot of effort then?'

'Because I was willing to fight for you.'

'Alright, so what if it's true? Maybe he got into trouble when he was younger and was too ashamed and embarrassed to admit it to me, or anyone. And he certainly wouldn't want people who work for him knowing something so personal. We've all done things we're not proud of, and some of us were lucky enough not to be caught.' I raise an eyebrow and remind him about the time he and his mates damaged a statue in the town centre.

'This is different, Vicki. It was serious. He was found guilty.'

'But you said he was only a child himself. Anyway, the Marc I know doesn't have a violent bone in his body. I'm telling you, if he did do it, he's learnt his lesson because he's not like that now. Or maybe you really are trying to split us up?'

'I'm not. He was sent to a Youth Offenders Institution.'

'I'd need to see proof to believe you. Do you even know what the conviction was for?' I flop down in the seat, deflated.

'All I know is that he was locked up for it.'

56

'If it really was him, you can't judge, because you don't know what it was for or the circumstances. What if he had no choice but to defend himself against his mother? I mean, she sounds like a right piece of work.' I sit back in the chair trying not to let it show on my face how shocked I am at what he's found out.

Lee sighs.

'You've had it in for Marc since the moment I started working in that office,' I remind him.

'Only because he had eyes for you from day one. He never liked me, and it was his opportunity to belittle me in front of all my colleagues. I can't believe you've fallen for the crap that comes out of his mouth. The big *I am* promising everyone fat bonuses if they worked their butts off, then back-tracking down the line, blaming us for not hitting our targets. Making sure you were by his side every day. He's done everything he can to make my life hell.'

'You're exaggerating. Why would he pick you out? What could he possibly have against you?'

Lee shakes his head. 'Isn't trying to take you away from me enough?' He shrugs.

'Look, if there's something else, then please tell me. If it would explain everything, why not just say?'

He's silent for a few seconds. 'Because it's not my story to tell and because it's not just me that would be affected by the consequences.' He holds my eyes with his.

'So there is something else,' I say.

Debbie taps the door lightly and looks round. 'Okay to come in?'

'Yeah, of course.' Lee opens his arms and Alfie and Bella run to him. They sit either side of him on the bed and I move my chair back to give them some time together, while I mull over what he's said.

I still don't accept that Lee is describing the person I've got to know and fallen in love with. I've never seen Marc hurt anyone or anything. He helped me with a bird I found wounded in the garden only a few days ago. It had broken its wing possibly hitting the window. He cancelled a meeting to drive me to a bird sanctuary while I cradled the poor thing in my hands.

'We need to go soon if we're going to catch a train home,' I tell the children.

'Do we have to?' Alfie says.

'I want to stay with Daddy.' Bella folds her arms.

'I'm afraid you can't. Daddy needs to stay in hospital and rest so he can get better.' I stand up.

'I can give you a lift,' Debbie says.

'No. But thank you. I expect you want to stay here with your brother.' I'm surprised she's offering after our argument and I'm not keen on spending another long car journey with her now I know she's been helping Lee smear Marc's name.

'I need to go home anyway,' Debbie says, 'to see to the animals. Rhona's not coping too well on her own. I can always come back up again,' she says, turning to Lee. I look from one to the other and can't help wondering if they're concocting another plan.

'But I need to go now really,' I say, expecting her to say she can't leave until later, because I honestly don't think she wants to spend another long car journey with me either. She side-eyes her brother, probably not thinking I've noticed. What are they up to?

'That's fine, I'm ready to go too,' Debbie says. 'What do you say, kids? Shall we go on another road trip? Who wants to pick some tunes for the journey?'

To my surprise, both children cheer, and I feel outnumbered. I suppose it will be easier than catching a train, and maybe I can use the time to my advantage.

I need to find out from Debbie what Lee won't tell me about Marc.

57

Awkward small talk between Debbie and I followed by a sing-along with the children lasts for a good half an hour into the drive home before my tablet rings, interrupting us.

'Hi Cassie, I'm on my way back. Any update?'

She sighs. 'The police have found Fran and Sean camping in some woods on the outskirts of the town, but Jess isn't with them.'

'Oh, Cassie! Won't they say where she is?'

'There was another girl with them, who said they didn't take Jess. They said the video was just a joke – Fran got Sean to put a blindfold on this other girl and film her, making out she was Jess. They'd heard she was missing and thought it would be a good prank to post on TikTok. With Fran holding a knife to her throat! Can you believe it?'

'What were they thinking? Do they realise the distress they've caused?'

'I don't suppose they care. All they're worried about is how many hits the video got, which is thousands apparently.'

'That's unbelievable. I mean a mock execution just for clicks? What is going on with these kids? So where is Jess?'

'The police still don't know, but they do think it's personal. So not a random attack on Olly, with her going missing as well.'

Unless it was Jess who attacked Olly, a little voice in my head says, but I dismiss it immediately.

'The police are questioning Fran and Sean as we speak, to see if they know where Jess's phone is, because they're not 100 per cent convinced she would have travelled up to Blackpool. Their theory is that Fran took Jess's phone from your house and sent someone else up to Blackpool who was going there anyway. The police are searching the area, just to cover all the bases. Dom's already up there with his mates.'

'I don't think they can have taken it because Jess phoned me after they'd left my house. Can you think of anyone else who could have had it in for Jess and Olly?' I ask.

'An anonymous call has come in from a neighbour who saw Jess talking with the Colin boy from across the road. It wasn't long before Olly was killed. The boy had left a small bunch of flowers for her on our doorstep, and she was seen having words with him. She was trying to give the flowers back apparently, so the police are looking into it. He's been obsessed with Jess for months, watching her from his bedroom window. I've always said it's a bit creepy. A quiet boy. Barely speaks. Jess says he's on the spectrum. She's insisted he's harmless, but I wish I'd taken it more seriously, because you never know what someone is capable of, do you? Oh God, Vicki, you don't think he's the one who's abducted her, do you?'

'It's hard to say. I don't know him, but I have seen him quite often standing at his bedroom window.'

'He's always staring at her. I wouldn't be surprised if he can see right into her bedroom from his. She was bothered about it to start with, but she's not mentioned it for a while.' Cassie sighs.

'Are the police aware? They should question him.'

'Yes, I think they plan to.'

'Please try and stay positive. I'll help you search Jess's room as soon as I get back.'

'Thank you, I'm really grateful. I can't even bear to go in there on my own not knowing where she is or what I'll find.' Her voice trails off.

'Is there something else?'

Cassie hesitates before answering. 'No, it's okay. It can wait. I'll tell you when you get here.'

I end the call and sit in silence.

'Haven't they found your babysitter yet?' Debbie asks. I twist round to see if the children are okay. They're both dozing off to sleep.

'Not yet, but they've found the teenagers who the police thought had kidnapped her. Seems like they were playing a sick prank. They posted images of it on social media. Filmed it in a derelict house and even got one of their friends to pretend to be Jess, wearing a blindfold and kneeling on the ground. This girl that's been bullying Jess posed with a knife as if they were about to execute her. Bastard bullies. It's the same two who had everyone invading my house.'

'That's disgusting. So the police still don't know where Jess is?'

'Not yet but they traced her mobile to Blackpool. Her boyfriend was found dead last night, and then she vanished. But what's really weird is she texted me last night. I think she may have had a fight with her boyfriend that got out of hand, and now she's gone into hiding.'

'It's possible.' Debbie nods.

'I don't really want to say that to her mum though.'

Debbie swings round to look at me. 'Or maybe she got scared by whoever attacked him and ran away? Especially if she saw what happened to him. She could be traumatised.'

'Apparently the police do think she was with him.'

'Sounds like it's enough to tip anyone over the edge, especially a hormonal teenage girl.' Debbie turns her face away and stares out of the windscreen again.

'Yeah, you're probably right.' I flick to Jess's name on my tablet and my thumb hovers over the call button. It's probably still switched off, but I promised Cassie I'd keep trying so I tap on it.

It starts to ring.

Then to my surprise, someone answers.

have chucked her phone in a river by now or taken the SIM card out.' Debbie glances at me then back at the busy road ahead.

'You're right. And I need to tell Cassie. Maybe this is the breakthrough we've been waiting for.'

I make a quick call to Cassie. She sounds lifted by the news that Jess appears to have answered her phone, even though she didn't speak.

'Thanks for this, Vicki, I'll let the police know so they can trace it,' Cassie says. 'If they can locate where this new signal came from, it might tell us whether Jess is still in the same area of Blackpool or not.' She thanks me and we end the call.

I lean back and shut my eyes. It's impossible to empty my head and go to sleep. Yet I must drift off because sometime later I open heavy eyelids and when I check the clock, it appears I have slept for over half an hour. I glance down at my tablet. There's a message from Marc saying he has to stay late at work to meet a client.

'You okay?' Debbie asks.

I nod, rubbing my eyes. I check the children over my shoulder. Bella is still asleep, her head to one side against her car seat. Alfie opens his eyes momentarily then closes them again. Marc isn't going to have time to check on his dog and her puppies if he's working late. Even if his gardener has looked in on them, they shouldn't have been left on their own overnight without at least making sure there's enough food and water for Milly.

'You really needed that nap, didn't you?' Debbie says.

'I think so,' I mumble. 'Didn't sleep well last night.'

'I'll drop you at your house in about ten minutes.'

'Actually, would you be able to take me to Marc's house quickly first and wait in the car with the kids? I need to go in and feed his dog for him.'

She says it's fine but doesn't look at me. I just need to make sure Milly and her litter are okay. I don't mention the puppies otherwise she's bound to want to come and see them, and I know he won't want her in there, and I can't leave the children in the car on their own.

'Thanks, Debbie. I appreciate it.' And I mean it. Despite our differences, she's always been helpful and reliable and it's not surprising that she defends Lee so vehemently as his big sister. They've always been close and now more so than ever because I sense they're holding a secret between them that I don't know about.

58

'Hello, Jess?' I say into my tablet. I can sense someone on the line, but they don't say anything. 'Jess, if you can't speak, please just make a noise so I know you're there, we're all so worried about you.'

I can just make out someone breathing because they're holding the phone close to their face.

'Jess, are you okay? Whatever it is, you're not in trouble, I want to help you.'

The line goes dead.

'Shit!' I slap my tablet. What she said comes back to me – about needing to tell Olly something important, something about trying to pick the right time because when he found out, he'd want to kill her. If they had a fight about it at the park, could she have killed him by mistake, defending herself?

'No answer?' Debbie asks.

'Someone did, I could hear them, but as soon as I spoke, the line cut off.' I try calling the number again. 'Now her phone is switched off.'

'At least she appears to have her phone with her.'

'Well, someone has it. I can't be sure if it was her answering or not.'

'If she's been taken, why would they have her mobile switched on? That doesn't make sense.'

'Good point. Possibly because they want me to *think* she's run away? Or Jess answered it but she's not ready to speak yet.'

'It must have been her then, because if it was someone else, they would

I text Marc to say I'm on the way to his house to feed the dogs. His reply comes straight back.

> No need. I'll call in later before I come over to you

> It'll be so late though. We are only two minutes away!

> Who is we??

> Debbie drove us home in the end but it's only me popping in

> It's really not necessary. You must be tired

> I had a nap in the car. Anyway, you've been away overnight. I need to make sure Milly is comfortable and has food and water. She needs to keep her energy up feeding all those pups.

> But I told you my gardener looks in on her

> Well, we're here now. It'll take five minutes. Surely you'd rather know from me that they're okay?

> Yes, of course, you're right. The food is in a tub on the shelf of the summer house and there's a tap next to the barbeque.

Debbie pulls up outside Marc's house. I hardly recognise it as I've only been here a couple of times before and that was earlier in the year when all the trees and plants were in full bloom. I double check I've got the right house number. That's strange. Marc said a couple of days ago that we couldn't come over because the roof repairs had started. I was expecting there to be builders here and scaffolding up outside.

There's no sign of either.

59

DEBBIE

The last place she wants to be is at Marc's house, but she's also curious and would like to go in. It's not where she thought someone like him would live. Turns out fairy tales are misleading: monsters are just ordinary-looking men and women who live among us.

It feels unfair that he owns a house like this *and* his own company – a life of privilege – while her brother is living in a camper van and has nothing.

Lee has risked everything for her. She's so grateful for what he's been doing, and now he's told her the truth about what has really been going on, it's time to take matters into her own hands. For them *and* for her niece and nephew. They can't spend their futures living with *him*.

She turns to gaze at their innocent sleeping faces, heads tipped together on the back seat. Sometimes she can hear echoes of her and Lee as children in their laughter or passing moments when she sees themselves in them.

One day they might thank her for saving them from a life based on lies.

The initial anger has stopped bubbling up for now, and a new calm and self-assurance has descended on her. Maybe it comes from cheating death like Lee has, but whatever higher power is looking over her, now is the time to take control and put things right.

60

VICKI

It feels strange opening Marc's front door without him here and I momentarily feel bad for being so pushy about coming, but after the weather we've had over the last twenty-four hours, I can't help but worry about Milly and her puppies being left on their own.

When we exchanged front door keys a couple of months ago, I took it as a sign that Marc was serious about our relationship and wanted me to visit his house more often, potentially with a view to moving in one day. But he's not invited me over, he always comes to mine. And now he's made it clear that he'd rather sell up and move into my small semi, I'm having doubts. Has he made an excuse about the roof damage just to put me off coming here? The only reason I can think of is that he's not as committed as I thought he was. Or am I overthinking it? Perhaps the roofer has let him down at the last minute and he's not thought to mention it to me with everything else going on.

I head straight across the hallway into the kitchen and take the back door key from a cabinet on the wall where he showed me. There's a plastic jug on the draining board which I fill with cool water and carry down the garden path.

Before I open the summer house door, I take a quick peek through the window. Milly is lying on a blanket with several of the puppies feeding from her. I slowly unlatch the door and go in. She looks up with her dopey spaniel eyes then flops her head down again in defeat. Her food bowl is empty and there's barely any water left. I top them both up. I'm glad I made the effort to check on her. When I was last here, she wasn't pregnant, so I'm not sure if it was something Marc planned using a stud, or she escaped when she was on heat.

I fold up the soiled puppy pads and lay down fresh ones. I'm tempted to hold one of the pups but they're only two weeks old and they're busy feeding, pushing their tiny pink and white paws into their mum's belly to draw the milk as they suckle. I crouch down and gently stroke Milly's head, telling her she's doing a good job.

The dog flap in the door rattles as I leave.

Back in the kitchen, I wash my hands and turn off the tap. A faint scratching sound stops me dead. I involuntarily shiver, suddenly aware I'm alone in such a big empty house. I'm so used to being in my small cosy home where I know every sound, this is alien to me. As I dry my hands, I listen again but all I can hear is the buzz of the fridge.

I use the downstairs toilet and as I'm coming out, I think I hear the scratching again. I'm not sure where it's coming from. We had a stray cat regularly visit our house when I was growing up. It would sneak in the front door when we least expected it.

I check around the kitchen and utility room, opening cupboards and drawers, but I don't find anything that could have made that noise. I can't help having a nosy around while I'm at it. I envy all the shiny cooking gadgets Marc owns, and the huge walk-in larder is to die for. I search around the whole of the downstairs: dining room, games room, living room and snug, but nothing. Then I hear it again. I check the time. I've been here a good ten minutes. Or is it longer? Wasn't it half past three when we arrived? I'm suddenly unsure. Time feels like it's warped. I text Debbie my apologies and promise I won't be long. She messages back saying not to worry, they're all having a nap.

Her reply gives me the green light to snoop around upstairs. I want to see how bad the water damage is for myself. Is it really so bad that we couldn't live here? I'm also curious to see what the rest of the house is like. I've only stayed over once and we arrived late in the evening and left early in the morning to get back for the kids, so I didn't have a chance to have a proper look round.

I count three double bedrooms and two singles leading off from the landing. All the doubles have en-suites. But one bedroom door is closed so I'm not sure how big it is. I try opening it but it's locked, so I put my ear up close. I can't hear anything scratching but there's a musty mouldy sort of smell coming from there. This must be the room that has the damage from the leaking roof. I'll have to ask Marc to show me, but I don't want him to know I've been snooping around.

Off the landing opposite is a huge family bathroom. I stand in the doorway in awe admiring it. I would give anything to live in a house like this. The solid fittings are gorgeous, boutique hotel quality, and the freestanding bath with scalloped feet is my idea of decadent luxury. Why is Marc so against us living here? Even for a few months would be incredible. I can just imagine waking up every morning on 500 thread count Egyptian cotton sheets, then plunging into this bath.

The scratching and tapping sound starts again. I spin round. It's coming from the locked room. Some sort of rodent must have got in there through the damage in the ceiling. I shudder.

Back in the car, everyone has just woken up and are in need of the bathroom, so they all troop into Marc's house and take turns. He won't be pleased, but I can hardly say no. Alfie swears at me when I let Bella go first, then stomps upstairs to the main bathroom.

'You could use one of the en-suites if you're desperate,' I say to Debbie.

'It's okay, I can wait,' she says, not hiding her interest in looking around.

Once they're all back in the car, I do a quick check round to make sure nothing is out of place. I'm nervous of Marc knowing I've let Debbie and the kids in when I promised I wouldn't.

As I'm about to leave, I notice a smear of mud on the stairs carpet. I don't remember seeing that before. A wave of panic crashes over me. I told Alfie to take his trainers off. Now Marc is going to know someone else has been in here. I can't do anything about it now. It will smear even more if I try and wipe it off.

I lock the front door and get back in the car. As Debbie sets off, I text Cassie that we'll be arriving in a few minutes.

When Debbie pulls up outside my house, Cassie is waiting for us on the pavement in floods of tears.

61

As soon as Debbie stops the car, I fling open the door and step down onto the pavement.

'Have they found her?' I ask, hoping it's good news but Cassie shakes her head. I pull her into a hug.

After a few seconds, she draws back. 'Come in and I'll tell you.'

I lift Bella out of her booster seat and Cassie unclips it and carries it onto the pavement. Debbie gets out, nudges a sleepy Alfie, and lifts our bags out of the boot.

'Thank you, Debbie. Please keep me updated on Lee's progress. All we want is for him to get better.'

'I know.' She gives me a quick hug, then the children, and we wave as she drives off. Cassie helps us dump the car seat and bags in our hallway, then we troop round to her house for a cup of tea. She switches the TV over to the cartoon channel and Bella curls up on the sofa with a glass of milk. Alfie slouches next to her with his phone and a can of cola.

'So what were you going to tell me?' I ask as Cassie drops teabags into two mugs and switches the kettle on.

She rubs her forehead and sits on a stool at their breakfast bar opposite me.

'The police went through our waste bin for clues, and found something in a bag of rubbish from Jess's room, and honestly, Vicki, now I don't know who my daughter is any more.' She covers her mouth as her eyes tear up. I put my arm around her.

'What did they find?' I ask gently.

'A pregnancy test. Can you even believe it?'

'Wow… that's a shock.' For a second, I'm so stunned I don't know what else to say.

'And it's positive.'

'Oh no, Cassie.' Poor Jess. Why didn't I spot any signs? I could have been there for her.

She starts crying again and my mind spins back to my own positive test only weeks ago. The utter horror of the result slams into me all over again. But for someone Jess's age, it's possibly an even more frightening experience.

'So do the police think she's taken off by herself because of it?'

Cassie nods. 'It must have been a nasty surprise for her. I just wish she could have come to me for help.' The kettle clicks as it finishes boiling.

'But it's understandable to run away. She probably didn't know what to do and didn't want to worry you.' I can't say it to Cassie, but I'm guessing Jess wouldn't have wanted to tell her because of Dom's reaction. He's going to go mad. It's a shame Jess didn't feel able to confide in me, especially after she helped me that day. Maybe that's why she tried to call me, now she's had time to think about it. Or maybe she didn't tell me because she thought it would bring back bad memories for me. Oh, Jess. I say a silent apology in my head.

Wherever she is, I hope she's okay.

'I assume Olly is the baby's father.' Cassie goes over to the kettle and pours boiling water into our mugs. 'Do you think she broke the news to him at the park, and he got upset with her and they argued?'

'I think so.' I turn away from Cassie so she can't see me wincing, picturing them having a heated argument.

'But Olly was a kind soul and not the sort to kick off.'

'That's the impression I got.' I nod and sigh inwardly. I really don't want to be the one to tell her Jess's secret.

'I think he genuinely loved her.' She finishes making our tea and hands me a mug. 'It's hard to imagine him getting angry with her, even if he didn't want a baby.'

I nod, although I didn't really know Olly, and I'm thinking that everyone has their breaking point.

'If only they could have come to us about it. Dom and I would have helped them. Jess can continue her education, if that's what she wants. I'd happily look after her baby. My grandchild. Why couldn't my own daughter come to me when she needed help?' Cassie takes a tissue from her pocket and cries into it.

Jess confided in me when she babysat a couple of weeks ago that she and Olly hadn't slept together yet. Although Cassie assumes the baby is Olly's, there was someone else in Jess's life that she's not told her about. Olly said he wanted to wait until after they got engaged, and Jess told me she wasn't sure that's what she wanted.

How can I tell Cassie this when she's so distraught? It will crush her even more. And if Jess did meet Olly at the park to tell him she was pregnant, he could easily have lost his temper with her, because he'd have known for certain she'd been unfaithful to him.

Which leaves me wondering, who did Jess sleep with behind Olly's back? And did that person kill Olly?

62

We finish drinking our tea and go upstairs to Jess's bedroom. It's straight ahead across the landing. One end of the room near the bed is lined with lilac, pink and silver striped wallpaper, and the other half is decorated in a more gothic style, with the wall behind her desk painted inky black peppered with neon Day of the Dead skull faces and books lined up on her shelves by authors such as Edgar Allen Poe, JB Priestly, and Dostoevsky.

Scanning the room, everywhere is essentially neat and tidy, except for where the bed has been stripped back, and drawers have been pulled out and left halfway open, presumably by police officers. Her desk is clear and clean, and a row of anime figurines are lined up behind where I'm guessing her laptop usually sits. Her school uniform is on a hanger on the back of the door and there's a small bolt lock high above the handle. I want to ask Cassie why a young girl needs to lock her bedroom door in her own home, but it seems intrusive, although my mind immediately switches to an image of Dom losing his temper.

'As I said, the police have already searched the house and taken her laptop and a few notebooks from her bedside table. They thought I should have a good look around too, see if I can spot anything they've missed that could indicate where she's gone. I told them I bought her a diary for Christmas, but they couldn't find it, so I expect that's what they're hoping I'll find. I tell you what though, if they can decipher the inner workings of a teenage girl's mind, then hats off to them.'

'It's got to be here somewhere. It's not the sort of thing you carry around with you.'

'She'd hate me even being in here, she's so private about what she gets up to in her own time, which is why I thought if you were with me, you could vouch for me being respectful of her things when she questions me about it.' Cassie stops abruptly and draws in a breath. 'Assuming she's found.' She presses her mouth with the back of her hand, trying to stop herself crying.

'They will find her.' I put my arm around her shoulders and give her a hug.

So Jess doesn't like to be disturbed doing whatever it is she does in here. Maybe that explains the lock on the inside of the door. But I'm still convinced it's to keep her father out.

* * *

Cassie peers into the already open top drawer of a narrow chest of drawers. It's full of a mixture of fluffy socks and school socks.

I check behind the half-opened curtains at a pile of Cassie's old CDs and player, as well as some Jess has been buying from charity shops. One has a piece of paper tucked into the case. I slip it out and read a note from Olly, promising to love Jess forever. She told me he's got his dad's old CD burner and loves making compilations of their favourite tunes, from Nirvana to Green Day. I show it to Cassie.

'He really did love her,' she says with sadness.

'Do you think it was mutual?'

'I think he was probably more keen on her.'

As I tuck the note back in the box, I notice a movement in the window of the house across the road. Colin is standing right up to the glass, staring at me. I'm sure he wasn't there a moment ago.

'That's a little bit creepy, isn't it? How often does he stand there?' I ask. I've occasionally seen him at his window from my house, but only in passing and I never thought that much about it until Jess went missing. The view into his bedroom is surprisingly clear through the sash window, unlike our modern PVC double glazing.

'Ah yes Colin, Jess's number one fan, after Olly of course. He gives me the shivers too. Like I said before, he's always leaving things for Jess on the doorstep. She's a kind girl and takes the time to talk to him. Since his diagnosis, his mother has pulled him out of mainstream school. Said they didn't have the facilities to support him. He was being bullied relentlessly, but the school failed to get it under control. According to Jess, his needs are complex. But she always takes the time to listen to him. I worried that he was getting a bit too obsessed with her at one point, watching out of his window all the time, but she always tells me I shouldn't be so judgy about someone who's a bit different.'

'Do you think it's possible he saw who Jess was last here with?'

'The police have spoken to him, so they must have asked him that.'

'I'm just thinking, if Olly called round for her, Colin may have seen them head off to the park. Would he have followed them?'

'I don't know.'

'Or maybe she was with someone else entirely.'

'Possibly, but the police will have asked him all those questions. Whether he saw her with Olly or another person, it doesn't really tell us much, except they may have been together when he died. They're not saying anything concrete at this point. For all we know they're watching Colin because they think he's the one to have taken her somewhere.'

'Oh God, yes.'

'I just want her found, alive and well.' Cassie sighs and opens the wardrobe, aimlessly flicking through the line of hanging clothes. 'Nothing is missing as far as I can tell.' She checks the pairs of shoes underneath. 'All here, except the black and white Converse trainers she usually wears.'

Cassie's mobile rings. Her eyes widen as she answers the call. I carry on searching around the room while she goes out to the landing to speak. A few minutes later she comes back, her face pale and drawn. She drops down on the bed, staring at the phone in her hands.

'What did they say?' I ask gently, guessing it was the police again. I sit next to her.

'They've found some stuff on Jess's laptop.' She heaves a big breath in and out. 'I'm her mother and I knew nothing about the pregnancy test and now this.' She points to her mobile.

'What have they found exactly?'

'You're not going to believe this. I mean, my Jessie? I thought I was a good mother. Not perfect you know, and Dom has a terrible temper; she's seen some fights between us. You've probably heard a few. But it's mainly been a happy house, with strong family values. We've always taught her what's right and wrong, so I don't know how this is possible.'

'Tell me what's happened.' I rest my hand on her arm, holding my breath.

She stares ahead almost in a trance. 'Apparently Jess has had an OnlyFans account, for almost six months. People are paying to watch her writhing about on her bed in... sexy outfits. I mean, she's only seventeen,' Cassie sobs.

'Seriously?' I lean back, stunned.

'The police say she's been careful not to show her face. She wears masks with cute cartoon animal faces or anime characters. There's a whole set of VIPs who pay her a premium for private online shows. And going by the last few messages they've found, which were sent just before she disappeared, one of her VIPs private messaged her to say they had a surprise for her.'

'Which was what?' I swallow, my mouth dry.

'Offering to pay her thousands of pounds to meet them at the park that evening and find out the identity of this particular VIP.'

'And she went even though it could be dangerous?'

'I suppose she felt she had no choice, because whoever this VIP is, they told her they know who she is: they know her real identity.'

63

'Shit, how did this person find out it was Jess?' I ask.

'The police said it looked like she filmed all her reels in her bedroom, so maybe there was something in here that gave her away.' Cassie looks around the room.

'It must be someone who knows her, who's been in here?'

'And assuming she had no idea who the VIP was, she'd have been nervous turning up to meet them on her own, so the police found out from her phone records that she contacted Olly to go to the park with her and confront this person.'

'Unless the VIP who messaged her *was* Olly?' There could easily have been a side to him we hadn't seen. He might not have liked his girlfriend flaunting herself online to other men.

'Oh God, do you really think so? He's been in here.' Cassie's hand goes to her mouth.

'He might not have agreed with what she was doing and been angry that she wouldn't give it up. She wouldn't have known he was the VIP until she got to the park, and then they probably had a fight about it.'

Cassie weaves her fingers together. 'And maybe she pushed him, he fell and hit his head. She panicked and ran off, not realising he was dead.'

'Wouldn't she have checked he was okay first though?'

'I'd have thought so. But why didn't she call an ambulance? She's done a first aid course,' Cassie says.

'Maybe she did check him, but it was already too late, so she panicked. She would have been in shock. People don't always behave rationally in an emergency.'

'I wonder if the police have come to the same conclusion – that she's not a runaway, she's on the run.'

Cassie gets down on her hands and knees and checks under the bed. She pulls out a canvas box and takes off the lid. There are all sorts of toys and books inside it from Jess's childhood. Cassie sifts through them in case the diary is tucked away amongst them, but it isn't.

Back at the wardrobe, I push Jess's clothes aside on the railing to get a better look at the space inside. At the back is a neat pile of clothes. I pull the top item out. It's a pink cropped halter-neck top attached to a short two-tier Ra-Ra skirt by two tiny gold-coloured chains front and back.

'I've never seen this before,' Cassie says, taking it from me.

I lift the rest of the outfits out onto the bed. While Cassie goes through them, I continue searching in the wardrobe.

A tiny triangle of white material at the back catches my eye. I lean in and run my hand over the smooth wood and find a dip around the edge of what feels like a loose panel. I pull my house keys out of my pocket and switch on the tiny keyring light and shine it in to see more clearly. It looks like a corner of cloth is caught in a secret hidey hole.

'What's this?' I say and Cassie comes over. She frowns then reaches in and pinches at the material, trying to pull it out, but it doesn't budge.

'Try this.' I hand her a metal clip from Jess's dressing table. She clicks it open and pokes one edge into the dip. After a couple of failed attempts, she hands the clip to me. I lever the hidey hole open by pressing down with both hands. Cassie shines the light on a white cloth wrapped around something. I draw it out, careful not to damage it. Cassie takes it from me and tears off the cloth, revealing the gold embossed word we were hoping for: Diary.

It naturally falls open on Sunday 27 October.

I can't believe it's Monday tomorrow. This has been the longest weekend in history. Somehow I have to avoid F and her gang, which seems the least of my probs right now. So glad I got to spend all today with Olly. He held me in his arms, and I felt safe. I wanted to tell him a million times, but I'm scared how he'll react. He has no idea, although he did say I was more lovey dovey than usual. I laughed at him saying that, and he told me his mum used to say it to his dad. I don't know how to tell him what happened. I'm sure he'll hate me.

'Do you think she meant tell him about the pregnancy?'

'I expect so.' I hesitate. Considering Olly is dead, and Jess is missing, I should tell her what I know. I swallow hard before I speak. 'I think there was someone else in her life.'

'Why do you say that?' Cassie frowns as though irritated with me.

'Because when she was here babysitting a couple of weeks ago, she was telling me that some of the girls at school were bragging about losing their virginity and how everyone says you'll know when you're ready. She said that she and Olly had never slept together.'

'What?' Cassie's eyes dart over my face. It's clearly something else Jess chose to confide in me rather than her mother. Cassie's phone rings. She shakes her head and carries her mobile onto the landing.

I take the opportunity to flick back a couple of pages of the diary. The entry for Friday 25 October, catches my eye. Jess was babysitting at my house.

V opened a bottle of wine when they got back from the dinner party. She offered me a glass, and we all sat watching an old episode of Doctor Who on iPlayer. I could tell they'd been drinking a lot already. V finished her drink, offered to top up my glass but I said I was going home. Then she staggered off to bed.

I can't even describe what happened, what I did! If V ever found out... she would kill me!

What is she talking about? I try to blink away the black dots appearing in my vision. I scan over and over the words, trying to work out what she means. What did she do? I need to know what happened.

I take my phone out of my pocket and photograph the page. The next day's entry is blank except for a deep violent scrawl in black ink which is imprinted on at least ten pages beneath it.

'They've traced your second call to Jess,' Cassie says, coming back in the room. I blink at her. Suddenly everything has changed.

'Was she in Blackpool?' I smooth over the cool diary pages with my hot palm, building up to showing Cassie the entry I've just read.

'No, her phone's signal was traced here, near home.'

'What?'

She shakes her head. 'I don't get it either. The police didn't say what their theory is, but they're going to focus their search around these streets now. I've told Dom and they're driving back here. How's it possible to have one call come from up there and one from here? She doesn't drive. Is someone deliberately trying to confuse us?'

'Maybe. Unless she has a good reason for not wanting to be found.'

As I hold out the diary to show her, a drip of blood splashes onto the page.

64

'What the hell is that?' I shout.

Cassie and I both look up at the ceiling, then at each other. Another drip splashes down, then another.

'Jesus! Is that blood?' Cassie frowns, holding out her hand to catch a drop.

I glance at her shocked face then sniff the liquid on the page. 'If it is, it's very watery.'

'Isn't it?' she says, peering at the liquid in her palm.

I'm not sure I want to know why something resembling blood is dripping from Jess's bedroom ceiling. I smell it again. It's musty and metallic, but not quite what I was expecting. I can't think what it reminds me of, but still, it brings bile to my throat which takes an effort to swallow down.

I pass Cassie my mini torch and she points it straight up above us. We both crane our necks and squint at the moving light until she's holding it steady enough to see a small black disc near the centre of the lampshade.

'Is that a hole?' Cassie says, grabbing the back of Jess's desk chair and dragging it to the middle of the room. 'How long's that been there?'

My lips part, but I can't seem to say anything coherent because my mind is sifting through the jumble of everything I know about Jess: the pregnancy, the unknown boyfriend, selling her body online, not wanting to tell me something she did, her boyfriend being killed, her going missing and now a hole in her bedroom ceiling and possibly blood dripping onto her diary.

Cassie climbs on the chair and points the torch again. Another drip lands on her face and she screams, shaking it off.

'I need to go into the loft, see where this is coming from.' She reaches out for my hand, and I help her step down. While she goes to the garage to get the ladders, I flick forward through Jess's diary. The bottom third of each page is dedicated to what I guess are appointments, presumably for her VIPs. The appointments list, in a kind of short-hand, includes the outfits they've requested for her to wear, a hashtag and a number but no names, only initials. I thumb through the pages to the last entry, two days ago and read:

> *Babysitting at V's tomorrow. Told Olly not to come over while I'm working.*
> *Can't talk to him right now. Take test with me so no one at home sees it.*
> *Need to know for SURE before it ruins my life. I will destroy HIM.*

Who is *HIM*? Did she invite a boy round that night before we got home? Could it have been Colin from across the road? Or another boy? I flick back through the pages to a couple of months ago, and the letter S springs out at me in several places.

> *S stared at me today in Physics.*

> *S asked if I could help him with his homework.*

> *S came up to me at break with a coffee for me.*

> *S is dangerously hot. When he looks at me, I think I'm going to faint.*

> *I feel so bad having feelings for S, but I can't help it. I love Olly but my body*
> *is full of desire every time I'm near him. How can that be right when I've*
> *promised myself to Olly?*

I try hard to think of anyone I know whose name begins with S. Isn't there a Simon who goes to school with her? No, it's something else. Then it comes to me, the boy the police mentioned, the one who was causing Jess trouble with Fran at our house, and then they thought she'd been kidnapped by them.

Wasn't his name Sean? Could this be him? Did he come to our house and sleep with Jess under our roof while my children were sleeping upstairs?

A rush of heat flashes through my body. This is what she meant when she said she thought I would kill her. I trusted Jess with my children, and she let some boy I don't know into the house. My guess is it's him behind the house invasion, although Fran's hardly blameless. They're probably in it together. Why did he sleep with Jess then gang up on her with her bully? Did she tell him it was a mistake, a one-off? Or did she tell him she was pregnant and he got angry with her?

'Could you give me a hand, please?' Cassie calls from the hall.

I put the diary on the bed and go and help her carry the ladders up. We position them under the loft hatch and stare each other out. Neither of us ever goes into the loft. Marc has been doing all my heavy lifting in that department, storing all the things I've sorted out that were Lee's, and getting the Christmas decorations down. Dom has vertigo so won't attempt to go up there unless absolutely necessary, hence they keep all their decorations and most of their junk in the garage.

'You know I'm scared of heights,' I say first.

'And you know I am too, but what choice do I have? I need to see what is dripping into my daughter's bedroom. I can't just wait for Dom to get home. He'll be ages yet and he won't want to go up a ladder. For all we know, Jess could be stuck up there unable to get down.'

My body shivers involuntarily, and I can't even disguise it. I need to step up and put my fears aside.

'I'll do it,' I tell her while I'm feeling brave.

'Are you sure?'

'Yeah.'

We open up the ladders into an inverted V shape and Cassie holds them steady on one side as I stand on the bottom rung with both feet. This doesn't feel so hard after all, it's only a few steps, but I can't seem to stop myself trembling. I hold onto the sides and climb up on the next rung, then the next, and before I know it, I need to push open the loft hatch or I'll hit my head on it.

My legs wobble on the narrow step even though Cassie is holding the ladders tightly. I take a deep breath and push the hatch up and over to one side then quickly grip the edge of the gap to steady myself. I go up one more step until the dark, draughty loft space is at my eye level.

A musty smell hits my nostrils but all I'm thinking about are spiders running around near my face or dropping into my hair. With the small amount of light coming up from the landing, I can just about make out several towering piles of boxes and bags, the usual overspill of stuff everyone has but can't part with.

'Can you see anything?' Cassie's face is looking up at me, worry etched all over it.

'Not much apart from boxes.'

'They've been there for years. We should probably have a clear out.'

'Shush a sec. I can hear something dripping.' But it's so faint, I can't see what it is or where it's coming from.

'Pass me the torch, please,' I call down to her. She plucks a torch from her pocket and passes it up to me. I can't help but look down at her to take it, and the disorientating fear of falling sweeps over me. I sway and gasp as I hang onto the ladders almost tipping them sideways.

'Bloody hell, Vicki, are you okay? Do you want me to go up?' she asks, steadying the ladders.

'I feel dizzy. Hang on. Let me have a quick look first.' I swallow hard, click the torch on and shine it into the darkness. 'There's rusty water dripping down from an old pipe. That must be what's coming through the ceiling. Looks like it's been knocked out of place and is possibly cracked.' I point the beam of light on the pipe, then around the walls. 'It looks like it's damaged. Oh, hang on, how did this happen?'

'What's that?' Cassie calls.

'There's a big hole in the wall that separates our houses.'

'Really? How did that get there?'

'I don't know. I've never been up here before.'

'And what do you mean big?'

'Big enough for someone to climb through,' I say.

65

'That can't be right. Let me have a look,' Cassie says, waving at me to climb down, which I gladly do.

At the bottom of the ladder, I hand her the torch while I steady the frame for her to climb up. She's quicker than me, her fear seems to have left her. At the top of the ladder, she stands on the platform and with the torch in her mouth, hauls herself into the space. I climb a few shaky steps up after her, until I can just see over the edge.

'We always meant to get a light put in up here, but never got round to it,' Cassie says as she flicks the torch around. The beam of light moves over the dark loft space, landing on the party wall between our two houses.

'I can't believe it.' She points the beam at it. 'It doesn't look like it could have crumbled away. It's been dismantled deliberately. Do you think Lee knocked through from your side? I mean, it's not us, we never come up here.'

'I suppose it could have been. He was annoyed when I asked him to move out, and he didn't leave for a few days. Maybe he wanted to sabotage my chances of selling the house after he'd gone.'

'Didn't he used to spend a lot of time in the loft?'

'When he insulated it, yes. Then he got Alfie to help him build shelves and storage to tidy it up so he could set up his old Scalextric set across the whole floor. The two of them spent hours up there, playing.'

'So I think we need to ask him about this, because it looks like someone has been spying on Jess in her bedroom.'

My jaw tightens at her insinuation. She moves the torch away and crouches down, aiming the light at the floorboards. 'There's definitely no blood, only rusty water dripping down and a couple of loose boards. I think that's where the hole is in her ceiling.'

'Why don't I go into Jess's room, shut the curtains to try and make it as dark as I can, then you shine the torch from here and I'll tell you if you can see it through the hole?'

'Good idea.'

'I'll call out to you when I'm ready,' I say and slowly climb down, trying not to make the ladders tip or sway any more than they already are.

In Jess's room, I note that Colin is no longer standing at his window. I wonder if he is still at home.

I'm not sure I trust him. But I'm probably being unfair. Just because I find it difficult to connect with someone with autism, doesn't make him guilty. I glance up and down the street, but there's no sign of him.

I draw the curtains shut, then stand in the middle of the room looking up at the black disc near the lampshade in the middle of the ceiling.

'I'm ready,' I call out to Cassie. A yellow beam lights up the tiny hole and shines straight down into my eyes. 'Yes, I can see it.' I blink and look away. The light goes off.

A few moments later, I meet Cassie on the landing, coming down the ladder.

'I could just about put my face to the hole and see through it, not easily though,' she says.

'Lee wouldn't spy on anyone, especially a child,' I say, still irritated that she could suggest he's behind it.

'Well why else would there be a massive gap in the wall that someone can fit through?'

'I don't know, but maybe you should ask Dom about it before you start pointing the finger.'

She glares at me. 'Alright, I will but you know he has vertigo, so he probably doesn't even know about this.'

'So how do any of us know for certain this wasn't already like it when we moved in? Maybe it was boarded over and Lee found it like that when he was up there?'

'The survey would have picked up on it.'

'We had one of the cheap ones and the woman who lived here before said the surveyor only had a quick look into the loft space from the top of the ladder, and that was it.'

'Maybe it's a coincidence then, but my daughter is still missing and someone has been secretly watching her.' Cassie makes a lot of noise folding the ladder and carries it downstairs. I follow with Jess's diary.

'I'll ask Marc if he noticed the hole when he put Lee's stuff in the loft, but he's not mentioned it.'

'Good. Thanks for helping me.'

'We will find her, I promise you.'

She nods but doesn't look convinced.

'Let's see what the police find in here.' I hand her the diary. I don't say, but flicking through it, Dom's name is highlighted a lot, and not in a good way.

Could he be spying on his daughter? The thought of what that would mean chills me to the core.

66

The following morning I'm woken by the alluring smell of cooking bacon. We always have a sausage or bacon roll on a Saturday morning and today is even more special than usual, because Alfie is officially a teenager.

Marc comes in with a mug of tea and puts it on my bedside table. He's already dressed in designer jeans and T-shirt.

'You're up early,' I say. 'I didn't hear you come in last night. Everything okay at work?' I half sit up and check the time. It's gone nine thirty.

'Yeah, the meeting with the new client went well. I ended up taking them out for dinner. Then I popped home to see Milly and the pups before coming here. Told you I would.' He smiles and points a finger at me.

'Glad to hear it, but if I hadn't called in earlier, they'd have been on their own for hours, even with the gardener checking in on them. Milly had no food left and hardly any water.'

'Fair enough. Were you there long?'

'No not really.' I instantly picture the smudge of mud on Marc's cream stair carpet and expect him to question me about who I let in, but he doesn't mention it.

'I was expecting to see scaffolding up and more of a mess from what you'd told me.' I pick up my tea and lean back against the headboard.

'Oh yeah, did I forget to say they've already fixed the hole in the roof? It didn't take as long as I thought because it wasn't that big after all. They're coming back next week to repair the floor and ceiling in the en-suite.'

'That's good news.' I blow the steam off my tea.

'Yeah, it is. Look, do you want me to grab Alfie's present and card from the wardrobe and let them come in? It's been hard keeping them amused, they've both been up since seven.'

'Yeah, why not. You could have woken me earlier; I wouldn't have minded.' This isn't quite the start to the day I had planned, and now I feel all out of sorts.

'I thought you might need a lie in after the last couple of days.' He opens the door, and Bella runs in and flops on the bed, followed by Alfie, who sidles in behind her, as though he's too cool to make a fuss about becoming a teenager.

Marc stacks the small pile of presents on the bed and we watch Alfie open them. The best I could afford from his wish list is an Xbox game which has just come out, and at over sixty pounds it's more than I wanted to spend. Alfie nods, admiring the cover and skimming the blurb. He barely says a word as he chucks it on the bed and opens the next gift.

When he's finished, he glances at Marc who raises an eyebrow, and Alfie dutifully thanks me and slopes off back to his room.

'Oh well, I suppose that's turning thirteen for you,' I say, unable to hide my disappointment at Alfie's lack of enthusiasm. I spent ages trying to pick things he would like, but nothing seems enough to please him these days.

I put my dressing gown on and go down to the kitchen for my bacon sandwich. They've all eaten theirs so I'm sitting on my own. Marc pours me a coffee from the cafetiere and tops his up.

'I need to pop back to mine this morning to see to the puppies and be there for a present for Alfie that's due to be delivered today.'

'Another present?' I sigh. 'You've already given him trainers.'

'I know but I couldn't resist.' He swallows a mouthful of coffee and lifts his eyebrows. His eyes widen and stare at me as though warning me not to question him. Then his face slackens into a smile.

'What did you get?' I squeeze a dollop of brown sauce onto my plate, dip my sandwich in and take a bite.

'Wait and see.' He grins, clearly pleased with himself. It's bound to be something that neither his dad nor I can possibly afford. But I smile back even though it feels like he's trying to win our son over with expensive gifts.

Upstairs I look in on Bella who is sitting on her bed reading a book. Alfie's bedroom door is firmly shut. Lately he starts swearing at me if I so much as look round the door at him. I presume he's playing an online game with his friends, but I really need to get in there to clean and collect empty plates and cups.

Before I get in the shower, I ping a quick text to Cassie to see if they've heard any news about Jess. A reply comes back instantly.

No, nothing.

I sigh deeply and get in the shower.

Once I'm dressed, I open my bedroom window and look down at the drive. Marc's car has already gone. My heart sinks. I thought he was going to wait for me to come down.

Then I notice Colin is standing on my front lawn.

67

Colin from across the road is in my front garden leaning over the rose bushes. I don't care what Jess says about him, sometimes I'm not sure what to make of his behaviour. I march downstairs and out of the front door where he's rummaging about in my flower beds.

'What are you doing?' I say in a stern voice.

He jolts and looks up at me, pale and frightened.

'I... I... Jess said...' His skin is so white, it's translucent. I've not noticed how thin he is before because he wears a thick baggy tracksuit.

'Jess said what?' Cassie strides out of her house and stands beside me, hands on hips.

'She hid something here,' he says quietly.

'Are you having us on? What have you done with Jess?' Cassie's voice deepens, on the verge of losing control.

'I haven't hurt her,' he whimpers. 'She's my best friend.'

He's trembling and there's real fear in his voice.

'It's okay, Colin. We're just worried about her. Can you tell me what she hid?' I ask gently.

Cassie glares at me and I imagine we're both thinking the same thing. Could it be something to do with Olly's death?

'I... I don't know, but she said' – he pauses and speaks slowly – 'if something happens to me, the evidence is in Vicki's garden, in a plastic bag buried near the rose bush.'

'Evidence of what? Do you know what's in the bag?'

Colin can't stop shaking his head.

'Right, I think you need to tell the police what you know. Is your mum home?' Cassie takes her phone out of her pocket.

'She's at work,' he says.

'What's going on?' Dom stands on his doorstep and tears at a piece of toast with his teeth.

'Colin thinks Jess buried some sort of evidence in Vicki's garden,' Cassie tells him.

He swallows down the last piece of toast. 'Don't talk daft, why would she do that?'

'I don't think he's making it up,' I say and Colin shakes his head furiously again.

Dom strides over. 'What are you going on about, boy? You've got a bit of a thing for my daughter, have you?'

Colin's cheeks flush.

'Leave him alone,' Cassie snaps.

'What have you done with her, eh?' Dom bellows only inches from Colin's red face.

'Stop it, Dom. He's trying to help,' Cassie says.

'He really thinks there's something buried here that will help us find her,' I add.

'Then let's call the police.' Dom folds his arms.

'I can't wait for them.' Cassie drops on her knees and starts digging. Dom pulls her away and uses his spade-like hands to scoop the earth away. It's not long before a clear plastic bag emerges in the dirt.

'There's something in it,' Dom says surprised, and Cassie locks eyes with him.

'Don't touch it. We need to preserve any DNA,' I remind them.

Cassie looks straight at me blinking rapidly, hand to her chest, nails caked in mud.

'You were right, Colin, thank you,' I say, and he smiles crookedly.

'Yes, thank you,' Cassie says. 'You're right, you are a good friend to our Jess.'

'Hang on, how do we know *he* didn't plant this here?' Dom says standing up.

'Just shut up!' Cassie shouts, waving her hands then clamps them over her mouth.

'Okay, okay.' Dom sighs.

'Do you have any idea what this is?' I crouch down and peer at a blood stain on a piece of blue-and-yellow patterned material. 'Could it be from the attack on Olly?'

Cassie shakes her head solemnly, her eyes red and full of tears.

'It's a pair of Jess's knickers.'

68

'Christ, Cassie. How do you know this isn't to do with Olly? He could have attacked Jess in the park, and she fought back? Or maybe it was Sean, and Olly tried to rescue her and got killed. Colin, please tell us anything you know,' I say, turning to him, a pang of guilt reverberating through me for assuming he'd hurt Jess.

He shakes his head and shrugs, his shoulders turning into himself.

Dom takes Cassie in his arms. It always surprises me what a hulk of a man he is next to petite Cassie.

'It's alright, we'll find her,' he says. 'And we'll find the bastard who did this to our girl, I promise you.' When he pulls back, I fill him in on what we found in the loft earlier.

'Isn't that the sort of thing Lee would do? He was mister DIY, always banging around up there.'

'Someone has been spying on our daughter,' Cassie says.

'Okay, well it's hard to believe Lee would do anything like that,' Dom says.

'I'll ask him why he didn't mention that the party wall had been knocked through on one side,' I say.

'It would have made quite a lot of noise, so whoever did it must have made sure we were all out at the time, and let's be honest, he's the only one it could be,' Dom says.

For a moment I don't know what to say. Why is he so quick to point the finger at Lee? Does he have something against Lee that I don't know about?

'And someone made that hole in Jess's ceiling with a drill,' Cassie adds. Dom puts his arm around her.

I blink at them, lost for words. Now I'm sure they're both thinking the same thing. After he got sacked, Lee was the only one of us who was at home during the day, which means he had every opportunity to knock the wall through. But he wouldn't do that. After we split up and he moved out, Marc started coming round and helped me move Lee's boxes of stuff up there. Surely if there was a gap big enough for someone to climb through to next door's loft, he would have mentioned it to me.

Unless the hole has been made much more recently than that. I slide a look across at Dom. Could he have knocked through the wall to make it look like Lee did it? He's conveniently not saying very much about his new job as an HGV Technician, how he often arrives home early in the mornings after night shifts. Is he trying to cover up what he's been doing? Perhaps Lee discovered what he'd been up to in the loft, and warned him he was going to tell me and Cassie about it? Dom certainly had the opportunity to drive up to the hospital in Blackpool to smother Lee, shut him up.

'And now you're the one who's at home during the day, just as everyone else is going to work and school,' I say, looking him right in the eye.

'And I told you that Dom suffers from vertigo.' Cassie folds her arms across her chest. How can she defend him when there have been so many arguments between him and Jess? Maybe she should question why there's so much tension between them.

'But *you* told me you were afraid of heights, yet you practically ran up those ladders yesterday.'

'Because my daughter's life is in danger,' Cassie shouts. Dom narrows his eyes at me and tightens his arm around his wife's shoulders. It only took a glance at the entries in Jess's diary to notice Dom's name at the centre of her anger, written in capital letters followed by violent scribblings with red pen about how much she hated him.

Are they normal father, daughter disagreements, or is Dom really capable of hurting his own daughter?

'Mum, where's Alfie?' Bella wails, appearing behind me on our doorstep.

I rush over and give her a hug. 'Alfie's in his room, sweetheart.'

'No, he's not, I just looked.'

'Oh.' I spin back to Cassie and Dom as if they'll know the answer. 'Maybe he's gone to Marc's.'

'Oh dear. Didn't he tell you where he was going?' Cassie's tone is sarcastic. She looks up at Dom's smug face.

I shake my head, baffled that they could turn on me, and Lee. How well do I really know them? Why has Jess been confiding in me instead of her mum, and why does she hate her dad? What has Dom done to her?

'Go, we'll manage just fine, the police are on their way.' Cassie's voice wavers as she glances down at the plastic bag still in the ground.

'I'm so sorry, Cass.'

'It's fine. I've got Dom here. Anyway, there's nothing else you can do,' Cassie says. 'You should be with Alfie celebrating his birthday.'

'Please let me know what the police say.'

She nods. 'Thanks for your help.'

I go inside with Bella and shut the door. Marc has left a note on the counter saying: *See you later*. Am I to assume he has taken Alfie with him? Why is Marc making decisions without me? Surely he could have waited five minutes for me to finish my shower and ask me if he could take Alfie with him? Much as I appreciate the interest and attention he's giving my son, he shouldn't be buying him big presents and taking him out with him without running it past me first. A tiny part of me wonders if he's doing it to spite Lee.

And what about Bella? I didn't know she'd been left on her own, even if I was only in the front garden.

I put the television on in the living room for Bella and run upstairs to check Alfie's bedroom. It's empty, but his computer is still on. The navy curtains are drawn, and the air is musty with the smell of unwashed clothes in the basket and strewn across the floor. There are a variety of dirty mugs and glasses next to the bed. It looks like he left in the middle of a game, which he hates to do. What was the hurry? There are several windows minimised on the screen, so I click on one to see what he's been doing.

I drop into his chair, unable to take in what I'm looking at. A YouTube video has been paused halfway through. I press play and a high-profile misogynist is spouting his toxic views to a group of boys, on how slutty girls and women are parading themselves like prostitutes online, on sites such as Instagram and OnlyFans. Another window is open. I click on it and a video of a scantily clad girl writhing on a bed has been paused. I know I shouldn't be shocked but I am. My son, barely a teenager, has been watching adult content. I turn away and I'm about to shut it down when I do a double take back at the screen. My mouth falls open. I recognise that stripy wallpaper.

But Alfie is still a child.

Yet here he is, watching a soft porn video of his babysitter on OnlyFans.

I blink several times at what I'm seeing. Jess is wearing a tiny bikini, her legs spread out on her bed. A Betty Boop mask is covering her face, but there's no hiding that lilac, pink and silver striped wallpaper. There's only one way I'm guessing Alfie knew she was doing this, and that's by spying on her in her bedroom.

I don't believe he's capable of knocking through the party wall by himself, but he could easily have drilled a hole in the ceiling. Lee's taught him how to put up shelves. Is he behind all this? I think of all the times I thought they were innocently playing Scalextric in the loft. Could they really have been up there spying on a teenage girl? The thought of it curdles my stomach and I taste sick in my mouth.

I take my phone out of my pocket and text Marc, asking where he and Alfie have gone. He replies straight away saying Alfie asked to go with him to his house. It's not like him to quit in the middle of a game. Maybe Marc teased him about this other present arriving for him.

> Okay, fine. Maybe let me know you're taking him with you next time? Is he alright?

> Sorry, I meant to message you. Yeah, he's fine.
> Playing on his new birthday present.

> What did you get him?

A PlayStation.

> That's too much on top of the trainers!

But I got a good deal for it through a friend, with a couple of games thrown in. I knew he'd love it, so I couldn't not get it!

> Okay, well there's something I need to ask you about. Will you be back soon?

Why don't you and Bella come over here? I'm baking cupcakes then later we could take the kids out for dinner? Although it's going to be hard to drag Alfie off his new console so maybe I'll cook.

It feels like I have no choice. It's sweet that he bought Alfie such a fantastic present, but two big ticket items are way too much, especially after everything I've just discovered on Alfie's computer. I'm not sure he deserves it.

> Okay, we'll be there soon.

I call Lee's mobile, but it goes straight to voice mail, so I leave a ranting message about the damage to the party wall in the loft and the hole in Jess's ceiling. At the end I ask him to call me back with a straight answer about whether he has anything to do with it or not, and if he knows the sort of garbage Alfie's been watching on his computer. If it isn't Lee who's behind this, the only other obvious person with access to my roof space apart from Dom and Alfie is Marc, and I can't think of one good reason why he would do anything like that.

71

I arrive at Marc's house with Bella, carrying Alfie's birthday cake in my arms. I've not had a chance to make one, so it's shop-bought in the shape of a games console; I hope Alfie likes it. After what I've seen on his computer, the last thing I feel like doing is celebrating. I need to have a serious chat with him, but not today. I don't want to spoil his thirteenth birthday.

We get out of the car and walk up the long drive to the double-fronted doors and I press the bell. I still think it's strange that there's no sign of any renovations despite what Marc's told me. If the roof has been fixed like he said, why didn't he tell me or invite me over sooner?

Marc answers the door in his chef's apron, cheeks flushed from the heat of the kitchen. He invites us into the spacious monochrome hall, which is bigger than my dining room, and kisses me on the lips as he takes the boxed cake from me.

'Phone,' he says, nodding at the wooden tray on the console table which already has his phone and Alfie's in it. He insisted on me sticking to this annoying rule when I first came here.

'But Cassie might need to call me, update me about Jess.'

'Then switch your phone off silent and you'll hear it ring, then you can answer it as though it were a house phone.'

I sigh and do as he asks. When he moves into my house, I won't let him implement this rule even though part of me knows it's a good thing not to be glued to our devices, but it still worries me. What if someone needs to contact me urgently and I don't hear it for some reason?

'Come and sit down, I've opened a bottle of Prosecco. These cupcakes will be ready shortly. Bella, I've got some freshly squeezed orange juice, can I get you a glass?'

Bella nods. She's not spoken much since her dad fell into the sea. I was hoping Alfie's birthday celebrations would cheer her up.

'Where is the birthday boy?' I ask, toying with the idea of having a quiet word with Alfie right now because I need answers and I'm not sure I can hold in my rage for a whole day.

'In the snug just down the corridor. I'm afraid you're going to struggle to get him off his PlayStation.' He pulls a mock guilty face, and I try not to show my annoyance at him buying another overly expensive present without consulting me first. It's way more than his dad can afford right now, and the last thing Alfie needs is more screen time. But I remind myself it's a kind and generous gift, so I keep my mouth shut. I don't want to seem ungrateful, especially as it feels like he's making a real effort to get to know the children. I do appreciate it because it will make life so much easier if and when we do all live together full time.

'You like dogs, don't you, Bella?' Marc asks as he hands her a glass of orange juice straight from the juicer. He smiles at me and I attempt to smile back but I'm still stressing about Alfie. I need to ask him outright why he's watching videos of Jess, how he even knew she was doing that, and why the hell he's watching that well-known woman-hater. Is it possible he didn't realise it was her? He'll say he clicked on the links by mistake. But I know in my gut that's not true.

Bella takes the drink and nods enthusiastically.

'Well, you've come to the right place at just the right time. My lovely Cocker Spaniel Milly, had a new litter of puppies about two weeks ago. Would you like to see them? I've made a den for them in the summer house.'

Bella nods, and it's so good to see her whole face brighten up. We troop outside to the garden, which must be at least half an acre in total, across the extensive patio and down to the summer house, tucked away in a wooded area near the bottom. Looking back at the house, it's much further away than I realised. Marc opens the door and the dog flap rattles. Seeing it again, I decide the space is probably bigger than my living room. Newspaper and puppy trainer pads cover every inch of the floor. Milly looks up at us from drinking water, with her sad spaniel eyes. I'd not noticed how thin she was before and how the skin from her teats and belly hang down like a half empty bag. She sways slowly back to her comfy looking rectangular pet bed on the ground and flops down. Her five puppies immediately start feeding from her.

'Aw, look at them, Mummy,' Bella exclaims, her eyes wide. 'Can I stroke them?'

I look to Marc to answer, and wonder why he didn't tell me about them as soon as they were born. If this was my beloved dog having puppies, I'd have been raving about it to everyone.

'If you sit near them, you can stroke them gently when they've finished feeding without upsetting the mother. You might even be able to pluck one away and sit it on your lap without her noticing. But if she gets agitated, you'd better put her back.' He laughs, glancing at me.

'Is this Milly's first litter?' I ask.

'No, no. This is her third.' He folds his arms and his expression is serious. 'She's young still, so has a few left in her yet.'

My mouth opens and shuts. I clear my throat. 'Oh, I see. You never mentioned you breed dogs.'

'It's just a hobby really. But she's my third spaniel. The females do love having a brood. Until I sell them of course, then I'll take her to a different stud and then we're off again.'

'What, you mean straight away?' Milly kicks her leg out and tries to shift, but the puppies are latched on like limpets. The silent agony of breastfeeding Alfie comes back to me.

'Yeah.' He pulls a face at my question.

'But aren't you supposed to let her body recover first?' I thought he loved dogs but he's not treating Milly with much care or dignity.

'She's a bitch. It's what they do.' He stares at me as though I'm stupid to even question him. I'm so shocked I can't speak. Could his mum have given his childhood dog away to save it from him? I only know his side of the story after all.

'But you won't be able to do this if you move into my house, you know that don't you?' I frown, not knowing why he's not discussed this with me. I don't have space for them and I'm not sure I agree with it.

'Okay, if you really don't want me to.' He shrugs.

'No, I don't.'

'Let's go in.' His voice is more serious now. He opens the door and ushers me out. My legs are trembling. I stumble onto the lawn. I've never seen this side of him before. I thought he cared about animals, but now it's started me questioning everything about him. It feels like I barely know him at all.

'I'll come and call you when the cupcakes are ready,' I tell Bella, although it's going to be difficult for her to hear me way down here. She sits on a cushion near the puppies and smiles at me for the first time in a couple of days. Now I'm confident she's going to be okay.

Marc curls his arm around my waist as we walk back up to the house. My heart is thumping in my chest. There's no sign at all of any workmen having done repairs on the roof, not even a spec of dirt or dust.

'When did you say they're starting work on the ceiling and floor?' My voice wavers. I'm not convinced there is any damage. The roof is modern and looks completely solid. But why would he lie? I think about the hole in Jess's ceiling and the damage to the party wall. He had access to my loft while I was out. How well do I really know him? Can I trust him? My children are in his house, but are they safe? Am I safe?

'They're hoping to start on the en-suite ceiling next week,' he says in a matter-of-fact way.

'Oh, I see.' The house is so huge, there are five sets of windows on the top floor alone. It's even bigger than I remember it. Seems an excessive amount of space for one person. I still don't understand why he hasn't suggested we move in. Surely we could live on one side while the other side is being repaired. Not that I feel like being with him at all right now. I need to ask him if he knows anything about the hole in the party wall and if so, why he's not mentioned it to me. This relationship won't work if he's been lying.

As we're nearing the patio, something draws my eye to an upstairs window. It was probably the shadow of a bird flying past. But no, it's there again. I'm not sure what it is.

'Is there someone in the bedroom up there?' I say and point to the window.

'No,' he laughs. 'It was probably my cockatoo. It's an empty room, the one with the water damage, so I thought I may as well let my cockatoo fly free in there during the day. She goes back in her cage at night.'

'That's a nice idea. I'd love to see it.' The bird must have been what I heard scratching and tapping. I wish he'd mentioned it because I'm not keen on having it in my house.

'It's safer to wait until it's dark, when it goes back to its cage for food. If I open the door when it's light, it's likely to escape.'

'Okay, well I don't mind waiting.'

'I'll take you up there later.' He winks at me.

His mood has lightened up again. Now's my chance to ask him about the loft. I stop and turn to him.

'Actually, before we go back in, there's something important I need to ask you.'

72

'Of course. What is it?' Marc asks, gently holding my arms.

'When you were taking the boxes up to the loft, you must have noticed the dividing wall to Cassie and Dom's had been partially knocked through? I was wondering why you hadn't mentioned it.'

His eyes flicker over mine. 'Yeah, I meant to tell you, but to be honest it seemed so odd, I didn't want to alarm you.' He puts his finger to his lips. 'Then I thought it must have been like that for a long time, otherwise I figured you'd have mentioned it to me.' He shrugs. 'With all this drama going on with Lee, I'm afraid I completely forgot to say.'

'There has been a lot going on. But are you saying you don't know how it got like that?' I frown at him, not sure how he could have forgotten to tell me something as odd as this.

'No, like I say, I assumed it had been like it for a while because it had been boarded over which is why I didn't notice it at first. But the last time I went up there this large sheet of plaster board had been moved across, so half the gap in the dividing wall was visible.'

'Someone must have moved it completely out of the way since then, because the gap was uncovered when I went up there with Cassie.'

'You and Cassie went up there?' Marc scratches his head.

'Yeah, we found a hole in Jess's ceiling.'

'Oh, that's odd.' He frowns. 'Because a few days ago, I woke up in the night and heard a scratching sound above the bathroom, and assumed it was a mouse. But I heard something else too, so I looked out of our bedroom door. The step-seat was on the landing below the open loft hatch.'

'What? In the middle of the night?' I frown, wondering why he's only just telling me now.

'I know, I thought I was dreaming. But I watched through a crack in the door and saw Alfie drop himself down from the loft onto the top of the steps and close the hatch. He climbed down, put the steps back into the bathroom and went to bed. At first I thought he might have been looking for something in one of the boxes I'd put up there, but I had a look the next day and found the board had been moved and there was a big gap in the party wall. I couldn't believe it.'

'So why didn't you wake me up, tell me straight away?'

'I almost did, but I didn't want to stress you out, especially in the middle of the night. It would have caused a huge commotion, and Alfie would have been so embarrassed.'

'But I don't understand what he was doing up there when he should have been asleep.' For a second my mind stops completely. I can hardly take it in.

Alfie's been watching Jess online, and now it looks like he's been spying on her too. What's happened to my little boy? I barely recognise the person he's become.

'Whatever it was, I guess he was trying to hide it.' Marc shrugs. I blink at him and although I'm hearing his words, I'm not able to absorb them. I can't believe this is happening.

'It can't have been him who broke through the party wall, so someone else must have done it.'

He tilts his head. 'And I think we both know who that is.'

'Mmm, maybe.'

'You don't think it was Lee who knocked it through?'

'Why would he?' I examine his face to see if he's keeping anything else from me. It feels like there's something he's holding back.

'I don't know, but then why is Alfie going into your loft in the middle of the night?' He tips his hands over.

'I think he's possibly been climbing through to next door's loft to spy on Jess.'

'Really?'

'Cassie and I found a tiny hole in Jess's bedroom ceiling. Alfie is quite handy with a drill.'

'But he's not like that, is he?'

'You should see the filth I found on his computer. He's been watching her on OnlyFans.'

He pulls a disgusted face. 'Is she aware of this?'

'I don't know.' I take a deep breath and tell him about the misogynist that Alfie's been watching online, spouting hate and condoning violence against women. The weight of it all is too much and I start crying.

'Vicki, I'm so sorry.' Marc draws me into his arms. 'That's shocking. I guess he's lost his father figure and is looking to this vile man for direction. It's not easy for his generation, not knowing how to be a young man in this new world, but that's no excuse.'

'I think you're right, but I don't want to bring it up with him today and ruin his birthday, so let's keep a lid on it for now, until tomorrow at least, okay?'

'That's fine, if you're sure?'

'Yes, although it's going to be hard to enjoy today, knowing what I've seen and what you've told me.'

We go inside. Marc goes back to the kitchen to check on the cupcakes, and I head towards the snug to find Alfie.

If Jess finds out what Alfie's been doing, she might press charges, and he could be locked up. Except, no one knows where she is. I can hardly bear to think it, but could Alfie have something to do with Olly's death and Jess's disappearance too?

I stand at the door for a few moments watching my son leaning towards a large screen playing a car racing game on his new PlayStation. How did she not spot the signs that he was changing so radically? They're always talking about young men being influenced by these preachers of hate towards women online and in the news, and she's always thought her boy was too grounded and respectful to ever treat women and girls like that, so how could this have happened?

'Are you having a good birthday?' I touch Alfie's shoulder, but he shrugs me off like I've given him an electric shock. He barely looks up at me from his game.

'You like your present then?' I try again. He shrugs. He's been so off since Lee moved out.

'Get lost.'

'What did you say?' I blink rapidly, astonished at this new level of disrespect.

'Just piss off and leave me alone.' He grimaces.

'Look at me and do not talk to me like that,' I demand, raising my voice.

He swivels round and gives me the finger. 'Now fuck off.'

I'm speechless and a bit tearful that he could be so rude to me. I understand he's angry with me and it's hard for him and Bella to adjust to life without their dad at home, but I'm going to insist Marc takes this present back if Alfie carries on like this. I wouldn't normally put up with such disgusting behaviour, but I don't want to cause a scene in Marc's house *and* ruin Alfie's birthday. I need to bring all of this up with Alfie again tomorrow, including what he's been watching online. I'll confiscate his bloody screens if necessary.

I go to the bathroom to calm down and when I come out, I take my shoes off and go to sit in the living room. I could have quite happily made this my home, but not now. I'm too confused and unsure about Marc. When I walk in, I notice he's topped up my glass of Prosecco and left it by the sofa with a folded blanket. He can be so thoughtful. Lee would never do anything like this for me without me having to ask. But then Lee would never treat an animal like a baby-making machine.

I drink a large mouthful of Prosecco and lie down on the sofa, covering myself up with the blanket. It's been such a long stressful few days and I've managed to read everyone so wrong. I feel so alone. I'm not sure who I can trust any more. No one close to me is who I thought they were, and I've missed so many things about Alfie. I shouldn't have spent so much time and energy on Marc because it's meant I've not paid enough attention to what my own son has been up to.

I meant to check my phone when I came out of the bathroom, but I'm too exhausted to get up now. Bubbly always relaxes me, makes me sleepy. I just need a ten-minute power nap, then I'll take the kids home. Cool things off with Marc for a while so I can spend time getting Alfie off the internet and back on track.

I snuggle under the blanket and shut my eyes.

A while later, I jolt awake to the sound of someone crying.

73

My first thought is it's Bella crying. Then I remember she's outside with the puppies. But maybe she's come in.

I try to sit up, but I must have slept for longer than a short nap because my head is heavy with sleep. There's almost a whole glass of Prosecco I haven't touched, and I really don't feel like it now. My legs wobble when I stand up and shuffle down the hall but there's no one around. Why hasn't Marc called me to say the cupcakes are ready? He's not in the kitchen and it looks like the oven has been switched off but the cakes are still inside.

Maybe he heard the crying too and has gone in the garden to check on Bella. But if it was her, I don't think we'd hear it in the house. I can't see anyone out there from the kitchen window. A mild panic creeps up my chest. I don't think it sounded like Alfie crying, so it must have been Bella. I check in the snug, but he's not there. His game is paused on the TV screen.

I need to check my phone while Marc's not around, see if there's any news about Jess, but it isn't in the dish on the hall console table. I'm sure I left it there with his and Alfie's. My head is so foggy. Where's it gone and where's Alfie?

The crying starts again; it's definitely coming from upstairs. Perhaps Bella hurt herself outside and Marc and Alfie are patching her up in the bathroom. I slowly climb the stairs, holding on tight because my head is throbbing so hard it hurts to open my eyes fully. I drank the Prosecco far too quickly, and on an empty stomach, it always goes straight to my head. But I only had two glasses. This feels different. Has Marc deliberately put something in my drink to help me sleep?

If one of them has had an accident, why didn't they wake me up? I'm no help to anyone like this. I won't be in a fit state to drive home.

At the top of the stairs, all the bedroom doors are ajar except one. The room that was locked when I was last here. Marc told me it was out of bounds because it's for his cockatoo. It seems extreme to me, letting a bird take over a whole bedroom, pooping and dropping feathers all over the place. I don't agree with caging birds, but that's no better. Is this the real reason why he doesn't want us to live here?

I'm about to open the bedroom door and shut it again quickly if the bird flies towards me, when I hear another cry. Someone is clearly in distress. It's coming from the other side of this door. Worse than that, I know immediately that it's Alfie.

I burst in but can't believe what I'm seeing.

74

DEBBIE

Debbie pulls up in her Land Rover a few doors up from Vicki's house. Usually, she can park outside or on the drive but there's police tape around the front garden and a policewoman standing guard.

'What's going on?' Lee sits up in the passenger seat, fumbling to undo his seat belt.

'You stay there, I'll find out what's happened,' Debbie says, patting his leg to reassure him while her heart is thumping right up into her throat. Now she knows for sure that she should have said something to Vicki. God, she swung backwards and forwards for the whole damn journey home, *yes she should tell her, no don't say a word*. When she eventually dropped Vicki and the kids at home, she wanted to speak out, but the words wouldn't come. Even so, as she drove away she'd felt enormous relief knowing her secret had stayed a secret. But then the guilt had kicked in. And now... If something has happened to them that she could have prevented, she'll never be able to live with herself.

'What's he gawping at?' Lee points to the house opposite Vicki's, where a boy is standing at his bedroom window staring out. 'He was always a strange one,' he adds, looking at her. The whites of Lee's eyes are bloodshot and the skin around them crinkly. He's aged so much in the last few days even though he was only in hospital for a short while. It feels to her like he died and came back to life. The doctor wanted him to stay in another day, but he discharged himself and called her to pick him up, insisting he couldn't miss Alfie's thirteenth birthday for anything, or anyone, even if Vicki won't let them spend time together. He said he couldn't have Alfie believing the lies about him. And he's right. He needs his son to know he's here for him, that he's made an effort.

She reaches for the birthday present from the back seat and climbs out, shutting the door quietly. The policewoman standing outside Vicki's house won't tell her anything, so she knocks on Cassie's door. Dom answers. He's wearing shorts and a T-shirt in this weather. Debbie explains that Lee has just come out of hospital and she's driven him here because he wants to drop Alfie's present off and say happy birthday.

'Do you know where Vicki is?' she adds.

Dom frowns at her for a moment or two, then looks out at Lee sitting in the car.

'Why is there a policewoman outside their house?' Debbie asks.

Dom glances over his shoulder, then says, 'You'd both better come in.'

'Okay, thanks, I'll go and get Lee.'

'I'll stick the kettle on and make you both a cuppa. You're gonna need it.' He pulls a face like he's eaten a sour cherry and she wonders what the hell's been going on in the short time since she dropped Vicki and the kids off yesterday.

She carries the present back to the car and helps Lee out, looping her arm through his to steady him. The boy is still standing at his bedroom window. Doesn't he have something better to do?

Cassie is sitting at the kitchen table. Dom brings the mugs of tea over and piles a packet of custard creams onto a plate in the middle.

'Thanks for this, just what we needed after the long drive,' Debbie says. The air is thick with everything that's not being said so she slices right through it. 'Where are Vicki and the kids?' She's tempted to crack a joke about needing the police because they set fire to the house with the birthday candles, but Alfie's only thirteen and Cassie and Dom don't look in the mood for laughing.

'They've gone to Marc's,' Cassie says.

'Should have known.' Lee tuts.

'So why the police?' Debbie asks again. A feeling of dread clutches her chest.

Cassie leans forward and waves her finger at Lee. 'Hang on, before we tell you anything, you need to explain what you've been doing in your loft.'

'What do you mean *doing*?' He looks at Dom then turns to Debbie, probably hoping one of them will explain.

'Alright, tell me when you last went up there and what you and Alfie used to get up to,' Cassie says, folding her arms.

'Why? I've not been up there for months. I used to go up there quite a bit with Alfie when I still lived there. We played on my old Scalextric, had the track right across the floor with loop the loops and all sorts, but you know that. It was a couple of years back. Then he discovered computer games and that was the end of that era.'

'But I want to know when you started the renovations?'

'What renovations?' He screws up his face. 'All I did was add insulation, knocked up a few shelves for storage and that's about it.'

'No knocking out chunks of the shared wall?' Dom folds his arms and tips back in his chair.

'No, of course not. Is this to do with the message Vicki left me?' Lee pulls a puzzled expression. 'Why would I do that?'

'A big chunk of the party wall has been knocked through,' Dom says, tilting his head, watching every move Lee makes. 'Big enough for someone to climb through if they wanted to.'

'Well, it wasn't me if that's what you're implying.' Lee narrows his eyes at Dom. 'You know me, I'd have come and spoken to you if I'd wanted to do anything that would affect a shared wall, fence, or whatever.'

'That's exactly what I said,' he says to Cassie as though that ends the matter.

'Vicki says she doesn't know who did it. But worse still, someone has drilled a little hole in Jess's bedroom ceiling, presumably to spy on her whenever they want to, and now her boyfriend Olly is dead, and she's gone missing.' Cassie throws her hands up in the air as if to say the situation is hopeless.

'Olly?' Lee says. He looks like he's seen a ghost.

A chill slides down Debbie's spine. She swivels her head until she's looking Lee in the eye. He blinks back at her.

'But why are the police outside Vicki's house?' Debbie asks. 'Is everyone okay?'

'They were when I saw them earlier.' Cassie explains Colin's story about Jess telling him she'd buried some evidence in Vicki's front garden, and to dig it up if anything happened to her.

'And sure enough, I dug up a clear plastic bag with a pair of my daughter's bloodied knickers in it. The police have taken them away to be examined, to see if it is her blood and if there's anything... anyone else's DNA on them. They're hoping it will give them a clue as to what happened to her before she disappeared.'

'On top of the pregnancy test kit they found in the rubbish bag from Jess's bedroom, I think it's pretty clear what's happened to her,' Dom says.

'But Jess told me that belonged to Vicki,' Lee says.

'Did she?' Cassie asks. 'When?'

'Day before yesterday when I got rid of all those teenagers at our house, I saw it in her bag and threatened to tell you two about it. She insisted it wasn't hers, but Vicki's.'

'Vicki's pregnant?' Debbie asks.

'Apparently so, although Marc didn't seem to know about it when I mentioned it to him up on the pier. I think that's why he let go of me.'

'He did that on purpose?' Dom looks flabbergasted.

'Yeah, nice guy eh?' Lee says.

'Vicki's not said anything to me about being pregnant.' Cassie frowns.

'Doesn't sound like she's told anyone except Jess.'

Debbie doesn't speak but she feels Lee's fingers rest on hers under the table.

'I was pretty mean about it to Jess if I'm being honest,' Lee says. 'Making her tell me. I told her I'd call you guys. I assumed she was pregnant and it was Olly's, although I seem to remember him telling me once that he wanted to wait until they'd got married first. He was old fashioned like that. I just assumed he must have cracked.'

'I didn't know you knew Olly,' Cassie says.

'Yeah, he was on work experience for a couple of weeks in the accounts department. A real whizz with figures.'

'Oh right, he never mentioned it to us. We didn't know him all that well really. Such a quiet boy.' Cassie frowns at Dom.

'Do you know what time Vicki and Alfie left?' Debbie asks.

'A good couple of hours ago. I think Vicki was a bit pissed off. Marc went off with Alfie without telling her. I think he decided to cook at his house, and celebrate Alfie's birthday there. She left in quite a hurry with Bella.'

'Do you know where Marc lives?' Lee asks. 'So we can take Alfie's present over.'

'I can pass it on for you,' Cassie says, holding out her hand for the gift, sitting up straight.

'Thanks, but I've come all this way to see my boy,' Lee says.

'But isn't it going to upset Vicki and potentially start another fight with Marc?'

'You wouldn't be saying that if...' Lee presses his lips together. Debbie pinches his leg.

'If what?' Dom asks.

'It's nothing. Just a bit of rivalry between two men.' Debbie tries to smile but her face aches with the effort.

'Vicki told me what happened on the pier. Said Marc tried to save you, but you say he let you fall?'

'Because he did,' Lee says.

'Come on, we're mates, aren't we? At least we used to be. What is it with him that you hate so much?' Dom leans his elbows on the table, palms outwards.

'He can't say,' Debbie says for him.

'Sorry, Debbie, but I want to hear it from Lee. We lived next door to each other for what eight, ten years?' He points his hand at Lee, eyebrows raised.

Lee glances at Debbie then rubs under his eye as though he's trying to stop himself crying. He blows out a breath and pauses before he speaks.

'Marc isn't who he says he is.'

75

VICKI

At the end of a four-poster bed, Alfie is kneeling, trousers and pants down with his back to me. Marc is at the head of the bed leaning over someone, holding them down. I can't see who it is with Alfie in the way, but they don't appear to be moving. I cling to the door frame, the room spinning.

'Alfie?' is all I can manage to say in a strange voice that doesn't sound like me. I try to think why his pants are round his ankles.

'Mum.' He yelps like a wounded animal as he turns in my direction, hauling his pants up, not quite looking at me but I can see there are tears in his scrunched-up eyes. A shiver runs down my spine.

'What's going on here?' I cry, and stagger towards Alfie, trying to see who's on the bed, but in seconds Marc has pounced forward and is blocking my view, gripping my hands tight.

I need to know who is on the bed lying flat, knees up, not moving. Are they alive and in danger too?

'Alfie,' I call and dig my heels in. My son is sobbing. He looks terrified.

'You don't need to be here, darling. Why don't you come and lie down, I can see you're not feeling well.' Marc spins me round and tries to steer me back out of the door.

'What are you doing to him? Why did he have his pants down?' I bellow, and try to elbow and wriggle out of his grasp.

'No really, come and have a nice lie down.' His grip tightens around my arms.

'Leave my son alone.' I struggle against him but he's too strong. 'Let go of me!'

'He's fine,' he says in a tight voice as he tries to shove me out of the door, but I grab hold of the handle with both hands.

'What's going on? Who's on the bed with him?' I fight against Marc and the fogginess in my head.

'It's Jess, Mum,' Alfie sobs, leaning to one side to let me see.

'What?' I yell and yank away from Marc as hard as I can, but I can't free myself and he squeezes me harder, his fingers pressing into my skin until it hurts.

'It's just a little birthday game we're playing,' Marc grumbles.

'*You* took her?' I scream. 'Why? What are you doing? Tell me what's going on?' I kick out at him but he moves his legs away and pushes his body against mine, squashing me against the door.

'Don't you worry, she's helping us out.' He shifts a few inches and I elbow him sharply in the stomach. He doubles over but doesn't let go of me and in that moment, I catch a glimpse of Jess's hair, the side of her head, an ear.

'What have you done to her? Leave her alone. Let her go.' I strain to catch a glimpse of her face, some sign that she's alive. She tries to lift her head from the pillow a few centimetres and make noises at me, but she's bound to the bed. Marc turns to look at her and I see her eyes bulging with the strain of wanting to speak, but her mouth is covered with grey tape.

'I don't want to do it, Mum,' Alfie sobs.

'Do what? What are you making him do?' I scream, my hands tightening on the handle while he tries to prise my fingers off.

'Now he's turned thirteen, I'm merely showing him how to become a man.'

'He doesn't need to know, he's just a boy,' I shout. 'Let them go!'

'But his father is useless, and he needs a good role model like me to show him how to navigate his way in this modern world.'

'What are you talking about? Why do you hate Lee *so* much?'

But Marc is no longer listening. 'All boys need to take the first opportunity they get, grab it firmly with both hands and shed the embarrassment of their virginity.'

'You're making him... rape her?' I glare at him, the words catching in my throat, but he won't look me in the eye.

'You need to let go now,' he orders and bashes down hard on my fingers with his fist. My hands spring off as I yelp in pain and twist my hands together.

'Get away from me,' I scream.

'Mum, don't leave me!' Alfie cries, twisting round.

Marc grips my shoulders and shoves me out of the door.

'Don't do this to them!' I plead with him, but he grunts something under his breath.

'Get out of there!' I shout to Alfie over my shoulder as Marc drags me down the corridor. I just hope he understands what I mean and is brave enough to act.

76

DEBBIE

Cassie writes Marc's address down for us on the back of an envelope.

'He lives in the old part of town. Maybe you should call Vicki and let her know you're coming?'

Debbie and Lee exchange a glance.

'No, it's okay, we'd rather surprise them.' Debbie pulls a tight smile.

'But if what you say about him is true, and he's not who he says he is, we should call the police and warn Vicki.'

'No way. They'll just bundle in and put her in danger. He can talk his way out of anything. Look what he's done to me. We need to handle this,' Lee says.

Dom narrows his eyes at him. 'You've just got out of hospital, mate. Can you seriously handle Marc between the two of you?'

'It's not about brute force,' Lee says.

'Then you need to tell us what this is about,' Dom says standing up. 'Because if it's anything to do with our Jess going missing...'

Lee glances questioningly at Debbie. He's leaving it up to her. Her breathing quickens. She bunches up the corner of her fleece in her hand. She's not spoken about it out loud once in all these years.

'We think it might be,' Debbie says slowly. She touches around her eye where the nerves have started twitching.

Lee gently squeezes Debbie's hand. 'Marc attacked Debbie when she was younger, but he had a different name then. He's changed his identity to mask who he is.'

'What he is,' Debbie adds and swallows, her mouth dry.

Cassie stands next to Dom, her face drained of colour. 'Then whether you like it or not, we're coming with you,' she says.

77

VICKI

Marc lifts me off my feet and carries me into another room with a double bed.

'You can't do this to them. Let them go!' I yell.

He lays me on the bed. I try to get up but he holds me there and covers me in a scratchy woollen blanket, tucking it in around me.

'I'm sorry you had to see that, Vicki. It wasn't for your eyes. But he needs to finish the job if he wants to become a real man. Too many boys are virgins these days through no fault of their own.'

'What do you mean? He's too young to worry about that. It's utter madness. Neither of them want to do it. You need to let them go.'

He pulls straps over the blanket and tightens them until my ankles flatten to the mattress turning my feet sideways, and I can't move them at all.

'You women can't be trusted. That's what it's come to, I'm afraid. Emasculating men, not wanting to get married, or have babies. Do you know how far the birth rate has dropped? Left to you, the human race would die out.'

'But women have more autonomy now and that's a good thing.'

The sound of metal-on-metal scraping makes me wince, the buckle of a belt or something like it is being pulled across my chest, pushing the air out of me.

'Is it? When were you going to tell me you were carrying my baby?' He stares down at me, eyebrows raised.

'I... I was going to tell you, when I'd got past twelve weeks.'

He swoops in close to my face. 'Liar!' A spray of spit covers my skin. His eyes are so wide they're almost bulging out of their sockets. 'Jess confirmed to me about the clinic, the abortion. I just knew there was something going on. All the whispering and secrets, and then I saw your messages about your appointment. Well, no matter, you're far too old anyway. But Jess isn't.' The side of his top lip hitches in a smirk.

He strides out before I can respond. The door clicks shut, and a key is turned in the lock.

78

'Where the hell has he gone?' Marc bellows on the landing only moments later. Then his footsteps thunder down the stairs. My boy must have got away! I've always reminded both children about the bravery of the mouse standing up to the Gruffalo, to remind them that no matter how big or frightening their opponent, they can use their intelligence and cunning to outwit them. I hope he manages to find his phone and call for help. If he runs down the garden, he'll find Bella in the summer house with the puppies. I hope he keeps her safe. She must be wondering where we all are by now.

I wriggle as hard as I can to get free but it's no good, I'm completely immobile except for my head and neck. I strain to hear a noise from the next room. Has Jess really been here locked away all this time? So is he the person who arranged to meet her online, then took her? Oh God, does that mean he killed Olly too? It must have been him who knocked through the partition wall during the day when everyone was out, so he could spy on Jess in her bedroom. I daren't think what she's already been through, after what was found in my front garden. And the positive pregnancy test. Was that Marc too? I scream out in frustration.

'We're going to get out of here, Jess!' I shout. I know she can't reply, but I don't want her to give up hope.

A shriek rises up from outside the bedroom window, and I immediately know it is Bella. My breathing quickens. He cannot touch my girl. He cannot hurt her. I will kill him. A few minutes later Marc unlocks the door and bursts into the room holding Bella under his arm and dragging Alfie by his. He dumps her at the bottom of the bed kicking and crying.

'Leave them alone!' I shout at him, but Marc doesn't even look at me. He grunts and takes a screaming Alfie away by the scruff of his neck.

The bedroom door slams shut.

79

DEBBIE

After a short drive across town, Debbie parks outside Marc's mansion. The front door is locked so Dom tries around the back, through a side gate. The back door is wide open. Dom leads them in. Alfie's birthday cake is still in the box on the side. The faint smell of burnt cakes is in the air.

'Where is everybody?' Debbie whispers.

'Hey, this is Vicki's phone, what's it doing here?' Cassie says, picking it up from the fruit bowl on the table. She turns it over to show Vicki's personalised cover – a photo of the kids. 'Where are Alfie and Bella? I've never known them to be so quiet.'

A burst of crying upstairs stops them in their tracks. Debbie puts her hand in her pocket. It's still there and despite her frazzled nerves, she takes comfort from the fact that this time she's in control.

'I'll go up first, Debbie and Lee, you stay here,' Dom says.

'No, I'm coming with you,' Debbie says. 'Cassie, can you stay with Lee, please?' She's not going to take no for an answer.

Cassie nods and Debbie is about to follow Dom up the stairs when Cassie starts whimpering into her hand.

'What is it?' Dom whispers.

'That's Jess's bag.' She points to her daughter's rucksack at the bottom of the stairs, partially hidden by pairs of shoes.

'Shit.' Dom grinds his teeth.

At the top of the stairs, they hear crying in the room to the left. Dom storms in, Debbie close behind. Marc is standing over Jess, who's lying stretched out on the bed, her wrists tied with rope, duct tape across her mouth. She's hardly wearing any clothes except skimpy lingerie and stockings.

'You fucking pervert,' Dom screams and punches Marc in the face. Before Marc recovers Dom hits him again, but this time Marc lunges forward, knees him in the groin and makes a dash for the door. Dom recovers quickly and charges straight at Marc's back, crashing him to the ground. The full force of Dom's weight and stature lands on top of him.

'You're going to be okay,' Debbie says to Jess as she unties her hands. She tosses the rope to Dom, and he ties Marc's hands behind his back. The crying starts again, and she realises it's coming from Alfie, who is curled up in a ball half naked at the end of the bed.

Debbie calls out to Cassie and Lee to come up.

'What have you done to our daughter, you piece of shit?' Dom turns Marc over on the ground and shakes his shoulders, banging his head on the carpet several times, then he holds him there with his foot.

'Jess!' Cassie runs in and straight over to her daughter, and takes her in her arms. Lee goes to Alfie and helps him pull up his pants and trousers, then hugs him tight. Debbie steps back, taking it all in. If she'd spoken up sooner, could she have prevented all this? She can't think about this now. She needs to focus on what she came here to do.

'Where's your mum and Bella?' Lee asks him.

'Locked in another room,' he says, and a new wave of crying takes over him.

'It's okay.' Lee rubs his back to soothe him.

'I got away when he took them in there, and ran into the garden. Bella was in the summer house,' Alfie says between sobs, 'I tried to call the police, but... but my phone died.'

Dom fishes a bunch of keys out of Marc's pocket and tosses them to Debbie. She nods at Lee to come with her. She's in charge now. Cassie stays with Jess and Alfie while Lee and Debbie go and find the other bedroom. There's only one locked and after trying a few keys, they find the right one.

Bella is trying to unbuckle the straps across Vicki on the bed. When she sees her dad, she dashes straight into his arms. Thank goodness they're alive. Debbie finishes unstrapping the belts across Vicki's body and helps her sit up.

Vicki leans into Debbie who puts her arm around her shoulders. As she joins the others in the main bedroom, Marc is still pinned to the floor, Dom sitting on top of his chest.

Cassie is carefully helping Jess take the tape off her mouth. She immediately starts bawling into her mother's arms.

'Tell me what he did to you baby,' Cassie says, stroking Jess's hair. She passes Lee a glass and he goes to the bathroom to fill it with fresh water. Jess takes a sip then clears her throat.

'He tricked me. He messaged me on OnlyFans saying he knew who I was. I asked Olly to come with me, just in case, but by the time I'd got there, he'd killed Olly then he kidnapped me,' she sobs.

'He... raped me.'

80

VICKI

We're all quiet, shell-shocked. Our worst fears confirmed. I grimace at Marc with disgust. I have no words. He was so convincing. I didn't pick up any clues that he was capable of rape and murder.

While Cassie comforts her daughter, I'm just grateful they're here to rescue us. I'm so cold I'm shivering, the tips of my nails are blue. I don't want to think about what Marc would have done to me and Bella, or Jess and Alfie.

'I know I should have told you,' Jess says to her mum, 'then none of this would have happened, but he threatened me. Told me if I breathed a word to anyone, he would set fire to our house.'

'How dare you!' Cassie screams at Marc and lunges towards him landing a kick in his ribs.

I feel like doing the same for what he's done. I can barely contain my anger.

'You utter piece of shit,' Dom bellows and pummels Marc with several punches to the body.

'When did he do this to you, sweetheart?' Cassie says to Jess gently. 'We found your hidden evidence in Vicki's front garden. Colin told us about it.'

'Bless him.' She sniffs, wiping her eyes, leaning like a rag doll on her mum's chest. 'He saw me upset that night... after Marc attacked me.'

'When was this?' I ask.

Jess blinks up at her mum and raises her hands to her mouth.

'Take your time,' Cassie says and rubs her arm.

'It was about six weeks ago, when I was babysitting for you. The night I lost my phone.' She dips her head. This isn't easy for her. 'You went to bed soon after you and Marc got back from your night out. But he stayed up and you'd given me another glass of wine, so I thought it was a bit rude to leave it. Then he topped it up without asking and I thought one more wouldn't hurt, and I felt I owed it to you to get to know him as he was staying at your place more often.' She draws in a breath and glances at her mum, her face filled with anguish. 'He was watching a film on TV I liked too, *Notting Hill*, and we were having a laugh about it, but he kept topping up my glass and then he started saying how much he fancied Julia Roberts, and all the things he wanted to do to her in bed, right down to graphic details.' Her eyes shut for a long second then she gulps down a mouthful of water. 'I was so shocked I could hardly move. And the next thing I knew, he was on top of me, but he was too strong, I couldn't get him off. I was frozen with fear,' she sobs.

'You fucker!' Dom yells and leans his arm hard across Marc's face, squashing his nose and lips to one side. Marc groans but Dom doesn't get off.

Cassie strokes Jess's hair as she cries.

'And that's why I found your phone under the sofa the next day,' I say, and Jess nods.

'The police found a pregnancy test in the bin liner from your bedroom,' Cassie tells her.

'I took the test when I babysat at Vicki's, but I got interrupted by Fran and her lot. I didn't find out until later that my test was positive.'

'Oh, Jess,' Cassie cries.

'I thought it was yours,' Lee says to me and explains how he saw Jess with it.

Jess looks down, then up at her mum and dad. 'I'm sorry, but he threatened to tell you, and I was scared what you'd say and do, so I told him it was yours, Vicki. I couldn't face telling anyone what Marc did to me.'

'It's okay, I understand,' I say.

Marc twists his head away from Dom's arm. 'But Vicki *was* pregnant, and she got rid of my child without even telling me,' he shouts, his voice strained. He wipes his bloodied lips on the carpet.

'I don't want any more children, especially now I've hit forty,' I say. 'I didn't want you pressuring me into keeping it. I've got everything I want in Alfie and Bella and my career. Why should I give that up for you, or anyone?'

'So you went off and had an abortion. You bitch.'

'And I'm glad I did because you are clearly not cut out to be a father, with your perverted mind.'

'You're all the same you women, and as for Jess, she was begging for it for weeks, giving me the eye every time I saw her.'

'That's a lie,' Jess shouts back, 'and Olly was innocent too. Why did you have to kill him?'

'It was an accident. You know that and I know that. He fell and hit his head on a rock. There's no evidence to say anything different.'

'Except he wasn't just Jess's boyfriend, was he?' Lee chips in.

Everyone looks at him. Marc narrows his eyes.

'Olly told me exactly what you did to frame me.'

81

DEBBIE

'What do you mean?' Vicki asks.

'Lee's talking a load of bullshit as usual. All those drugs have addled his little brain,' Marc says.

'Olly told me all about Marc bribing him at the office when he was there on work experience. What was the deal? If he planted drugs in my drawer as a prank, you'd make sure he was in the running for a full-time job there when he graduated? If he *didn't* do it, he'd have to leave that day. Poor kid believed you. Except when he heard that I'd got the sack over it, he felt so guilty that he came and told me what you made him do.'

'He should have kept quiet then, shouldn't he?' Marc says.

'So it wasn't an accident,' Jess shouts.

'And that wasn't the only reason you had it in for Olly, was it?' Lee says.

'What are you going on about?'

'While he was working in the accounts department, he noticed some of the invoices didn't look quite right. One was for a company his grandmother has shares in. He rang them up and discovered they'd never had any dealings with you or your company. He found a few others too, and it was the same story every time. What it adds up to is you falsely claiming VAT and defrauding HMRC. I helped Olly report you, so you should expect a visit from the tax man and the police any time soon.' Lee folds his arms and grins.

'You bastard!' Marc spits blood.

'It's the least I could do. It's what you deserve. You were so determined to destroy me, turn my family against me and make sure Vicki cut me out of her life and the kids' lives.' Lee wipes his hands together.

'You're welcome to her. I've got no use for her any more.'

'You disgust me,' Vicki yells at him.

'Has anyone called the police?' Lee asks. Everyone shakes their heads. 'Well don't bother just yet,' he tells us.

'Why not?' Vicki asks, pulling Bella and Alfie closer to her.

'Because Debbie has some unfinished business of her own with Marc.'

'What are you talking about?' Vicki frowns at him then at Debbie.

Lee hesitates. Debbie nods at him to continue. Her little brother is always there to protect her, putting her first. They all need to know what he did to her. By not being brave and speaking up sooner she's been protecting Marc, she can see that now. Well, no more.

'Our paths first crossed way back, although I'm sure he doesn't remember me.'

'What's this all about?' Vicki asks. Lee gives her a hard stare then focuses back on his sister.

'I tried to warn him off you, Vicki,' Lee says. 'I took him aside at work and told him I knew exactly what he'd done, but he started coming for me.'

'Why didn't you tell me?' she asks.

'Because you would have believed him over me.'

'That's not true,' Vicki protests.

'It's taken a long time to track him down, because he changed his name when he came out of youth offenders.'

'Don't listen to him, he's full of shit,' Marc says.

'But here we are, despite you trying to kill me.' Lee sneers at him.

'Can someone please tell us what this is about?' Dom says.

'He tried to push me off the pier, then smother me with a pillow. All to silence me.'

'But why?' Vicki cries.

'Because I found out his real identity. The one he's been trying to cover up since his conviction for attacking my sister.' Lee's chin wobbles as he speaks. As far as Debbie knows, he's never said it aloud before either.

Everyone looks at Debbie, aghast.

'Go ahead. This is your moment,' Lee says to her, raising a fist, eyes bright.

'I've waited a long time for this, Kevin Young,' Debbie says as she pulls a hand gun out of her pocket, and aims it at Marc's head.

82

VICKI

'What the fuck?' Marc shrinks away from Debbie, eyes wide.

'Don't shoot, Debbie. He's not worth it,' I gasp and tighten my hold on Alfie and Bella, making sure my body is shielding theirs. Dom curses under his breath as he stands up and moves in front of Cassie and Jess.

Marc kicks his feet out trying to manoeuvre himself in a position to get up, but because his hands are tied, he can't.

'You don't remember me, do you?' Debbie tilts her head.

'You're not my type.' Marc's lip curls and he looks away.

'We remember you,' Lee says. 'Go on. Take a good look at her. She's a lot older now, but there must be something about her you remember.' Debbie points the gun between Marc's eyes, making him stare at her face.

'Can someone please tell me what's going on,' I say, but everyone is silent, watching Debbie and Marc's every move.

'I used to have a nickname, Beebee. Ring any bells?' Debbie tips her head down, staring right at him.

Marc shakes his head then turns his gaze to the ground.

I wrack my brains. I've seen that name before. It was written on the harness of the vintage rocking horse Debbie gave Bella when she was born.

'Why did she call you Kevin?' I snap at Marc.

'I don't bloody know,' he says.

'Tell me what happened, Lee?' I ask.

'Kevin Young changed his name to Marc Summers when he was just sixteen, after he came out of Youth Offenders.'

'So you lied to me about who you are?' I yell, not that it matters, not on top of all the other things he's done. But still, I believed him.

Marc's jaw stiffens except the muscle pulsing in the side of his cheek.

'What was he locked up for?' I ask. Nausea slithers up my throat because part of me has already guessed.

'He raped me when I was eleven.' Debbie's voice cracks. 'It was in the sea on holiday.' She blinks rapidly and steadies her hands, still pointing the gun at his head.

'You?' Marc says in a quiet tone, staring at her.

'Oh, Debbie,' I say mournfully, but she doesn't look my way or even flinch.

'Yes, little old me.' She points the gun at Marc's groin, and he shuffles on the carpet to try and get away. I squint and cover the children's eyes, imagining her practicing for this moment in one of the derelict barns at her farm.

'*You* were only thirteen years old. We met one hot day on the beach. I was happily building sandcastles, do you remember? You pretended to like me, but all the time you must have been plotting what you were going to do to me. It was you who suggested we go for a swim to cool down, but then you lured me into deeper waters even though I told you I was scared of being out of my depth. *Hold on to my arm*, you said. But then you swam out even further with me clinging to you, and I was petrified. When we were far enough out and no one could see, you forced yourself on me, stole away my innocence.' Debbie sniffs, tears running down her cheeks. 'And then you swam off, leaving me there to drown.'

'You were ripe for the taking, untouched.' He smirks but Lee kicks him in the stomach. Marc gasps for breath and curls into a ball.

'I was lucky that someone on a jet ski saw me in time, and saved me,' Debbie continues, 'but it's taken me a lifetime to get over the trauma and find my confidence again, especially in water. I never wanted to feel that fear again, so I joined a swimming club and gradually overcame it and became stronger. I'm so glad I persevered because it meant I could save my brother from you.'

'You're a pervert.' Dom kicks him in the back. Marc groans.

'I don't know you at all, do I? This whole time you've lied to me about who you are,' I say. 'Why did you do it?'

Marc coughs a spray of blood onto the cream carpet and squints up at me, cowering like a naughty child. 'Lots of boys at school had done it by that age,' he says in a hoarse voice, his body shaking. 'I was made to feel like a right nancy being the only virgin, and this old PE teacher at school said he'd help me get my confidence, give me extra classes after school. Except it wasn't sport he taught me. He said it was important to learn life lessons, be ready to go out into the world. I didn't know any different, so I let him do it to me. That's why I didn't want your boy to feel the odd one out like me. I wanted to help him, pass on the baton so to speak. Become a real man. Can't you see that?'

'What happened to you is despicable, but you can't expect me to forgive you for repeating the abuse,' I say. 'How dare you even think of grooming my son. You disgust me.' I hug Alfie tighter.

'And don't forget he let go of Lee on the pier, and then tried to smother him with a pillow in his hospital bed,' Debbie says.

'Is that true?' I shout. He's been so convincing. I believed he was a good person.

'What if it is?' Marc grunts.

'We seriously need to call the police,' Cassie says.

Lee glances at Debbie and nods.

'This scumbag needs locking up for the rest of his life,' Dom says, taking his phone out of his pocket and leaving the room.

'How did I let such a monster into our lives?' I say to Cassie.

'Because he never showed us this side of himself, this damaged view he has of the world and of women, of his right as a male to take what he wants.'

'He convinced us all,' Jess says.

I swallow down the urge to be sick and lean forward at the real possibility I won't be able to control it. I turn to Lee and Debbie.

'Why did neither of you warn me about him?'

'I tried to, but you wouldn't believe me and clung onto him even more,' Lee says.

'I'm so sorry for what he put you through,' I say to Debbie.

'I've never spoken about what happened to me before and I forbade Lee to tell anyone, even you. He knew it would be too distressing for me. I didn't know Lee had found him until we were in hospital,' Debbie says.

'You're a bloody menace, digging into my business and into my past.' Marc kicks out at Lee, but he steps back.

'I've been searching for Kevin Young on and off over the years...' Lee swallows and pauses for a couple of seconds. 'So when I discovered he'd changed his name, I managed to find him online. He was setting up a new property renovation business two years ago, so I applied for a contract job, became indispensable to him so he offered me a permanent position. Then I was able to keep a closer eye on him. But about ten months later Vicki applied for the role of Marc's PA. I tried to put her off, but I couldn't stop her. As soon as Marc met her, I knew he'd offer her the position because she's the best there is, but then he made a play for her. Without telling him I was Debbie's brother, I confronted him with what I knew about his conviction. Threatened to go public with it if he didn't back off from Vicki. It wasn't long after that he set me up with the weed in my desk drawer, probably because it was the easiest way to get rid of me.'

'I wish you could have told me what he'd done to Debbie. I'd never have gone for the job, or dated him,' I say.

'I couldn't do that to Debbie, I'm sorry, I had to protect her. She didn't want anyone knowing, no matter how blameless she was. She was in therapy half her life, and had been doing really well so I couldn't risk putting her back in that dark place. I made a promise to her and to Mum.' Lee looks down. 'I'm sorry. I genuinely didn't think you were in danger.'

'Anyone else knowing would have tipped me over the edge. It's been hard for me to cope with,' Debbie says.

I nod, and try to imagine how awful it must have been for her, but it still doesn't forgive that Lee knowingly put me and our kids in harm's way by not telling us. Keeping this secret from me was a huge mistake I'm not going to be able to forgive or forget in a hurry. I turn back to Marc. 'So you even lied about going to work and went straight back up to the hospital instead.'

Marc ignores me and shuts his eyes.

'He came in and threatened me to keep quiet or he'd kill me,' Lee says, 'then he said he'd kill the kids too if I said a word about the VAT or his past to anyone. And I'm guessing that when Olly turned up at the park, he warned Marc not to expose Jess's online identity, or he'd tell HMRC what he'd found out about his deception. But Marc probably threatened him in the same way and punched him, causing him to fall and hit his head. I don't suppose Olly knew about the rape and the pregnancy though, did he?'

Jess shakes her head. 'I couldn't tell him. It would have broken his heart.'

Lee turns to Marc again. 'Whether you intended to kill Olly or not, you punched him so hard he fell and hit his head on a rock, and left him for dead. You then kidnapped his girlfriend to continue your sordid abuse of her. And before this you were grooming my son right under Vicki's nose, getting him to spy on Jess through a hole in the ceiling, watch her on OnlyFans, and view all sorts of disgusting misogynistic and pornographic material on the internet.'

Debbie waves the gun at him. 'You tried so hard to hide who you were. But you haven't changed at all, have you?'

I cover Alfie and Bella's eyes, bracing myself, trembling all over. This is madness. There's nowhere to hide. She could hit any of us by mistake. I didn't even know Debbie owned a gun. I presume she uses it at the farm. But bringing it here? This is premeditated. I think she means to kill Marc.

'And you just go to prove that women are cruel bitches who need sorting out,' he laughs bitterly.

'Well, you're not getting away with anything this time,' Debbie says and pulls the trigger, shooting Marc's foot. He screams and grasps hold of his leg, his whole body shaking, blood spray over the carpet.

Bella screams. Jess starts crying again. I turn Alfie and Bella's heads away, my hands shaking, holding them tightly against me. Jesus Christ. This is insane. What is Debbie thinking?

'It's okay, it'll be okay,' I say quietly to the children over and over. I cannot believe she shot him.

Everyone is talking and shouting, and I just want to get the kids out of here, but I daren't move while Debbie still has a gun in her hand. Cassie is comforting Jess. I'm shocked to see a satisfied look on her face, but I suppose Marc deserves it.

'Accidents happen.' Dom shrugs and slaps Lee on the back. Debbie hands the gun to Lee and he puts it in his pocket. Dom shakes her hand.

I sigh with relief at the sound of police sirens approaching.

'Just be grateful I'm leaving you intact,' Debbie tells Marc and kicks him in the groin.

EPILOGUE

VICKI

One year later

'Time to open some presents,' I say, carrying a tray of tea into the living room. Alfie and Bella are still in their pyjamas and Lee is in his dressing gown.

'Shall I pass the presents out?' Alfie says, kneeling on the carpet by the Christmas tree. He's grown so much in the last year and his behaviour has improved 100 per cent.

'Yes, go for it,' I say.

'This one's for you, Mum, from all of us.' Alfie smiles and hands me a rectangular present.

'Open it, Mummy.' Bella claps her hands.

I rip the shiny snowman paper off to find the back of a picture frame. I turn it over. It's a photograph of the four of us that Debbie took on our last holiday of the summer. We hired a motor home and spent three weeks travelling along the south coast of England, stopping off to meet up with Debbie and her partner Rhona at their farm near Brixham on the way. She'd claimed to the police that her shooting Marc was an act of self-defence, that Marc tried to take the gun from her resulting in her shooting his foot, and with all our witness statements, this claim was upheld by the judge.

Marc is to serve his sentence under close supervision due to threats on his life. He was convicted of Olly's manslaughter, one count of rape against Jess, and one count of kidnap and false imprisonment. He's unlikely to see the light of day again for a long time.

'I hope you like it, Mum,' Alfie says and gives me a hug. He's matured a lot since last Christmas, and he isn't shy of showing us affection any more. He's told us that in PSHE lessons at school they've been discussing the dangers of misogyny online, and how women and girls deserve to be treated with respect.

It's been a long year, but he's made such good progress in his private counselling sessions. They've helped us as a family, to face head on what Marc put us through and navigate a way forward.

Jess is doing well after having had an abortion. A DNA sample confirmed Marc was the father, which helped to convict him. She's started college now and has come off social media completely. Her friends helped her set up a fund for a memorial stone and remembrance gathering for the first anniversary of Olly's death.

Bella insisted on keeping one of the puppies from the litter at Marc's house. The rest of them went to an animal rescue centre and have all found good homes. Milly is being cared for by one of the women who works there. I worried the puppy would be a constant reminder of what happened to us, but Bella said she wanted to 'save' one of them. So when he was old enough to leave his mum, Bailey came to live with us and now we can't imagine life without him.

After Marc was arrested, Lee went to rehab. After he came out, we had an honest chat about how far Marc had manipulated the narrative surrounding Lee's addiction. I acknowledged my part in believing him and allowing him to manipulate me too, convincing me Lee had become a hardened drug addict and bad father, when deep down I knew that couldn't be true. I told Lee how much I regret stopping him seeing our children and believing Marc's lies.

Now Lee's back living with us, so we can co-parent in harmony, be there for our children at all times. I hadn't realised what squalor he'd been living in. For now he and I have separate rooms. I don't know whether we'll reconnect as a couple, but that's not my priority right now, our children are. We both start new jobs in the New Year, and we're looking forward to this new chapter in our lives.

'A present for you, Dad,' Alfie says, passing him a box wrapped in Father Christmas paper.

Lee rips the paper off and opens a cardboard lid. Inside something is wrapped in tissue paper.

'Open it, Dad,' Bella cries excitedly.

I don't know what it is because Alfie bought it himself with his pocket money, earned from chores.

Lee carefully unwraps a mug decorated with the words, Best Dad Ever. He looks choked up, so they both go over and jump on him, giving him hugs.

Seeing them happy and reunited like this makes me grateful to have my family back together.

It's a new beginning for us all.

* * *

MORE FROM RUBY SPEECHLEY

Another book from Ruby Speechley, *The Daughter You Left*, is available to order now here:

https://mybook.to/TheDaughterYouLeft

ACKNOWLEDGEMENTS

Once again, I'm indebted to the incredible team at Boldwood for bringing this book into the world. Enormous thanks to my brilliant editor, Emily Yau, for your trust and belief in my stories and for helping me elevate them until they shine. Thanks to my copy editor, Candida Bradford, for spotting any errors. You truly are a lifesaver. And thank you to Rachel Sargeant for your sharp-eyed proofreading skills.

None of it would be possible without my agent, Jo Bell, supporting and encouraging me at every stage. Huge thanks to you and everyone at Bell Lomax Moreton.

Thank you to my writer friends for the chats, advice and listening to my novel ideas and woes. You know who you are.

One of the biggest highlights of being a writer is meeting readers, and I've met many this year at library events around Cheshire. It really does make all the hard work worthwhile, so thank you to readers near and far.

Finally, my family keep me going through all the ups and downs of life while I write and edit my books. Special thanks as always to my husband Richard, and my three children, Charlie, Edward and Sophie, who continue to give me astonishing levels of love, energy and purpose.

ABOUT THE AUTHOR

Ruby Speechley is a bestselling psychological thriller writer, whose titles include *Someone Else's Baby*. Previously published by Hera, she has been a journalist and worked in PR and lives in Cheshire.

Download your exclusive bonus content from Ruby Speechley here:

Visit Ruby's website: www.rubyspeechley.com

Follow Ruby on social media:

facebook.com/Ruby-Speechley-Author-100063999185095

x.com/rubyspeechley

instagram.com/rubyjtspeechley

ALSO BY RUBY SPEECHLEY

Gone

Missing

Guilty

The Uninvited Guest

Someone Else's Baby

Stolen

The Daughter You Left

THE *Murder* LIST

THE MURDER LIST IS A NEWSLETTER DEDICATED TO SPINE-CHILLING FICTION AND GRIPPING PAGE-TURNERS!

SIGN UP TO MAKE SURE YOU'RE ON OUR HIT LIST FOR EXCLUSIVE DEALS, AUTHOR CONTENT, AND COMPETITIONS.

SIGN UP TO OUR NEWSLETTER

BIT.LY/THEMURDERLISTNEWS

Boldwood

Boldwood Books is an award-winning fiction publishing company seeking out the best stories from around the world.

Find out more at www.boldwoodbooks.com

Join our reader community for brilliant books, competitions and offers!

Follow us

@BoldwoodBooks

@TheBoldBookClub

Sign up to our weekly deals newsletter

https://bit.ly/BoldwoodBNewsletter

www.ingramcontent.com/pod-product-compliance
Lightning Source LLC
Chambersburg PA
CBHW011759010726
47497CB00012B/3208